I0553496

Another Sheaf by John Galsworthy

John Galsworthy was born at Kingston Upon Thames in Surrey, England, on August 14th 1867 to a wealthy and well established family. His schooling was at Harrow and New College, Oxford before training as a barrister and being called to the bar in 1890. However, Law was not attractive to him and he travelled abroad becoming great friends with the novelist Joseph Conrad, then a first mate on a sailing ship.

In 1895 Galsworthy began an affair with Ada Nemesis Pearson Cooper, the wife of his cousin Major Arthur Galsworthy. The affair was kept a secret for 10 years till she at last divorced and they married on 23rd September 1905.

Galsworthy first published in 1897 with a collection of short stories entitled "The Four Winds". For the next 7 years he published these and all works under his pen name John Sinjohn. It was only upon the death of his father and the publication of "The Island Pharisees" in 1904 that he published as John Galsworthy.

His first play, The Silver Box in 1906 was a success and was followed by "The Man of Property" later that same year and was the first in the Forsyte trilogy. Whilst today he is far more well know as a Nobel Prize winning novelist then he was considered a playwright dealing with social issues and the class system. Here we publish Villa Rubein, a very fine story that captures Galsworthy's unique narrative and take on life of the time.

He is now far better known for his novels, particularly The Forsyte Saga, his trilogy about the eponymous family of the same name. These books, as with many of his other works, deal with social class, upper-middle class lives in particular. Although always sympathetic to his characters, he reveals their insular, snobbish, and somewhat greedy attitudes and suffocating moral codes. He is now viewed as one of the first from the Edwardian era to challenge some of the ideals of society depicted in the literature of Victorian England.

In his writings he campaigns for a variety of causes, including prison reform, women's rights, animal welfare, and the opposition of censorship as well as a recurring theme of an unhappy marriage from the women's side. During World War I he worked in a hospital in France as an orderly after being passed over for military service.

He was appointed to the Order of Merit in 1929, after earlier turning down a knighthood, and awarded the Nobel Prize in 1932 though he was too ill to attend.

John Galsworthy died from a brain tumour at his London home, Grove Lodge, Hampstead on January 31st 1933. In accordance with his will he was cremated at Woking with his ashes then being scattered over the South Downs from an aeroplane.

Index of Contents

ANOTHER SHEAF

THE ROAD

The road stretched in a pale, straight streak, narrowing to a mere thread at the limit of vision—the only living thing in the wild darkness. All was very still. It had been raining; the wet heather and the pines gave forth scent, and little gusty shivers shook the dripping birch trees. In the pools of sky, between broken clouds, a few stars shone, and half of a thin moon was seen from time to time, like the fragment of a silver horn held up there in an invisible hand, waiting to be blown.

Hard to say when I first became aware that there was movement on the road, little specks of darkness on it far away, till its end was blackened out of sight, and it seemed to shorten towards me. Whatever was coming darkened it as an invading army of ants will darken a streak of sunlight on sand strewn with pine needles. Slowly this shadow crept along till it had covered all but the last dip and rise; and still it crept forward in that eerie way, as yet too far off for sound.

Then began the voice of it in the dripping stillness, a tramping of weary feet, and I could tell that this advancing shadow was formed of men, millions of them moving all at one speed, very slowly, as if regulated by the march of the most tired among them. They had blotted out the road, now, from a few yards away to the horizon; and suddenly, in the dusk, a face showed.

Its eyes were eager, its lips parted, as if each step was the first the marcher had ever taken; and yet he was stumbling, almost asleep from tiredness. A young man he was, with skin drawn tight over his heavy cheek-bones and jaw, under the platter of his helmet, and burdened with all his soldier's load. At first I saw his face alone in the darkness, startlingly clear; and then a very sea of helmeted faces, with their sunken eyes shining, and their lips parted. Watching them pass—heavy and dim and spectre-like in the darkness, those eager dead-beat men—I knew as never before how they had longed for this last march, and in fancy seen the road, and dreamed of the day when they would be trudging home. Their hearts seemed laid bare to me, the sickening hours they had waited, dreaming and longing, in boots rusty with blood. And the night was full of the loneliness and waste they had been through....

Morning! At the edge of the town the road came arrow-straight to the first houses and their gardens, past them, and away to the streets. In every window and at each gate children, women, men, were looking down the road. Face after face was painted, various, by the sunlight, homely with line and wrinkle, curve and dimple, pallid or ruddy, but the look in the eyes of all these faces seemed the same. "I have waited so long," it said, "I cannot wait any more—I cannot!" Their hands were clasped, and by the writhing of those hands I knew how they had yearned, and the madness of delight waiting to leap from them—wives, mothers, fathers, children, the patient hopers against hope.

Far out on the road something darkened the sunlight. They were coming!

THE SACRED WORK

The Angel of Peace, watching the slow folding back of this darkness, will look on an earth of cripples. The field of the world is strewn with half-living men. That loveliness which is the creation of the æsthetic human spirit; that flowering of directed energy which we know as civilisation; that manifold and mutual service which we call progress—all stand mutilated and faltering. As though, on a pilgrimage to the dreamed-of Mecca, water had failed, and by the wayside countless muffled forms sat waiting for rain; so will the long road of mankind look to-morrow.

In every township and village of our countries men stricken by the war will dwell for the next half-century. The figure of Youth must go one-footed, one-armed, blind of an eye, lesioned and stunned, in the home where it once danced. The half of a generation can never again step into the sunlight of full health and the priceless freedom of unharmed limbs.

So comes the sacred work.

Can there be limit to the effort of gratitude? Niggardliness and delay in restoring all of life that can be given back is sin against the human spirit, a smear on the face of honour.

Love of country, which, like some little secret lamp, glows in every heart, hardly to be seen of our eyes when the world is at peace—love of the old, close things, the sights, sounds, scents we have known from birth; loyalty to our fathers' deeds and our fathers' hopes; the clutch of Motherland—this love sent our soldiers and sailors forth to the long endurance, to the doing of such deeds, and the bearing of so great and evil pain as can never be told. The countries for which they have dared and suffered have now to play their part.

The conscience of to-day is burdened with a load well-nigh unbearable. Each hour of the sacred work unloads a little of this burden.

To lift up the man who has been stricken on the battlefield, restore him to the utmost of health and agility, give him an adequate pension, and re-equip him with an occupation suited to the forces left him—that is a process which does not cease till the sufferer fronts the future keen, hopeful, and secure. And such restoration is at least as much a matter of spirit as of body. Consider what it means to fall suddenly out of full vigour into the dark certainty that you can never have full strength again, though you live on twenty, forty, sixty years. The flag of your courage may well be down half-mast! Apathy—that creeping nerve disease—is soon your bed-fellow and the companion of your walks. A curtain has fallen before your vision; your eyes no longer range. The Russian "Nichevo"—the "what-does-it-matter?" mood—besets you. Fate seems to say to you: "Take the line of least resistance, friend—you are done for!" But the sacred work says to Fate: "Retro, Satanas! This our comrade is not your puppet. He shall yet live as happy and as useful—if not as active—a life as he ever lived before. You shall not crush him! We shall tend him from clearing station till his discharge better than wounded soldier has ever yet been tended. In special hospitals, orthopædic, paraplegic, phthisic, neurasthenic, we shall give him back functional ability, solidity of nerve or lung. The flesh torn away, the lost sight, the broken ear-drum, the destroyed nerve, it is true, we cannot give back; but we shall so re-create and fortify the rest of him that he shall leave hospital ready for a new career. Then we shall teach him how to tread the road of it, so that he fits again into the national life, becomes once more a workman with pride in his work, a stake in the country, and the consciousness that, handicapped though he be, he runs the race level with his fellows, and is by that so much the better man than they. And beneath the feet of this new workman we shall put the firm plank of a pension."

The sacred work fights the creeping dejections which lie in wait for each soul and body, for the moment stricken and thrown. It says to Fate: "You shall not pass!"

And the greatest obstacle with which it meets is the very stoicism and nonchalance of the sufferer! To the Anglo-Saxon, especially, those precious qualities are dangerous. That horse, taken to the water, will too seldom drink. Indifference to the future has a certain loveability, but is hardly a virtue when it makes of its owner a weary drone, eking out a pension with odd jobs. The sacred work is vitally concerned to defeat this hand-to-mouth philosophy. Side by side in man, and especially in Anglo-Saxon, there live two creatures. One of them lies on his back and smokes; the other runs a race; now one, now the other, seems to be the whole man. The sacred work has for its end to keep the runner on his feet; to proclaim the nobility of running. A man will do for mankind or for his country what he will not do for himself; but mankind marches on, and countries live and grow, and need our services in peace no less than in war. Drums do not beat, the flags hang furled, in time of peace; but a quiet music is ever raising its call to service. He who in war has flung himself, without thought of self, on the bayonet and braved a hail of bullets often does not hear that quiet music. It is the business of the sacred work to quicken his ear to it. Of little use to man or nation would be the mere patching-up of bodies, so that, like a row of old gossips against a sunlit wall, our disabled might sit and weary out their days. If that were all we could do for them, gratitude is proven fraudulent, device bankrupt; and the future of our countries must drag with a lame foot.

To one who has watched, rather from outside, it seems that restoration worthy of that word will only come if the minds of all engaged in the sacred work are always fixed on this central truth: "Body and spirit are inextricably conjoined; to heal the one without the other is impossible." If a man's mind, courage and interest be enlisted in the cause of his own salvation, healing goes on apace, the sufferer is remade. If not, no mere surgical wonders, no careful nursing, will avail to make a man of him again. Therefore I would say: "From the moment he enters hospital, look after his mind and his will; give them food; nourish them in subtle ways, increase that nourishment as his strength increases. Give him interest in his future; light a star for him to fix his eyes on. So that, when he steps out of hospital, you shall not have to begin to train one who for months, perhaps years, has been living, mindless and will-less, the life of a half-dead creature."

That this is a hard task none who knows hospital life can doubt.

That it needs special qualities and special effort quite other than the average range of hospital devotion is obvious. But it saves time in the end, and without it success is more than doubtful. The crucial period is the time spent in hospital; use that period to re-create not only body, but mind and will-power, and all shall come out right; neglect to use it thus, and the heart of many a sufferer, and of many a would-be healer, will break from sheer discouragement.

The sacred work is not departmental; it is one long organic process from the moment when a man is picked up from the field of battle to the moment when he is restored to the ranks of full civil life. Our eyes must not be fixed merely on this stressful present, but on the world as it will be ten years hence. I see that world gazing back, like a repentant drunkard at his own debauch, with a sort of horrified amazement and disgust. I see it impatient of any reminiscence of this hurricane; hastening desperately to recover what it enjoyed before life was wrecked and pillaged by these blasts of death. Hearts, which now swell with pity and gratitude when our maimed soldiers pass the streets, will, from sheer familiarity, and through natural shrinking from reminder, be dried to a stony indifference. "Let the dead past bury its dead" is a saying terribly true, and perhaps essential to the preservation of mankind. The world of ten years hence will shrug its shoulders if it sees maimed and useless men crawling the streets of its day, like winter flies on a windowpane.

It is for the sacred work to see that there shall be no winter flies. A niche of usefulness and self-respect exists for every man, however handicapped; but that niche must be found for him. To carry the process of restoration to a point short of this is to leave the cathedral without spire.

Of the men and women who have this work in hand I have seen enough—in France and in my own country, at least—to know their worth, and the selfless idealism which animates them. Their devotion, courage, tenacity, and technical ability are beyond question or praise. I would only fear that in the hard struggle they experience to carry each day's work to its end, to perfect their own particular jobs, all so important and so difficult, vision of the whole fabric they are helping to raise must often be obscured. And I would venture to say: "Only by looking upon each separate disabled soldier as the complete fabric can you possibly keep that vision before your eyes. Only by revivifying in each separate disabled soldier the will to live can you save him from the fate of merely continuing to exist."

There are wounded men, many, whose spirit is such that they will march in front of any effort made for their recovery. I well remember one of these—a Frenchman—nearly paralysed in both legs. All day long he would work at his "macramé," and each morning, after treatment, would demand to try and stand. I can see his straining efforts now, his eyes like the eyes of a spirit; I can hear his daily words: "Il me semble que j'ai un peu plus de force dans mes jambes ce matin, Monsieur!" though, I fear, he never had. Men of such indomitable initiative, though not rare, are but a fraction. The great majority have rather the happy-go-lucky soul. For them it is only too easy to postpone self-help till sheer necessity drives, or till some one in whom they believe inspires them. The work of re-equipping these with initiative, with a new interest in life, with work which they can do, is one of infinite difficulty and complexity. Nevertheless, it must be done.

The great publics of our countries do not yet, I think, see that they too have their part in the sacred work. So far they only seem to feel: "Here's a wounded hero; let's take him to the movies, and give him tea!" Instead of choking him with cheap kindness each member of the public should seek to reinspire the disabled man with the feeling that he is no more out of the main stream of life than they are themselves; and each, according to his or her private chances, should help him to find that special niche which he can best, most cheerfully, and most usefully fill in the long future.

The more we drown the disabled in tea and lip gratitude the more we unsteel his soul, and the harder we make it for him to win through, when, in the years to come, the wells of our tea and gratitude have dried up. We can do a much more real and helpful thing. I fear that there will soon be no one of us who has not some personal friend disabled. Let us regard that man as if he were ourselves; let us treat him as one who demands a full place in the ranks of working life, and try to find it for him.

In such ways alone will come a new freemasonry to rebuild this ruined temple of our day. The ground is rubbled with stones—fallen, and still falling. Each must be replaced; freshly shaped, cemented, and mortised in, that the whole may once more stand firm and fair. In good time, to a clearer sky than we are fortunate enough to look on, our temple shall rise again. The birds shall not long build in its broken walls, nor lichens moss it. The winds shall not long play through these now jagged windows, nor the rain drift in, nor moonlight fill it with ghosts and shadows. To the glory of man we will stanchion, and raise and roof it anew.

Each comrade who for his Motherland has, for the moment, lost his future is a miniature of that shattered temple.

To restore him, and with him the future of our countries, that is the sacred work.

THE BALANCE SHEET OF THE SOLDIER-WORKMAN

Let the reader take what follows with more than a grain of salt. No one can foretell—surely not this writer—with anything approaching certainty what will be the final effect of this war on the soldier-workman. One can but marshal some of the more obvious and general liabilities and assets, and try to strike a balance. The whole thing is in flux. Millions are going into the crucible at every temperature; and who shall say at all precisely what will come out or what conditions the product issuing will meet with, though they obviously cannot be the same as before the war? For in considering this question, one must run into the account on either side not only the various effects of the war on the soldier-workman, but the altered influences his life will encounter in the future, so far as one can foresee; and this is all navigation in uncharted waters.

Talking with and observing French soldiers during the winter of 1916-1917, and often putting to them this very question: How is the war going to affect the soldier-workman? I noticed that their answers followed very much the trend of class and politics. An adjutant, sergeant, or devout Catholic considered that men would be improved, gain self-command, and respect for law and order, under prolonged discipline and daily sacrifice. A freethinker of the educated class, or a private of Socialistic tendencies, on the other hand, would insist that the strain must make men restless, irritable, more eager for their rights, less tolerant of control. Each imagined that the war would further the chances of the future as they dreamed of it. If I had talked with capitalists—there are none among French soldiers—they would doubtless have insisted that after-war conditions were going to be easier, just as the "sans-sous" maintained that they were going to be harder and provocative of revolution. In a word, the wish was father to the thought.

Having observed this so strongly, the writer of these speculations says to himself: "Let me, at all events, try to eliminate any bias, and see the whole thing as should an umpire—one of those pure beings in white coats, purged of all the prejudices, passions, and predilections of mankind. Let me have no temperament for the time being, for I have to set down—not what would be the effect on me if I were in their place, or what would happen to the future if I could have my way, but what would happen all the same if I were not alive. Only from an impersonal point of view, if there be such a thing, am I going to get even approximately at the truth."

Impersonally, then, one notes the credit facts and probabilities towards the future's greater well-being; and those on the debit side, of retrogression from the state of well-being, such as it was, which prevailed when war was declared.

First, what will be the physical effect of the war on the soldier-workman? Military training, open-air life, and plentiful food are of such obvious physical advantage in the vast majority of cases as to need no pointing out. And how much improvement was wanted is patent to any one who has a remnant left of the old Greek worship of the body. It has made one almost despair of industrialised England to see the great Australians pass in the streets of London. We English cannot afford to neglect the body any longer; we are becoming, I am much afraid, a warped, stunted, intensely plain people. On that point I refuse to speak with diffidence, for it is my business to know something about beauty, and in our masters and pastors I see no sign of knowledge and little inkling of concern, since there is no public opinion to drive them forward to respect beauty. One-half of us regard good looks as dangerous and savouring of immorality; the other half look upon them as "swank," or at least superfluous. Any interest manifested in such a subject is confined to a few women and a handful of artists. Let any one who has an eye for looks take the trouble to observe the people who pass in the streets of any of our big towns, he will count perhaps one in five—not beautiful—but with some pretensions to being not absolutely plain; and one can say this without fear of hurting any feelings, for all will think themselves exceptions. Frivolity apart, there is a dismal lack of good looks and good physique in our population; and it will be all to the good to have had this physical training. If that training had stopped short of the fighting line it would be physically entirely beneficial; as it is, one has unfortunately to set against its advantages—leaving out wounds and mutilation altogether—a considerable number of overstrained hearts and nerves, not amounting to actual disablement; and a great deal of developed rheumatism.

Peace will send back to their work very many men better set up and hardier; but many also obviously or secretly weakened. Hardly any can go back as they were. Yet, while training will but have brought out strength which was always latent, and which, unless relapse be guarded against, must rapidly decline, cases of strain and rheumatism will for the most part be permanent, and such as would not have taken place under peace conditions. Then there is the matter of venereal disease, which the conditions of military life are carefully fostering—no negligible factor on the debit side; the health of many hundreds must be written off on that score. To credit, again, must be placed increased personal cleanliness, much greater handiness and resource in the small ways of life, and an even more complete endurance and contempt of illness than already characterised the British workman, if that be possible. On the whole I think that, physically, the scales will balance pretty evenly.

Next, what will be the effect of the war on the mental powers of the soldier-workman? Unlike the French (sixty per cent. of whose army are men working on the land), our army must contain at least ninety per cent. of town workers, whose minds in time of peace are kept rather more active than those of workers on the land by the ceaseless friction and small decisions of town life. To gauge the result of two to five years' military life on the minds of these town workers is a complicated and stubborn problem. Here we have the exact converse of the physical case. If the army life of the soldier-workman stopped short of service at the front one might say at once that the effect on his mind would be far more disastrous than it is. The opportunity for initiative and decision, the mental stir of camp and depôt life is nil compared with that of service in the fighting line. And for one month at the front a man spends perhaps five at the rear. Military life, on its negative side, is more or less a suspension of the usual channels of mental activity. By barrack and camp life the normal civilian intellect is, as it were, marooned. On that desert island it finds, no doubt, certain new and very definite forms of activity, but any one who has watched old soldiers must have been struck by the "arrested" look which is stamped on most of them—by a kind of remoteness, of concentrated emptiness, as of men who by the conditions of their lives have long been prevented from thinking of anything outside a ring fence. Two to five years' service will not be long enough to set the old soldier's stamp on a mind, but one can see the process beginning; and it will be quite long enough to encourage laziness in minds already disposed to lying fallow. Far be it from this pen to libel the English, but a feverish mental activity has never been their vice; intellect, especially in what is known as the working-class, is leisurely; it does not require to be encouraged to take its ease. Some one has asked me: "Can the ordinary worker think less in the army than when he wasn't in the army?" In other words: "Did he ever think at all?" The British worker is, of course, deceptive; he does not look as if he were thinking. Whence exactly does he get his stolidity—from climate, self-consciousness, or his competitive spirit? All the same, thought does go on in him, shrewd and "near-the-bone"; life-made rather than book-made thought. Its range is limited by its vocabulary; it starts from different premises, reaches different conclusions from those of the "pundit," and so is liable to seem to the latter non-existent. But let a worker and an educated man sit opposite each other in a railway carriage without exchanging a word, as is the fashion with the English, and which of their two silent judgments on the other will be superior? I am not sure, but I rather think the worker's. It will have a kind of deadly realism. In camp and depôt life the mind standing-at-ease from many civilian frictions and needs for decision, however petty, and shaken away from civilian ruts, will do a good deal of thinking of a sort, be widened, and probably re-value many things—especially when its owner goes abroad and sees fresh types, fresh manners, and the world. But actual physical exertion, and the inertia which follows it, bulk large in military service, and many who "never thought at all" before they became soldiers will think still less after! I may be cynical, but it seems to me that the chief stimulus to thought in the ordinary mind is money, the getting and the spending thereof; that what we call "politics," those social interests which form at least half the staple of the ordinary worker's thought, are made up of concern as to the wherewithal to live. In the army money is a fixed quantity which demands no thought, neither in the getting nor the spending; and the constant mental activity which in normal life circles round money of necessity dries up.

But against this indefinite general rusting of mind machinery in the soldier-workman's life away from the fighting line certain definite considerations must be set. Many soldiers will form a habit of reading—in the new armies the demand for books is great; some in sheer boredom will have begun an all-round cultivation of their minds; others again will be chafing continually against this prolonged holding-up of their habitual mental traffic—and when a man chafes he does not exactly rust; so that, while the naturally lazy will have been made more lazy, the naturally eager may be made very eager.

The matter of age, too, is not unimportant. A soldier of twenty, twenty-five, even up to thirty, probably seldom feels that the mode of life from which he has been taken is set and permanent. He may be destined to do that work all his days, but the knowledge of this has not so far bitten him; he is not yet in the swing and current of his career, and feels no great sense of dislocation. But a man of thirty-five or forty, taken from an occupation which has got grip on him, feels that his life has had a slice carved out of it. He may realise the necessity better than the younger man, take his duty more seriously, but must have a sensation as if his springs were let down flat. The knowledge that he has to resume his occupation again in real middle age, with all the steam escaped, must be profoundly discouraging; therefore I think his mental activity will suffer more than that of the younger man. The recuperative powers of youth are so great that very many of our younger soldiers will unrust quickly and at a bound regain all the activity lost. Besides, a very great many of the younger men will not go back to the old job.

But older men, though they will go back to what they were doing before more readily than their juniors, will go back with diminished hope and energy, and a sort of fatalism. At forty, even at thirty-five, every year begins to seem important, and several years will have been wrenched out of their working lives just, perhaps, when they were beginning to make good.

Turning to the spells of service at the front—there will be no rusting there—the novelty of sensation, the demand for initiative and adaptability are too great. A soldier said to me: "My two years in depôt and camp were absolutely deadening; that eight weeks at the front before I was knocked over were the best eight weeks I ever had." Spells at the front must wipe out all or nearly all the rust; but against them must be set the deadening spells of hospital, which too often follow, the deadening spells of training which have gone before; and the more considerable though not very permanent factor—that laziness and dislocation left on the minds of many who have been much in the firing line. As the same young soldier put it: "I can't concentrate now as I could on a bit of work—it takes me longer; all the same, where I used to chuck it when I found it hard, I set my teeth now." In other words, less mental but more moral grip.

On the whole, then, so far as mental effect goes, I believe the balance must come out on the debit side.

And, now, what will be the spiritual effect of the war on the soldier-workman? And by "spiritual" I mean the effect of his new life and emotional experience, neither on his intellect, nor exactly on his "soul"—for very few men have anything so rarefied—but on his disposition and character.

Has any one the right to discuss this who has not fought? It is with the greatest diffidence that I hazard any view. On the other hand, the effects are so various, and so intensely individual, that perhaps only such a one has a chance of forming a general judgment unbiassed by personal experience and his own temperament. What thousands of strange and poignant feelings must pass through even the least impressionable soldier who runs the gamut of this war's "experience"! And there will not be too many of our soldier-workmen returning to civil life without having had at least a taste of everything. The embryo Guardsman who sticks his bayonet into a sack, be he never so unimaginative, with each jab of that bayonet pictures dimly the body of a "Hun," and gets used to the sensation of spitting it. On every long march there comes a time that may last hours when the recruit feels done up, and yet has to go on "sticking it." Never a day passes, all through his service, without some moment when he would give his soul to be out of it all and back in some little elysium of the past; but he has to grit his teeth and try to forget. Hardly a man who, when he first comes under fire, has not a struggle with himself which amounts to a spiritual victory. Not many who do not arrive at a "Don't care" state of mind that is almost equal to a spiritual defeat. No soldier who does not rub shoulders during his service with countless comrades strange to him, and get a wider understanding and a fuller tolerance. Not a soul in the trenches, one would think, who is not caught up into a mood of comradeship and self-suppression which amounts almost to exaltation. Not one but has to fight through moods almost reaching extinction of the very love of life. And shall all this—and the many hard disappointments, and the long yearning for home and those he loves, and the chafing against continual restraints, and the welling-up of secret satisfaction in the "bit done," the knowledge that Fate is not beating, cannot beat him; and the sight of death all round, and the looking into Death's eyes—staring those eyes down; and the long bearing of pain; and the pity for his comrades bearing pain—shall all this pass his nature by without marking it for life? When all is over, and the soldier-workman back in civil life, will his character be enlarged or shrunken? The nature of a man is never really changed, no more than a leopard's skin, it is but developed or dwarfed. The influences of the war will have as many little forms as there are soldiers, and to attempt precision of summary is clearly vain. It is something of a truism to suggest that the war will ennoble and make more serious those who before the war took a noble and serious view of life; and that on those who took life callously it will have a callousing effect. The problem is rather to discover what effect, if any, will be made on that medium material which was neither definitely serious nor obviously callous. And for this we must go to consideration of main national characteristics. It is—for one thing—very much the nature of the Briton to look on life as a game with victory or defeat at the end of it, and to feel it impossible that he can be defeated. He is not so much concerned to "live" as to win this life match. He is combative from one minute to the next, reacts instantly against any attempt to down him. The war for him is a round in this great personal match of his with Fate, and he is completely caught up in the idea of winning it. He is spared that double consciousness of the French soldier who wants to "live," who goes on indeed superbly fighting "pour la France" out of love for his country, but all the time cannot help saying to himself: "What a fool I am—what sort of life is this?" I have heard it said by one who ought to know, if any one can, that the British soldier hardly seems to have a sense of patriotism, but goes through it all as a sort of private "scrap" in which he does not mean to be beaten, and out of loyalty to his regiment, his "team," so to speak. This is partly true, but the Briton is very deep, and there are feelings at the bottom of his well which never see the light. If the British soldier were fighting on a line which ran from Lowestoft through York to Sunderland, he might show very different symptoms. Still, at bottom he would always, I think, feel the business to be first in the nature of a contest with a force which was trying to down him personally. In this contest he is being stretched, and steeled—that is, hardened and confirmed—in the very quality of stubborn combativeness which was already his first characteristic.

Take another main feature of the national character—the Briton is ironic. Well, the war is deepening his irony. It must, for it is a monstrously ironic business.

Some—especially those who wish to—believe in a religious revival among the soldiers. There's an authentic story of two convalescent soldiers describing a battle. The first finished thus: "I tell you it makes you think of God." The second—a thoughtful type—ended with a pause, and then these words: "Who could believe in God after that?" Like all else in human life, it depends on temperament. The war will speed up "belief" in some and "disbelief" in others. But, on the whole, comic courage shakes no hands with orthodoxy.

The religious movement which I think is going on is of a subtler and a deeper sort altogether. Men are discovering that human beings are finer than they had supposed. A young man said to me: "Well, I don't know about religion, but I know that my opinion of human nature is about fifty per cent. better than it was." That conclusion has been arrived at by countless thousands. It is a great factor—seeing that the belief of the future will be belief in the God within; and a frank agnosticism concerning the great "Why" of things. Religion will become the exaltation of self-respect, of what we call the divine in man. "The Kingdom of God" is within you. That belief, old as the hills, and reincarnated by Tolstoi years ago, has come into its own in the war; for it has been clearly proved to be the real faith of modern man, underneath all verbal attempts to assert the contrary. This—the white side of war—is an extraordinarily heartening phenomenon; and if it sent every formal creed in the world packing there would still be a gain to religion.

Another main characteristic of the Briton, especially of the "working" Briton, is improvidence—he likes, unconsciously, to live from hand to mouth, careless of the morrow. The war is deepening that characteristic too—it must, for who could endure if he fretted over what was going to happen to him, with death so in the wind?

Thus the average soldier-workman will return from the war confirmed and deepened in at least three main national characteristics: His combative hardihood, his ironic humour, and his improvidence. I think he will have more of what is called "character"; whether for good or evil depends, I take it, on what we connote by those terms, and in what context we use them. I may look on "character" as an asset, but I can well imagine politicians and trades union leaders regarding it with profound suspicion. Anyway, he will not be the lamb that he was not even before the war. He will be a restive fellow, knowing his own mind better, and possibly his real interest less well; he will play less for safety, since safety will have become to him a civilian sort of thing, rather contemptible. He will have at once a more interesting and a less reliable character from the social and political point of view.

And what about his humanity? Can he go through all this hell of slaughter and violence untouched in his gentler instincts? There will be—there must be—some brutalisation. But old soldiers are not usually inhumane—on the contrary, they are often very gentle beings. I distrust the influence of the war on those who merely write and read about it. I think editors, journalists, old gentlemen, and women will be brutalised in larger numbers than our soldiers. An intelligent French soldier said to me of his own countrymen: "After six months of civil life, you won't know they ever had to 'clean up' trenches and that sort of thing." If this is true of the Frenchman, it will be more true of the less impressionable Briton. If I must sum up at all on what, for want of a better word, I have called the "spiritual" count, I can only say that there will be a distinct increase of "character," and leave it to the reader to decide whether that falls on the debit or the credit side.

On the whole then, an increase of "character," a slight loss of mental activity, and neither physical gain nor loss to speak of.

We have now to consider the rather deadly matter of demobilisation. One hears the suggestion that not more than 30,000 men shall be disbanded per week; this means two years at least. Conceive millions of men whose sense of sacrifice has been stretched to the full for a definite object which has been gained—conceive them held in a weary, and, as it seems to them, unnecessary state of suspense. Kept back from all they long for, years after the reality of their service has departed! If this does not undermine them, I do not know what will. Demobilisation—they say—must be cautious. "No man should be released till a place in the industrial machine is ready waiting for him!" So, in a counsel of perfection, speak the wise who have not been deprived of home life, civil liberty, and what not for a dismal length of two, three, and perhaps four years. No! Demobilisation should be as swift as possible, and risks be run to make it swift. The soldier-workman who goes back to civil life within two or three months after peace is signed goes back with a glow still in his heart. But he who returns with a rankling sense of unmerited, unintelligible delay—most prudently, of course, ordained—goes back with "cold feet" and a sullen or revolting spirit. What men will stand under the shadow of a great danger from a sense of imminent duty, they will furiously chafe at when that danger and sense of duty are no more. The duty will then be to their families and to themselves. There is no getting away from this, and the country will be well advised not to be too coldly cautious. Every one, of course, must wish to ease to the utmost the unprecedented economic and industrial confusion which the signing of peace will bring, but it will be better to risk a good deal of momentary unemployment and discontent rather than neglect the human factor and keep men back long months in a service of which they will be deadly sick. How sick they will be may perhaps be guessed at from the words of a certain soldier: "After the war you'll have to have conscription. You won't get a man to go into the army without!" What is there to prevent the Government from beginning now to take stock of the demands of industry, from having a great land settlement scheme cut and dried, and devising means for the swiftest possible demobilisation? The moment peace is signed the process of re-absorption into civil life should begin at once and go on without interruption as swiftly as the actual difficulties of transport permit. They, of themselves, will hold up demobilisation quite long enough. The soldier-workman will recognise and bear with the necessary physical delays, but he will not tolerate for a moment any others for his so-called benefit.[A]

And what sort of civil life will it be which awaits the soldier-workman? I suppose, if anything is certain, a plenitude, nay a plethora, of work is assured for some time after the war. Capital has piled up in hands which will control a vast amount of improved and convertible machinery. Purchasing power has piled up in the shape of savings out of the increased national income. Granted that income will at once begin to drop all round, shrinking perhaps fast to below the pre-war figures, still at first there must be a rolling river of demand and the wherewithal to satisfy it. For years no one has built houses, or had their houses done up; no one has bought furniture, clothes, or a thousand other articles which they propose buying the moment the war stops. Railways and rolling stock, roads, housing, public works of all sorts, private motor cars, and pleasure requirements of every kind have been let down and starved. Huge quantities of shipping must be replaced; vast renovations of destroyed country must be undertaken; numberless repairs to damaged property; the tremendous process of converting or re-converting machinery to civil uses must be put through; State schemes to deal with the land, housing, and other problems will be in full blast; a fierce industrial competition will commence; and, above all, we must positively grow our own food in the future. Besides all this we shall have lost at least a million workers through death, disablement, and emigration; indeed, unless we have some really attractive land scheme ready we may lose a million by emigration alone. In a word, the demand for labour, at the moment, will be overwhelming, and the vital question only one of readjustment. In numberless directions women, boys, and older men have replaced the soldier-workman. Hundreds of thousands of soldiers, especially among the first three million, have been guaranteed reinstatement. Hundreds of thousands of substitutes will, therefore, be thrown out of work. With the exception of the skilled men who have had to be retained in their places all through, and the men who step back into places kept for them, the whole working population will have to be refitted with jobs. The question of women's labour will not be grave at first because there will be work for all and more than all, but the jigsaw puzzle which industry will have to put together will try the nerves and temper of the whole community. In the French army the peasant soldier is jealous and sore because he has had to bear the chief burden of the fighting, while the mechanic has to a great extent been kept for munition making, transport, and essential civil industry. With us it is if anything the other way. In the French army, too, the feeling runs high against the "embusqué," the man who—often unjustly—is supposed to have avoided service. I do not know to what extent the same feeling prevails in our army, but there is certainly an element of it, which will not make for content or quietude.

Another burning question after the war will be wages. We are assured they are going to keep up. Well, we shall see. Certain special rates will, of course, come down at once. And if, in general, wages keep up, it will not, I think, be for very long. Still, times will be good at first for employers and employed. At first—and then!

Some thinkers insist that the war has to an appreciable extent been financed out of savings which would otherwise have been spent on luxury. But the amount thus saved can easily be exaggerated—the luxurious class is not really large, and against their saving must be set the spending by the working classes, out of increased wages, on what in peace years were not necessities of their existence. In other words, the luxurious or investing class has cut off its peace-time fripperies, saved and lent to the Government; the Government has paid the bulk of this money to the working class, who have spent most of it in what to them would be fripperies in time of peace. It may be, it is, all to the good that luxurious tastes should be clipped from the wealthy, and a higher standard of living secured to the workers, but this is rather a matter of distribution and social health than of economics in relation to the financing of the war.

There are those who argue that because the general productive effort of the country during the war has been speeded up to half as much again as that of normal times, by tapping women's labour, by longer hours and general improvement in machinery and industrial ideas, the war will not result in any great economic loss, and that we may with care and effort avoid the coming of bad times after the first boom. The fact remains, and anybody can test it for himself, that there is a growing shortage of practically everything except—they say—cheap jewellery and pianos. I am no economist, but that does seem to indicate that this extra production has not greatly compensated for the enormous application of labour and material resources to the quick-wasting ends of war instead of to the slow-wasting ends of civil life. In other words, a vast amount of productive energy and material is being shot away. Now this, I suppose, would not matter, in fact might be beneficial to trade by increasing demand, if the purchasing power of the public remained what it was before the war. But in all the great countries of the world, even America, the peoples will be faced with taxation which will soak up anything from one-fifth to one-third of their incomes, and, even allowing for a large swelling of those incomes from war savings, so that a great deal of what the State takes with one hand she will return to the investing public with the other, the diminution of purchasing power is bound to make itself increasingly felt. When the reconversion of machinery to civil ends has been completed, the immediate arrears of demand supplied, shipping and rolling-stock replaced, houses built, repairs made good, and so forth, this slow shrinkage of purchasing power in every country will go hand in hand with shrinkage of demand, decline of trade and wages, and unemployment, in a slow process, till they culminate in what one fears may be the worst "times" we have ever known. Whether those "times" will set in one, two, or even six years after the war, is, of course, the question. A certain school of thought insists that this tremendous taxation after the war, and the consequent impoverishment of enterprise and industry, can be avoided, or at all events greatly relieved, by national schemes for the development of the Empire's latent resources; in other words, that the State should even borrow more money to avoid high taxation and pay the interests on existing loans, should acquire native lands, and swiftly develop mineral rights and other potentialities. I hope there may be something in this, but I am a little afraid that the wish is father to the thought, and that the proposition contains an element akin to the attempt to lift oneself up by the hair of one's own head; for I notice that many of its disciples are recruited from those who in old days were opposed to the State development of anything, on the ground that individual energy in free competition was a still greater driving power.

However we may wriggle in our skins and juggle with the chances of the future, I suspect that we shall have to pay the piper. We have without doubt, during the war, been living to a great extent on our capital. Our national income has gone up, out of capital, from twenty-two hundred to about three thousand six hundred millions, and will rapidly shrink to an appropriate figure. Wealth may, I admit, recover much more quickly than deductions from the past would lead us to expect. Under the war's pressure secrets have been discovered, machinery improved, men's energies and knowledge brightened and toned up. The Prime Minister not long ago said: "If you insist on going back to pre-war conditions, then God help this country!" A wise warning. If the country could be got to pull together in an effort to cope with peace as strenuous as our effort to cope with the war has been one would not view the economic future with disquietude. But one is bound to point out that if the war has proved anything it has proved that the British people require a maximum of danger dangled in front of their very noses before they can be roused to any serious effort, and that danger in time of peace has not the poster-like quality of danger in time of war; it does not hit men in the eye, it does not still differences of opinion, and party struggles, by its scarlet insistence. I hope for, but frankly do not see, the coming of an united national effort demanding extra energy, extra organising skill, extra patience, and extra self-sacrifice at a time when the whole nation will feel that it has earned a rest, and when the lid has once more been taken off the political cauldron. I fancy, dismally, that a people and a Press who have become so used to combat and excitement will demand and seek further combat and excitement, and will take out this itch amongst themselves in a fashion even more strenuous than before the war. I am not here concerned to try to cheer or depress for some immediate and excellent result, as we have all got into the habit of doing during the war, but to try to conjure truth out of the darkness of the future. The vast reconstructive process which ought to be, and perhaps is, beginning now will, I think, go ahead with vigour while the war is on, and for some little time after; but I fear it will then split into pro and con, see-saw, and come to something of a standstill.

These, so sketchily set down, are a few of the probable items—credit and debit—in the industrial situation which will await the soldier-workman emerging from the war. A situation agitated, cross-currented, bewildering, but busy, and by no means economically tight at first, slowly becoming less bewildering, gradually growing less and less busy, till it reaches ultimately a bad era of unemployment and social struggle. The soldier-workman will go back, I believe, to two or three years at least of good wages and plentiful work. But when, after that, the pinch begins to come, it will encounter the quicker, more resentful blood of men who in the constant facing of great danger have left behind them all fear of consequences; of men who in the survival of one great dislocation to their lives, have lost the dread of other dislocations. The war will have implanted a curious deep restlessness in the great majority of soldier souls. Can the workmen of the future possibly be as patient and law-abiding as they were before the war, in the face of what seems to them injustice? I don't think so. The enemy will again be Fate—this time in the form of capital, trying to down them; and the victory they were conscious of gaining over Fate in the war will have strengthened and quickened their fibre to another fight, and another conquest. The seeds of revolution are supposed to lie in war. They lie there because war generally brings in the long run economic stress, but also because of the recklessness or "character"—call it what you will—which the habitual facing of danger develops. The self-control and self-respect which military service under war conditions will have brought to the soldier-workman will be an added force in civil life; but it is a fallacy, I think, to suppose, as some do, that it will be a force on the side of established order. It is all a question of allegiance, and the allegiance of the workman in time of peace is not rendered to the State, but to himself and his own class. To the service of that class and the defence of its "rights" this new force will be given. In measuring the possibilities of revolution, the question of class rides paramount. Many hold that the war is breaking down social barriers and establishing comradeship, through hardship and danger shared. For the moment this is true. But whether that new comradeship will stand any great pressure of economic stress after direct regimental relationship between officer and man has ceased and the war is becoming just a painful memory, is to me very doubtful. But suppose that to some extent it does stand, we have still the fact that the control of industry and capital, even as long as ten years after the war, will be mainly in the hands of men who have not fought, of business men spared from service either by age or by their too precious commercial skill. Towards these the soldier-workman will have no tender feelings, no sense of comradeship. On the contrary—for somewhere back of the mind of every workman there is, even during his country's danger, a certain doubt whether all war is not somehow hatched by the aristocrats and plutocrats of one side, or both. Other feelings obscure this instinct during the struggle, but it is never quite lost, and will spring up again the more confirmed for its repression. That we can avoid a straitened and serious time a few years hence I believe impossible. Straitened times dismally divide the classes. The war-investments of the working class may ease things a little, but war-savings will not affect the outlook of the soldier-workman, for he will have no war-savings, except his life, and it is from him that revolution or disorder will come, if it come at all.

Must it come? I think most certainly, unless between now and then means be found of persuading capital and labour that their interests and their troubles are identical, and of overcoming secrecy and suspicion between them. There are many signs already that capital and labour are becoming alive to this necessity. But to talk of unity is an amiable distraction in which we all indulge these days. To find a method by which that talk may be translated into fact within a few years is perhaps more difficult. One does not change human nature; and unless the interests of capital and labour are in reality made one, true co-operation established, and factory conditions transformed on the lines of the welfare system—no talk of unity will prevent capitalist and working man from claiming what seem to them their rights. The labour world is now, and for some time to come will be, at sixes and sevens in matters of leadership and responsibility; and this just when sagacious leadership and loyal following will be most needed. The soldier-workman was already restive under leadership before the war; returned to civil life, he will be far more restive. Yet, without leadership, what hope is there of co-operation with capital; what chance of finding a golden mean of agreement? But even if the problems of leadership are solved, and councils of capitalists and labour leaders established, whose decisions will be followed—one thing is still certain: no half-measures will do; no seeming cordialities with mental reservations; no simulated generosity which spills out on the first test; nothing but genuine friendliness and desire to pull together. Those hard business heads which distrust all sentiment as if it were a poison are the most short-sighted heads in the world. There is a human factor in this affair, as both sides will find to their cost if they neglect it. Extremists must be sent to Coventry, "caste" feeling dropped on the one hand, and suspicion dropped on the other; managers, directors, and labour leaders, all must learn that they are not simply trustees for their shareholders or for labour, but trustees of a national interest which embraces them all—or worse will come of it.

But I am not presumptuous enough to try to teach these cooks how to make their broth, neither would it come within the scope of these speculations, which conclude thus: The soldier-workman, physically unchanged, mentally a little weakened, but more "characterful" and restive, will step out through a demobilisation—heaven send it be swift, even at some risk!—into an industrial world, confused and busy as a beehive, which will hum and throb and flourish for two or three years, and then slowly chill and thin away into, may be, the winter ghost of itself, or at best an autumn hive. There, unless he be convinced, not by words but facts, that his employer is standing side by side with him in true comradeship, facing the deluge, he will be quick to rise, and with his newly-found self-confidence take things into his own hands. Whether, if he does, he will make those things better for himself would be another inquiry altogether.

1917.

[A] Since these words were written one hears of demobilization schemes ready to the last buttons. Let us hope the buttons won't come off.—J. G.

THE CHILDREN'S JEWEL FUND

The mere male novelist who takes pen to write on infants awaits the polished comment: "He knows nothing of the subject—rubbish; pure rubbish!" One must run that risk.

In the report of the National Baby Week it is written:—"Is it worth while to destroy our best manhood now unless we can ensure that there will be happy, healthy citizens to carry on the Empire in the future?" I confess to approaching this subject from the point of view of the infant citizen rather than of the Empire. And I have wondered sometimes if it is worth while to save the babies, seeing the conditions they often have to face as grown men and women. But that, after all, would be to throw up the sponge, which is not the part of a Briton. It is written also:—"After the war a very large increase in the birth-rate may be looked for." For a year or two, perhaps; but the real after-effect of the war will be to decrease the birth-rate in every European country, or I am much mistaken. "No food for cannon, and no extra burdens," will be the cry. And little wonder! This, however, does not affect the question of children actually born or on their way. If not quantity, we can at all events have quality.

I also read an account of the things to be done to keep "baby" alive, which filled me with wonder how any of us old babies managed to survive, and I am afraid that unless we grow up healthy we are not worth the trouble. The fact is: The whole business of babies is an activity to be engaged in with some regard to the baby, or we commit a monstrous injustice, and drag the hands of the world's clock backwards.

How do things stand? Each year in this country about 100,000 babies die before they have come into the world; and out of the 800,000 born, about 90,000 die. Many mothers become permanently damaged in health by evil birth conditions. Many children grow up mentally or physically defective. One in four of the children in our elementary schools are not in a condition to benefit properly by their schooling. What sublime waste! Ten in a hundred of them suffer from malnutrition; thirty in the hundred have defective eyes; eighty in the hundred need dental treatment; twenty odd in the hundred have enlarged tonsils or adenoids. Many, perhaps most, of these deaths and defects are due to the avoidable ignorance, ill-health, mitigable poverty, and other handicaps which dog poor mothers before and after a baby's birth. One doesn't know which to pity most—the mothers or the babies. Fortunately, to help the one is to help the other. In passing I would like to record two sentiments: my strong impression that we ought to follow the example of America and establish Mothers' Pensions; and my strong hope that those who visit the sins of the fathers upon illegitimate children will receive increasingly the contempt they deserve from every decent-minded citizen.

On the general question of improving the health of mothers and babies I would remind readers that there is no great country where effort is half so much needed as here; we are nearly twice as town and slum ridden as any other people; have grown to be further from nature and more feckless about food; we have damper air to breathe, and less sun to disinfect us. In New Zealand, with a climate somewhat similar to ours, the infant mortality rate has, as a result of a widespread educational campaign, been reduced within the last few years to 50 per 1,000 from 110 per 1,000 a few years ago. It is perhaps too sanguine to expect that we, so much more town-ridden, can do as well here, but we ought to be able to make a vast improvement. We have begun to. Since 1904, when this matter was first seriously taken in hand, our infant mortality rate has declined from 145 per 1,000 to 91 per 1,000 in 1916. This reduction has been mainly due to the institution of infant welfare centres and whole-time health visitors. Of centres there are now nearly 1,200. We want 5,000 more. Of visitors there are now hardly 1,500. We want, I am told, 2,000 more. It is estimated that the yearly crop of babies, 700,000, if those of the well-to-do be excepted, can be provided with infant welfare centres and whole-time health visitors by expenditure at the rate of £1 a head per year. The Government, which is benevolently disposed towards the movement, gives half of the annual expenditure; the other half falls on the municipalities. But these 5,000 new infant welfare centres and these extra 2,000 health visitors must be started by voluntary effort and subscription. Once started, the Government and the municipalities will have to keep them up; but unless we start them, the babies will go on dying or growing up diseased. The object of the Jewel Fund, therefore, is to secure the necessary money to get the work into train.

What are these Infant Welfare Centres, and have they really all this magic? They are places where mothers to be, or in being, can come for instruction and help in all that concerns birth and the care of their babies and children up to school age. "Prevention is better than cure," is the motto of these Centres. I went to one of the largest in London. It has about 600 entries in the year. There were perhaps 40 babies and children and perhaps 30 mothers there. About 20 of these mothers were learning sewing or knitting. Five of them were sitting round a nurse who was bathing a three-weeks-old baby. The young mother who can wash a baby to the taste and benefit of the baby by the light of nature must clearly be something of a phenomenon. In a room downstairs were certain little stoics whose health was poor; they were brought there daily to be watched. One was an air-raid baby, the thinnest little critter ever seen; an ashen bit of a thing through which the wind could blow; very silent, and asking "Why?" with its eyes. They showed me a mother who had just lost her first baby. The Centre was rescuing it from a pauper's funeral. I can see her now, coming in and sitting on the edge of a chair; the sudden puckering of her dried-up little face, the tears rolling down. I shall always remember the tone of her voice—"It's my baby." Her husband is "doing time"; and want of food and knowledge while she was "carrying it" caused the baby's death. Several mothers from her street come to the Centre; but, "keeping herself to herself," she never heard of it till too late. In a hundred little ways these Centres give help and instruction. They, and the Health Visitors who go along with them, are doing a great work; but there are many districts all over the country where there are no Centres to come to; no help and instruction to be got, however desperately wanted. Verily this land of ours still goes like Rachel mourning for her children. Disease, hunger, deformity, and death still hound our babes, and most of that hounding is avoidable. We must and shall revolt against the evil lot, which preventible ignorance, ill health, and poverty bring on hundreds of thousands of children.

It is time we had more pride. What right have we to the word "civilised" till we give mothers and children a proper chance? This is but the Alpha of decency, the first step of progress. We are beginning to realise that; but, even now, to make a full effort and make it at once—we have to beg for jewels.

What's a jewel beside a baby's life? What's a toy to the health and happy future of these helpless little folk?

You who wear jewels, with few exceptions, are or will be mothers—you ought to know. To help your own children you would strip yourselves. But the test is the giving for children not one's own. Beneath all flaws, fatuities, and failings, this, I solemnly believe, is the country of the great-hearted. I believe that the women of our race, before all women, have a sense of others. They will not fail the test.

Into the twilight of the world are launched each year these myriads of tiny ships. Under a sky of cloud and stars they grope out to the great waters and the great winds—little sloops of life, on whose voyaging the future hangs. They go forth blind, feeling their way. Mothers, and you who will be mothers, and you who have missed motherhood, give them their chance, bless them with a gem—light their lanterns with your jewels!

1917.

FRANCE, 1916-1917

It was past eleven, and the packet had been steady some time when we went on deck and found her moving slowly in bright moonlight up the haven towards the houses of Le Havre. A night approach to a city by water has the quality of other-worldness. I remember the same sensation twice before: coming in to San Francisco from the East by the steam-ferry, and stealing into Abingdon-on-Thames in a rowing-boat. Le Havre lay, reaching up towards the heights, still and fair, a little mysterious, with many lights which no one seemed using. It was cold, but the air already had a different texture, drier, lighter than the air we had left, and one's heart felt light and a little excited. In the moonlight the piled-up, shuttered houses had colouring like that of flowers at night—pale, subtle, mother-o'-pearl. We moved slowly up beside the quay, heard the first French voices, saw the first French faces, and went down again to sleep.

In the Military Bureau at the station, with what friendly politeness they exchanged our hospital passes for the necessary forms; but it took two officials ten minutes of hard writing! And one thought: Is victory possible with all these forms? It is so throughout France—too many forms, too many people to fill them up. As if France could not trust herself without recording in spidery handwriting exactly where she is, for nobody to look at afterwards. But France could trust herself. A pity!

Our only fellow-traveller was not a soldier, but had that indefinable look of connection with the war wrapped round almost everyone in France. A wide land we passed, fallow under the November sky; houses hidden among the square Normandy court-yards of tall trees; not many people in the fields.

Paris is Paris, was, and ever shall be! Paris is not France. If the Germans had taken Paris they would have occupied the bodily heart, the centre of her circulatory system; but the spirit of France their heavy hands would not have clutched, for it never dwelt there. Paris is hard and hurried; France is not. Paris loves pleasure; France loves life. Paris is a brilliant stranger in her own land. And yet a lot of true Frenchmen and Frenchwomen live there, and many little plots of real French life are cultivated.

At the Gare de Lyon poilus are taking trains for the South. This is our first real sight of them in their tired glory. They look weary and dusty and strong; every face has character, no face looks empty or as if its thought were being done by others. Their laughter is not vulgar or thick. Alongside their faces the English face looks stupid, the English body angular and—neat. They are loaded with queer burdens, bread and bottles bulge their pockets; their blue-grey is prettier than khaki, their round helmets are becoming. Our Tommies, even to our own eyes, seem uniformed, but hardly two out of all this crowd are dressed alike. The French soldier luxuriates in extremes; he can go to his death in white gloves and dandyism—he can glory in unshavenness and patches. The words in extremis seem dear to the French soldier; and, con amore, he passes from one extreme to the other. One of them stands gazing up at the board which gives the hours of starting and the destinations of the trains. His tired face is charming, and has a look that I cannot describe—lost, as it were, to all surroundings; a Welshman or a Highlander, but no pure Englishman, could look like that.

Our carriage has four French officers; they talk neither to us nor to each other; they sleep, sitting well back, hardly moving all night; one of them snores a little, but with a certain politeness. We leave them in the early morning and get down into the windy station at Valence. In pre-war days romance began there when one journeyed. A lovely word, and the gate of the South. Soon after Valence one used to wake and draw aside a corner of the curtain and look at the land in the first level sunlight; a strange land of plains, and far, yellowish hills, a land with a dry, shivering wind over it, and puffs of pink almond blossom. But now Valence was dark, for it was November, and raining. In the waiting-room were three tired soldiers trying to sleep, and one sitting up awake, shyly glad to share our cakes and journals. Then on through the wet morning by the little branch line into Dauphiné. Two officers again and a civilian, in our carriage, are talking in low voices of the war, or in higher voices of lodgings at Valence. One is a commandant, with a handsome paternal old face, broader than the English face, a little more in love with life, and a little more cynical about it, with more depth of colouring in eyes and cheeks and hair. The tone of their voices, talking of the war, is grave and secret. "Les Anglais ne lâcheront pas" are the only words I plainly hear. The younger officer says: "And how would you punish?" The commandant's answer is inaudible, but by the twinkling of his eyes one knows it to be human and sagacious. The train winds on in the windy wet, through foothills and then young mountains, following up a swift-flowing river. The chief trees are bare Lombardy poplars. The chief little town is gathered round a sharp spur, with bare towers on its top. The colour everywhere is a brownish-grey.

We have arrived. A tall, strong young soldier, all white teeth and smiles, hurries our luggage out, a car hurries us up in the rainy wind through the little town, down again across the river, up a long avenue of pines, and we are at our hospital.

Round the long table, at their dinner-hour, what a variety of type among the men! And yet a likeness, a sort of quickness and sensibility, common to them all. A few are a little méfiant of these newcomers, with the méfiance of individual character, not of class distrustfulness, nor of that defensive expressionless we cultivate in England. The French soldier has a touch of the child in him—if we leave out the Parisians; a child who knows more than you do perhaps; a child who has lived many lives before this life; a wise child, who jumps to your moods and shows you his "sore fingers" readily when he feels that you want to see them. He has none of the perverse and grudging attitude towards his own ailments that we English foster. He is perhaps a little inclined to pet them, treating them with an odd mixture of stoic gaiety and gloomy indulgence. It is like all the rest of him; he feels everything so much quicker than we do—he is so much more impressionable. The variety of type is more marked physically than in our country. Here is a tall Savoyard cavalryman, with a maimed hand and a fair moustache brushed up at the ends, big and strong, with grey eyes, and a sort of sage self-reliance; only twenty-six, but might be forty. Here is a real Latin, who was buried by an explosion at Verdun; handsome, with dark hair and a round head, and colour in his cheeks; an ironical critic of everything, a Socialist, a mocker, a fine, strong fellow with a clear brain, who attracts women. Here are two peasants from the Central South, both with bad sciatica, slower in look, with a mournful, rather monkeyish expression in their eyes, as if puzzled by their sufferings. Here is a true Frenchman, a Territorial, from Roanne, riddled with rheumatism, quick and gay, and suffering, touchy and affectionate, not tall, brown-faced, brown-eyed, rather fair, with clean jaw and features, and eyes with a soul in them, looking a little up; forty-eight—the oldest of them all—they call him Grandpère. And here is a printer from Lyon with shell-shock; medium-coloured, short and roundish and neat, full of humanity and high standards and domestic affection, and so polite, with eyes a little like a dog's. And here another with shell-shock and brown-green eyes, from the "invaded countries"; méfiant, truly, this one, but with a heart when you get at it; neat, and brooding, quick as a cat, nervous, and wanting his own way. But they are all so varied. If there are qualities common to all they are impressionability and capacity for affection. This is not the impression left on one by a crowd of Englishmen. Behind the politeness and civilised bearing of the French I used to think there was a little of the tiger. In a sense perhaps there is, but that is not the foundation of their character—far from it! Underneath the tiger, again, there is a man civilised for centuries. Most certainly the politeness of the French is no surface quality, it is a polish welling up from a naturally affectionate heart, a naturally quick apprehension of the moods and feelings of others; it is the outcome of a culture so old that, underneath all differences, it binds together all those types and strains of blood—the Savoyard, and the Southerner, the Latin of the Centre, the man from the North, the Breton, the Gascon, the Basque, the Auvergnat, even to some extent the Norman, and the Parisian—in a sort of warm and bone-deep kinship. They have all, as it were, sat for centuries under a wall with the afternoon sun warming them through and through, as I so often saw the old town gossips sitting of an afternoon. The sun of France has made them alike; a light and happy sun, not too southern, but just southern enough.

And the women of France! If the men are bound in that mysterious kinship, how much more so are the women! What is it in the Frenchwoman which makes her so utterly unique? A daughter in one of Anatole France's books says to her mother: "Tu es pour les bijoux, je suis pour les dessous." The Frenchwoman spiritually is pour les dessous. There is in her a kind of inherited, conservative, clever, dainty capability; no matter where you go in France, or in what class—country or town—you find it. She cannot waste, she cannot spoil, she makes and shows—the best of everything. If I were asked for a concrete illustration of self-respect I should say—the Frenchwoman. It is a particular kind of self-respect, no doubt, very much limited to this world; and perhaps beginning to be a little frayed. We have some Frenchwomen at the hospital, the servants who keep us in running order—the dear cook whom we love not only for her baked meats, proud of her soldier son once a professor, now a sergeant, and she a woman of property, with two houses in the little town; patient, kind, very stubborn about her dishes, which have in them the essential juices and savours which characterise all things really French. She has great sweetness and self-containment in her small, wrinkled, yellowish face; always quietly polite and grave, she bubbles deliciously at any joke, and gives affection sagaciously to those who merit. A jewel, who must be doing something pour la France. And we have Madame Jeanne Camille, mother of two daughters and one son, too young to be a soldier. It was her eldest daughter who wanted to come and scrub in the hospital, but was refused because she was too pretty. And her mother came instead. A woman who did not need to come, and nearly fifty, but strong, as the French are strong, with good red blood, deep colouring, hair still black, and handsome straight features. What a worker! A lover of talk, too, and of a joke when she has time. And Claire, of a languissante temperament, as she says; but who would know it? Eighteen, with a figure abundant as that of a woman of forty, but just beginning to fine down; holding herself as French girls learn to hold themselves so young; and with the pretty eyes of a Southern nymph, clear-brown and understanding, and a little bit wood-wild. Not self-conscious—like the English girl at that age—fond of work and play; with what is called "a good head" on her, and a warm heart. A real woman of France.

Then there is the "farmeress" at the home farm which gives the hospital its milk; a splendid, grey-eyed creature, doing the work of her husband who is at the front, with a little girl and boy rounder and rosier than anything you ever saw; and a small, one-eyed brother-in-law who drinks. My God, he drinks! Any day you go into the town to do hospital commissions you may see the hospital donkey-cart with the charming grey donkey outside the Café de l'Univers or what not, and know that Charles is within. He beguiles our poilus, and they take little beguiling. Wine is too plentiful in France. The sun in the wines of France quickens and cheers the blood in the veins of France. But the gift of wine is abused. One may see a poster which says—with what truth I know not—that drink has cost France more than the Franco-Prussian War. French drunkenness is not so sottish as our beer-and-whiskey-fuddled variety, but it is not pleasant to see, and mars a fair land.

What a fair land! I never before grasped the charm of French colouring; the pinkish-yellow of the pan-tiled roofs, the lavender-grey or dim green of the shutters, the self-respecting shapes and flatness of the houses, unworried by wriggling ornamentation or lines coming up in order that they may go down again; the universal plane trees with their variegated trunks and dancing lightness—nothing more charming than plane trees in winter, their delicate twigs and little brown balls shaking against the clear pale skies, and in summer nothing more green and beautiful than their sun-flecked shade. Each country has its special genius of colouring—best displayed in winter. To characterise such genius by a word or two is hopeless; but one might say the genius of Spain is brown; of Ireland green; of England chalky blue-green; of Egypt shimmering sandstone. For France amethystine feebly expresses the sensation; the blend is subtle, stimulating, rarefied—at all events in the centre and south. Walk into an English village, however beautiful—and many are very beautiful—you will not get the peculiar sharp spiritual sensation which will come on you entering some little French village or town—the sensation one has looking at a picture by Francesca. The blue wood-smoke, the pinkish tiles, the grey shutters, the grey-brown plane trees, the pale blue sky, the yellowish houses, and above all the clean forms and the clear air. I shall never forget one late afternoon rushing home in the car from some commission. The setting sun had just broken through after a misty day, the mountains were illumined with purple and rose-madder, and snow-tipped against the blue sky, a wonderful wistaria blue drifted smoke-like about the valley; and the tall trees—poplars and cypresses—stood like spires. No wonder the French are spirituel, a word so different from our "spiritual," for that they are not; pre-eminently citizens of this world—even the pious French. This is why on the whole they make a better fist of social life than we do, we misty islanders, only half-alive because we set such store by our unrealised moralities. Not one Englishman in ten now really believes that he is going to live again, but his disbelief has not yet reconciled him to making the best of this life, or laid ghosts of the beliefs he has outworn. Clear air and sun, but not so much as to paralyse action, have made in France clearer eyes, clearer brains, and touched souls with a sane cynicism. The French do not despise and neglect the means to ends. They face sexual realities. They know that to live well they must eat well, to eat well must cook well, to cook well must cleanly and cleverly cultivate their soil. May France be warned in time by our dismal fate! May she never lose her love of the land; nor let industrialism absorb her peasantry, and the lure of wealth and the cheap glamour of the towns draw her into their uncharmed circles. We English have rattled deep into a paradise of machines, chimneys, cinemas, and halfpenny papers; have bartered our heritage of health, dignity, and looks for wealth, and badly distributed wealth at that. France was trembling on the verge of the same precipice when the war came; with its death and wind of restlessness the war bids fair to tip her over. Let her hold back with all her might! Her two dangers are drink and the lure of the big towns. No race can preserve sanity and refinement which really gives way to these. She will not fare even as well as we have if she yields; our fibre is coarser and more resistant than hers, nor had we ever so much grace to lose. It is by grace and self-respect that France had her pre-eminence; let these wither, as wither they must in the grip of a sordid and drink-soothed industrialism, and her star will burn out. The life of the peasant is hard; peasants are soon wrinkled and weathered; they are not angels; narrow and over-provident, suspicious, and given to drink, they still have their roots and being in the realities of life, close to nature, and keep a sort of simple dignity and health which great towns destroy. Let France take care of her peasants and her country will take care of itself.

Talking to our poilus we remarked that they have not a good word to throw to their députés—no faith in them. About French politicians I know nothing; but their shoes are unenviable, and will become too tight for them after the war. The poilu has no faith at all now, if he ever had, save faith in his country, so engrained that he lets the life-loving blood of him be spilled out to the last drop, cursing himself and everything for his heroic folly.

We had a young Spaniard of the Foreign Legion in our hospital who had been to Cambridge, and had the "outside" eyes on all things French. In his view je m'en foutism has a hold of the French army. Strange if it had not! Clear, quick brains cannot stand Fate's making ninepins of mankind year after year like this. Fortunately for France, the love of her sons has never been forced; it has grown like grass and simple wild herbs in the heart, alongside the liberty to criticise and blame. The poilu cares for nothing, no, not he! But he is himself a little, unconscious bit of France, and, for oneself, one always cares. State-forced patriotism made this war—a fever-germ which swells the head and causes blindness. A State which teaches patriotism in its schools is going mad! Let no such State be trusted! They who, after the war, would have England and France copy the example of the State-drilled country which opened these flood-gates of death, and teach mad provincialism under the nickname of patriotism to their children, are driving nails into the coffins of their countries. Je m'en foutism is a natural product of three years of war, and better by far than the docile despair to which so many German soldiers have been reduced. We were in Lyon when the Russian Revolution and the German retreat from Bapaume were reported. The town and railway station were full of soldiers. No enthusiasm, no stir of any kind, only the usual tired stoicism. And one thought of what the poilu can be like; of our Christmas dinner-table at the hospital under the green hanging wreaths and the rosy Chinese lanterns, the hum, the chatter, the laughter of free and easy souls in their red hospital jackets. The French are so easily, so incorrigibly gay; the dreary grinding pressure of this war seems horribly cruel applied to such a people, and the heroism with which they have borne its untold miseries is sublime. In our little remote town out there—a town which had been Roman in its time, and still had bits of Roman walls and Roman arches—every family had its fathers, brothers, sons, dead, fighting, in prison, or in hospital. The mothers were wonderful. One old couple, in a ferblanterie shop, who had lost their eldest son and whose other son was at the front, used to try hard not to talk about the war, but sure enough they would come to it at last, each time we saw them, and in a minute the mother would be crying and a silent tear would roll down the old father's face. Then he would point to the map and say: "But look where they are, the Boches! Can we stop? It's impossible. We must go on till we've thrown them out. It is dreadful, but what would you have? Ah! Our son—he was so promising!" And the mother, weeping over the tin-tacks, would make the neatest little parcel of them, murmuring out of her tears: "Il faut que ça finisse; mais la France—il ne faut pas que la France—Nos chers fils auraient été tués pour rien!" Poor souls! I remember another couple up on the hillside. The old wife, dignified as a duchess—if duchesses are dignified—wanting us so badly to come in and sit down that she might the better talk to us of her sons: one dead, and one wounded, and two still at the front, and the youngest not yet old enough. And while we stood there up came the father, an old farmer, with that youngest son. He had not quite the spirit of the old lady, nor her serenity; he thought that men in these days were no better than des bêtes féroces. And in truth his philosophy—of an old tiller of the soil—was as superior to that of emperors and diplomats as his life is superior to theirs. Not very far from that little farm is the spot of all others in that mountain country which most stirs the æsthetic and the speculative strains within one. Lovely and remote, all by itself at the foot of a mountain, in a circle of the hills, an old monastery stands, now used as a farm, with one rose window, like a spider's web, spun delicate in stone tracery. There the old monks had gone to get away from the struggles of the main valley and the surges of the fighting men. There even now were traces of their peaceful life; the fish-ponds and the tillage still kept in cultivation. If they had lived in these days they would have been at the war, fighting or bearing stretchers, like the priests of France, of whom eleven thousand, I am told—untruthfully, I hope—are dead. So the world goes forward—the Kingdom of Heaven comes!

We were in the town the day that the 1918 class received their preliminary summons. Sad were the mothers watching their boys parading the streets, rosetted and singing to show that they had passed and were ready to be food for cannon. Not one of those boys, I dare say, in his heart wanted to go; they have seen too many of their brethren return war-worn, missed too many who will never come back. But they were no less gay about it than those recruits we saw in the spring of 1913, at Argelès in the Pyrenees, singing along and shouting on the day of their enrolment.

There were other reminders to us, and to the little town, of the blood-red line drawn across the map of France. We had in our hospital men from the invaded countries without news of wives and families mured up behind that iron veil. Once in a way a tiny word would get through to them, and anxiety would lift a little from their hearts; for a day or two they would smile. One we had, paralysed in the legs, who would sit doing macramé work and playing chess all day long; every relative he had—wife, father, mother, sisters—all were in the power of the German. As brave a nature as one could see in a year's march, touchingly grateful, touchingly cheerful, but with the saddest eyes I ever saw. There was one little reminder in the town whom we could never help going in to look at whenever we passed the shop whose people had given her refuge. A little girl of eight with the most charming, grave, pale, little, grey-eyed face; there she would sit, playing with her doll, watching the customers. That little refugee at all events was beloved and happy; only I think she thought we would kidnap her one day—we stared at her so hard. She had the quality which gives to certain faces the fascination belonging to rare works of art.

With all this poignant bereavement and long-suffering amongst them it would be odd indeed if the gay and critical French nature did not rebel, and seek some outlet in apathy or bitter criticism. The miracle is that they go on and on holding fast. Easily depressed, and as easily lifted up again, grumble they must and will; but their hearts are not really down to the pitch of their voices; their love of country, which with them is love of self—the deepest of all kinds of patriotism—is too absolute. These two virtues or vices (as you please)—critical faculty and amour propre or vanity, if you prefer it—are in perpetual encounter. The French are at once not at all proud of themselves and very proud. They destroy all things French, themselves included, with their brains and tongues, and exalt the same with their hearts and by their actions. To the reserved English mind, always on the defensive, they seem to give themselves away continually; but he who understands sees it to be all part of that perpetual interplay of opposites which makes up the French character and secures for it in effect a curious vibrating equilibrium. "Intensely alive" is the chief impression one has of the French. They balance between head and heart at top speed in a sort of electric and eternal see-saw. It is this perpetual quick change which gives them, it seems to me, their special grip on actuality; they never fly into the cloud-regions of theories and dreams; their heads have not time before their hearts have intervened, their hearts not time before their heads cry: "Hold!" They apprehend both worlds, but with such rapid alternation that they surrender to neither. Consider how clever and comparatively warm is that cold thing "religion" in France. I remember so well the old curé of our little town coming up to lunch, his interest in the cooking, in the practical matters of our life, and in wider affairs too; his enjoyment of his coffee and cigarette; and the curious suddenness with which something seemed "to come over him"—one could hear his heart saying: "O my people, here am I wasting my time; I must run to you." I saw him in the court-yard talking to one of our poilus, not about his soul, but about his body; stroking his shoulder softly and calling him mon cher fils. Dear old man! Even religion here does not pretend to more than it can achieve—help and consolation to the bewildered and the suffering. It uses forms, smiling a little at them.

The secret of French culture lies in this vibrating balance; from quick marriage of mind and heart, reason and sense, in the French nature, all the clear created forms of French life arise, forms recognised as forms with definite utility attached. Controlled expression is the result of action and reaction. Controlled expression is the essence of culture, because it alone makes a sufficiently clear appeal in a world which is itself the result of the innumerable interplay of complementary or dual laws and forces. French culture is near to the real heart of things, because it has a sort of quick sanity which never loses its way; or, when it does, very rapidly recovers the middle of the road. It has the two capital defects of its virtues. It is too fond of forms and too mistrustful. The French nature is sane and cynical. Well, it's natural! The French lie just halfway between north and south; their blood is too mingled for enthusiasm, and their culture too old.

I never realised how old France was till we went to Arles. In our crowded train poilus were packed, standing in the corridors. One very weary, invited by a high and kindly colonel into our carriage, chatted in his tired voice of how wonderfully the women kept the work going on the farms. "When we get a fortnight's leave," he said, "all goes well, we can do the heavy things the women cannot, and the land is made clean. It wants that fortnight now and then, mon colonel; there is work on farms that women cannot do." And the colonel vehemently nodded his thin face. We alighted in the dark among southern forms and voices, and the little hotel omnibus became enmeshed at once in old, high, very narrow, Italian-seeming streets. It was Sunday next day; sunny, with a clear blue sky. In the square before our hotel a simple crowd round the statue of Mistral chattered or listened to a girl singing excruciating songs; a crowd as old-looking as in Italy or Spain, aged as things only are in the South. We walked up to the Arena. Quite a recent development in the life of Arles, they say, that marvellous Roman building, here cut down, there built up, by Saracen hands. For a thousand years or more before the Romans came Arles flourished and was civilised. What had we mushroom islanders before the Romans came? What had barbaric Prussia? Not even the Romans to look forward to! The age-long life of the South stands for much in modern France, correcting the cruder blood which has poured in these last fifteen hundred years. As one blends wine of very old stock with newer brands, so has France been blended and mellowed. A strange cosmic feeling one had, on the top of the great building in that town older than Rome itself, of the continuity of human life and the futility of human conceit. The provincial vanity of modern States looked pitiful in the clear air above that vast stony proof of age.

In many ways the war has brought us up all standing on the edge of an abyss. When it is over shall we go galloping over the edge, or, reining back, sit awhile in our saddles looking for a better track? We were all on the highway to a hell of material expansion and vulgarity, of cheap immediate profit, and momentary sensation; north and south in our different ways, all "rattling into barbarity." Shall we find our way again into a finer air, where self-respect, not profit, rules, and rare things and durable are made once more?

From Arles we journeyed to Marseilles, to see how the first cosmopolitan town in the world fared in war-time. Here was an amazing spectacle of swarming life. If France has reason to feel the war most of all the great countries, Marseilles must surely feel it less than any other great town; she flourishes in a perfect riot of movement and colour. Here all the tribes are met, save those of Central Europe—Frenchman, Serb, Spaniard, Algerian, Greek, Arab, Khabyle, Russian, Indian, Italian, Englishman, Scotsman, Jew, and Nubian rub shoulders in the thronged streets. The miles of docks are crammed with ships. Food of all sorts abounds. In the bright, dry light all is gay and busy. The most æsthetic, and perhaps most humiliating, sight that a Westerner could see we came on there: two Arab Spahis walking down the main street in their long robe uniforms, white and red, and their white linen bonnets bound with a dark fur and canting slightly backwards. Over six feet high, they moved unhurrying, smoking their cigarettes, turning their necks slowly from side to side like camels of the desert. Their brown, thin, bearded faces wore neither scorn nor interest, only a superb self-containment; but, beside them, every other specimen of the human race seemed cheap and negligible. God knows of what they were thinking—as little probably as the smoke they blew through their chiselled nostrils—but their beauty and grace were unsurpassable. And, visioning our western and northern towns and the little, white, worried abortions they breed, one felt downcast and abashed.

Marseilles swarmed with soldiers; Lyon, Valence, Arles, even the smallest cities swarmed with soldiers, and this at the moment when the Allied offensive was just beginning. If France be nearing the end of her man-power, as some assert, she conceals it so that one would think she was at the beginning.

From Marseilles we went to Lyon. I have heard that town described as lamentably plain; but compared with Manchester or Sheffield it is as heaven to hell. Between its two wide rolling rivers, under a line of heights, it has somewhat the aspect of an enormous commercialised Florence. Perhaps in foggy weather it may be dreary, but the sky was blue and the sun shone, a huge Foire was just opening, and every street bustled in a dignified manner.

The English have always had a vague idea that France is an immoral country. To the eye of a mere visitor France is the most moral of the four Great Powers—France, Russia, England, Germany; has the strongest family life and the most seemly streets. Young men and maidens are never seen walking or lying about, half-embraced, as in puritanical England. Fire is not played with—openly, at least. The slow-fly amorousness of the British working classes evidently does not suit the quicker blood of France. There is just enough of the South in the French to keep demonstration of affection away from daylight. A certain school of French novelist, with high-coloured tales of Parisian life, is responsible for his country's reputation. Whatever the Frenchman about town may be, he seems by no means typical of the many millions of Frenchmen who are not about town. And if Frenchwomen, as I have heard Frenchmen say, are légères, they are the best mothers in the world, and their "lightness" is not vulgarly obtruded. They say many domestic tragedies will be played at the conclusion of the war. If so, they will not be played in France alone; and compared with the tragedies of fidelity played all these dreadful years they will be as black rabbits to brown for numbers. For the truth on morality in France we must go back, I suspect, to that general conclusion about the French character—the swift passage from head to heart and back again, which, prohibiting extremes of puritanism and of licence, preserves a sort of balance.

From this war France will emerge changed, though less changed very likely than any other country. A certain self-sufficiency that was very marked about French life will have sloughed away. I expect an opening of the doors, a toleration of other tastes and standards, a softening of the too narrow definiteness of French opinion.

Even Paris has opened her heart a little since the war; and the heart of Paris is close, hard, impatient of strangers. We noticed in our hospital that whenever we had a Parisian he introduced a different atmosphere, and led us a quiet or noisy dance. We had one whose name was Aimé, whose skin was like a baby's, who talked softly and fast, with little grunts, and before he left was quite the leading personality. We had another, a red-haired young one; when he was away on leave we hardly knew the hospital, it was so orderly. The sons of Paris are a breed apart, just as our Cockneys are. I do not pretend to fathom them; they have the texture and resilience of an indiarubber ball. And the women of Paris! Heaven forfend that I should say I know them! They are a sealed book. Still, even Parisians are less intolerant than in pre-war days of us dull English, perceiving in us, perhaps, a certain unexpected usefulness. And, à propos! One hears it said that in the regions of our British armies certain natives believe we have come to stay. What an intensely comic notion! And what a lurid light it throws on history, on the mistrust engendered between nations, on the cynicism which human conduct has forced deep into human hearts. No! If a British Government could be imagined behaving in such a way, the British population would leave England, become French citizens, and help to turn out the damned intruders!

But we did not encounter anywhere that comic belief. In all this land of France, chockful of those odd creatures, English men and women, we found only a wonderful and touching welcome. Not once during those long months of winter was an unfriendly word spoken in our hearing; not once were we treated with anything but true politeness and cordiality. Poilus and peasants, porters and officials, ladies, doctors, servants, shop-folk, were always considerate, always friendly, always desirous that we should feel at home. The very dogs gave us welcome! A little black half-Pomeranian came uninvited and made his home with us in our hospital; we called him Aristide. But on our walks with him we were liable to meet a posse of children who would exclaim, "Pom-pom! Voilà, Pom-pom!" and lead him away. Before night fell he would be with us again, with a bit of string or ribbon, bitten through, dangling from his collar. His children bored him terribly. We left him in trust to our poilus on that sad afternoon when "Good-bye" must be said, all those friendly hands shaken for the last time, and the friendly faces left. Through the little town the car bore us, away along the valley between the poplar trees with the first flush of spring on their twigs, and the magpies flighting across the road to the river-bank.

The heart of France is deep within her breast; she wears it not upon her sleeve. But France opened her heart for once and let us see the gold.

And so we came forth from France of a rainy day, leaving half our hearts behind us.

1917.

ENGLISHMAN AND RUSSIAN

It has been my conviction for many years that the Russian and the Englishman are as it were the complementary halves of a man. What the Russian lacks the Englishman has; what the Englishman lacks, that has the Russian. The works of Gogol, Turgenev, Dostoievsky, Tolstoi, Tchekov—the amazing direct and truthful revelations of these masters—has let me, I think, into some secrets of the Russian soul, so that the Russians I have met seem rather clearer to me than men and women of other foreign countries. For their construing I have been given what schoolboys call a crib. Only a fool pretends to knowledge—the heart of another is surely a dark forest; but the heart of a Russian seems to me a forest less dark than many, partly because the qualities and defects of a Russian impact so sharply on the perceptions of an Englishman, but partly because those great Russian novelists in whom I have delighted, possess, before all other gifts, so deep a talent for the revelation of truth. In following out this apposition of the Russian and the Englishman, one may well start with that little matter of "truth." The Englishman has what I would call a passion for the forms of truth; his word is his bond—nearly always; he will not tell a lie—not often; honesty, in his idiom, is the best policy. But he has little or no regard for the spirit of truth. Quite unconsciously he revels in self-deception and flies from knowledge of anything which will injure his intention to "make good," as Americans say. He is, before all things, a competitive soul who seeks to win rather than to understand or to "live." And to win, or, shall we say, to maintain to oneself the illusion of winning, one must carefully avoid seeing too much. The Russian is light hearted about the forms of truth, but revels in self-knowledge and frank self-declaration, enjoys unbottoming the abysses of his thoughts and feelings, however gloomy. In Russia time and space have no exact importance, living counts for more than dominating life, emotion is not castrated, feelings are openly indulged in; in Russia there are the extremes of cynicism, and of faith; of intellectual subtlety, and simplicity; truth has quite another significance; manners are different; what we know as "good form" is a meaningless shibboleth. The Russian rushes at life, drinks the cup to the dregs, then frankly admits that it has dregs, and puts up with the disillusionment. The Englishman holds the cup gingerly and sips, determined to make it last his time, not to disturb the dregs, and to die without having reached the bottom.

These are the two poles of that instinctive intention to get out of life all there is in it—which is ever the unconscious philosophy guiding mankind. To the Russian it is vital to realise at all costs the fulness of sensation and reach the limits of comprehension; to the Englishman it is vital to preserve illusion and go on defeating death until death so unexpectedly defeats him.

What this wide distinction comes from I know not, unless from the difference of our climates and geographical circumstances. Russians are the children of vast plains and forests, dry air, and extremes of heat and cold; the English, of the sea, small, uneven hedge-rowed landscapes, mist, and mean temperatures. By an ironical paradox, we English have achieved a real liberty of speech and action, even now denied to Russians, who naturally far surpass us in desire to turn things inside out and see of what they are made. The political arrangements of a country are based on temperament; and a political freedom which suits us, an old people, predisposed to a practical and cautious view of life, is proving difficult, if not impossible, for Russians, a young people, who spend themselves so freely. But what Russia will become, politically speaking, he would be rash who prophesied.

I suppose what Russians most notice and perhaps envy in us is practical common sense, our acquired instinct for what is attainable, and for the best and least elaborate means of attaining it. What we ought to envy in Russians is a sort of unworldliness—not the feeling that this world is the preliminary of another, nothing so commercial; but the natural disposition to live each moment without afterthought, emotionally. Lack of emotional abandonment is our great deficiency. Whether we can ever learn to have more is very doubtful. But our imaginative writings, at all events, have of late been profoundly modified by the Russian novel, that current in literature far more potent than any of those traced out in Georg Brandes' monumental study. Russian writers have brought to imaginative literature a directness in the presentation of vision, a lack of self-consciousness, strange to all Western countries, and particularly strange to us English, who of all people are the most self-conscious. This quality of Russian writers is evidently racial, for even in the most artful of them—Turgenev—it is as apparent as in the least sophisticated. It is part, no doubt, of their natural power of flinging themselves deep into the sea of experience and sensation; of their self-forgetfulness in a passionate search for truth.

In such living Russian writers as I have read, in Kuprin, Gorky, and others, I still see and welcome this peculiar quality of rendering life through—but not veiled by—the author's temperament; so that the effect is almost as if no ink were used. When one says that the Russian novel has already profoundly modified our literature, one does not mean that we have now nearly triumphed over the need for ink, or that our temperaments have become Russian; but that some of us have become infected with the wish to see and record the truth and obliterate that competitive moralising which from time immemorial has been the characteristic bane of English art. In other words, the Russian passion for understanding has tempered a little the English passion for winning. What we admire and look for in Russian literature is its truth and its profound and comprehending tolerance. I am credibly informed that what Russians admire and look for in our literature is its quality of "no nonsense" and its assertive vigour. In a word, they are attracted by that in it which is new to them. I venture to hope that they will not become infected by us in this matter; that nothing will dim in their writers spiritual and intellectual honesty of vision or tinge them with self-consciousness. It is still for us to borrow from Russian literary art, and learn, if we can, to sink ourselves in life and reproduce it without obtrusion of our points of view, except in that subtle way which gives to each creative work its essential individuality. Our boisterousness in art is too self-conscious to be real, and our restraint is only a superficial legacy from Puritanism.

Restraint in life and conduct is another matter altogether. There Russians can learn from us, who are past-masters in control of our feelings. In all matters of conduct, indeed, we are, as it were, much older than the Russians; we were more like them, one imagines, in the days of Elizabeth.

Either similarity, or great dissimilarity, is generally needful for mutual liking. Our soldiers appear to get on very well with Russians. But only exceptional natures in either country could expect to understand each other thoroughly. The two peoples are as the halves of a whole; different as chalk from cheese; can supplement, intermingle, but never replace each other. Both in so different ways are very vital types of mankind, very deep sunk in their own atmospheres and natures, very insulated against all that is not Russian, or is not English; deeply unchangeable and impermeable. It is almost impossible to de-Anglicise an Englishman; as difficult to de-Russianise a Russian.

1916.

AMERICAN AND BRITON

On the mutual understanding of each other by Britons and Americans the future happiness of nations depends more than on any other world cause.

I have never held a whole-hearted brief for the British character. There is a lot of good in it, but much which is repellent. It has a kind of deliberate unattractiveness, setting out on its journey with the words: "Take me or leave me." One may respect a person of this sort, but it is difficult either to know or to like him. I am told that an American officer said recently to a British staff officer in a friendly voice: "So we're going to clean up Brother Boche together!" and the British staff officer replied "Really!" No wonder Americans sometimes say: "I've got no use for those fellows."

The world is consecrate to strangeness and discovery, and the attitude of mind concreted in that "Really!" seems unforgivable, till one remembers that it is manner rather than matter which divides the hearts of American and Briton.

In a huge, still half-developed country, where every kind of national type and habit comes to run a new thread into the rich tapestry of American life and thought, people must find it almost impossible to conceive the life of a little old island where traditions persist generation after generation without anything to break them up; where blood remains undoctored by new strains; demeanour becomes crystallised for lack of contrasts; and manner gets set like a plaster mask. The English manner of to-day, of what are called the classes, is the growth of only a century or so. There was probably nothing at all like it in the days of Elizabeth or even of Charles II. The English manner was still racy when the inhabitants of Virginia, as we are told, sent over to ask that there might be despatched to them some hierarchical assistance for the good of their souls, and were answered: "D—n your souls, grow tobacco!" The English manner of to-day could not even have come into its own when that epitaph of a lady, quoted somewhere by Gilbert Murray, was written: "Bland, passionate, and deeply religious, she was second cousin to the Earl of Leitrim; of such are the Kingdom of Heaven." About that gravestone motto was a certain lack of the self-consciousness which is now the foremost characteristic of the English manner.

But this British self-consciousness is no mere fluffy gaucherie, it is our special form of what Germans would call "Kultur." Behind every manifestation of thought or emotion the Briton retains control of self, and is thinking: "That's all I'll let them see"; even: "That's all I'll let myself feel." This stoicism is good in its refusal to be foundered; bad in that it fosters a narrow outlook; starves emotion, spontaneity, and frank sympathy; destroys grace and what one may describe roughly as the lovable side of personality. The English hardly ever say just what comes into their heads. What we call "good form," the unwritten law which governs certain classes of the Briton, savours of the dull and glacial; but there lurks within it a core of virtue. It has grown up like callous shell round two fine ideals—suppression of the ego lest it trample on the corns of other people, and exaltation of the maxim: "Deeds before words." Good form, like any other religion, starts well with some ethical truth, but soon gets commonised and petrified till we can hardly trace its origin, and watch with surprise its denial and contradiction of the root idea.

Without doubt good form had become a kind of disease in England. A French friend told me how he witnessed in a Swiss Hotel the meeting between an Englishwoman and her son, whom she had not seen for two years; she was greatly affected—by the fact that he had not brought a dinner-jacket. The best manners are no "manners," or at all events no mannerisms; but many Britons who have even attained to this perfect purity are yet not free from the paralytic effects of "good form"; are still self-conscious in the depths of their souls, and never do or say a thing without trying not to show what they are feeling. All this guarantees a certain decency in life; but in intimate intercourse with people of other nations who have not this particular cult of suppression, we English disappoint, and jar, and often irritate. Nations have their differing forms of snobbery. At one time the English all wanted to be second cousins to the Earl of Leitrim, like that lady bland and passionate. Nowadays it is not so simple. The Earl of Leitrim has become etherealised. We no longer care how a fellow is born so long as he behaves as the Earl of Leitrim would have, never makes himself conspicuous or ridiculous, never shows too much what he's really feeling, never talks of what he's going to do, and always "plays the game." The cult is centred in our public schools and universities.

At a very typical and honoured old public school the writer of this essay passed on the whole a happy time; but what a curious life, educationally speaking! We lived rather like young Spartans; and were not encouraged to think, imagine, or see anything that we learned in relation to life at large. It's very difficult to teach boys, because their chief object in life is not to be taught anything, but I should say we were crammed, not taught at all. Living as we did the herd-life of boys with little or no intrusion from our elders, and they men who had been brought up in the same way as ourselves, we were debarred from any real interest in philosophy, history, art, literature and music, or any advancing notions in social life or politics. I speak of the generality, not of the few black swans among us. We were reactionaries almost to a boy. I remember one summer term Gladstone came down to speak to us, and we repaired to the Speech Room with white collars and dark hearts, muttering what we would do to that Grand Old Man if we could have our way. But he contrived to charm us, after all, till we cheered him vociferously. In that queer life we had all sorts of unwritten rules of suppression. You must turn up your trousers; must not go out with your umbrella rolled. Your hat must be worn tilted forward; you must not walk more than two-a-breast till you reached a certain form, nor be enthusiastic about anything, except such a supreme matter as a drive over the pavilion at cricket, or a run the whole length of the ground at football. You must not talk about yourself or your home people, and for any punishment you must assume complete indifference.

I dwell on these trivialities because every year thousands of British boys enter these mills which grind exceeding small, and because these boys constitute in after life the great majority of the official, military, academic, professional, and a considerable proportion of the business classes of Great Britain.

They become the Englishmen who say: "Really!" and they are for the most part the Englishmen who travel and reach America. The great defence I have always heard put up for our public schools is that they form character. As oatmeal is supposed to form bone in the bodies of Scotsmen, so our public schools are supposed to form good, sound moral fibre in British boys. And there is much in this plea. The life does make boys enduring, self-reliant, good-tempered and honourable, but it most carefully endeavours to destroy all original sin of individuality, spontaneity, and engaging freakishness. It implants, moreover, in the great majority of those who have lived it the mental attitude of that swell, who when asked where he went for his hats, replied: "Blank's, of course. Is there another fellow's?"

To know all is to excuse all—to know all about the bringing-up of English public school boys makes one excuse much. The atmosphere and tradition of those places is extraordinarily strong, and persists through all modern changes. Thirty-seven years have gone since I was a new boy, but cross-examining a young nephew who left not long ago, I found almost precisely the same features and conditions. The war, which has changed so much of our social life, will have some, but no very great, effect on this particular institution. The boys still go there from the same kind of homes and preparatory schools and come under the same kind of masters. And the traditional unemotionalism, the cult of a dry and narrow stoicism, is rather fortified than diminished by the times we live in.

Our universities, on the other hand, are now mere ghosts of their old selves. At a certain old college in Oxford, last term, they had only two English students. In the chapel under the Joshua Reynolds window, through which the sun was shining, hung a long "roll of honour," a hundred names and more. In the college garden an open-air hospital was ranged under the old city wall, where we used to climb and go wandering in the early summer mornings after some all-night spree. Down on the river the empty college barges lay void of life. From the top of one of them an aged custodian broke into words: "Ah! Oxford'll never be the same again in my time. Why, who's to teach 'em rowin'? When we do get undergrads again, who's to teach 'em? All the old ones gone, killed, wounded and that. No! Rowin'll never be the same again—not in my time." That was the tragedy of the war for him. Our universities will recover faster than he thinks, and resume the care of our particular "Kultur," and cap the products of our public schools with the Oxford accent and the Oxford manner.

An acute critic tells me that Americans reading such deprecatory words as these by an Englishman about his country's institutions would say that this is precisely an instance of what an American means by the Oxford manner. Americans whose attitude towards their own country is that of a lover to his lady or a child to its mother, cannot—he says—understand how Englishmen can be critical of their own country, and yet love her. Well, the Englishman's attitude to his country is that of a man to himself, and the way he runs her down is but a part of that special English bone-deep self-consciousness. Englishmen (the writer amongst them) love their country as much as the French love France and the Americans America; but she is so much a part of them that to speak well of her is like speaking well of themselves, which they have been brought up to regard as "bad form." When Americans hear Englishmen speaking critically of their own country, let them note it for a sign of complete identification with that country rather than of detachment from it. But on the whole it must be admitted that English universities have a broadening influence on the material which comes to them so set and narrow. They do a little to discover for their children that there are many points of view, and much which needs an open mind in this world. They have not precisely a democratic influence, but taken by themselves they would not be inimical to democracy. And when the war is over they will surely be still broader in philosophy and teaching. Heaven forbid that we should see vanish all that is old, and has, as it were, the virginia-creeper, the wistaria bloom of age upon it; there is a beauty in age and a health in tradition, ill dispensed with. What is hateful in age is its lack of understanding and of sympathy; in a word—its intolerance. Let us hope this wind of change may sweep out and sweeten the old places of our country, sweep away the cobwebs and the dust, our narrow ways of thought, our mannikinisms. But those who hate intolerance dare not be intolerant with the foibles of age; we should rather see them as comic, and gently laugh them out. I pretend to no proper knowledge of the American people; but, though amongst them there are doubtless pockets of fierce prejudice, I have on the whole the impression of a wide and tolerant spirit. To that spirit one would appeal when it comes to passing judgment on the educated Briton. He may be self-sufficient, but he has grit; and at bottom grit is what Americans appreciate more than anything. If the motto of the old Oxford college, "Manners makyth man," were true, one would often be sorry for the Briton. But his manners do not make him; they mar him. His goods are all absent from the shop window; he is not a man of the world in the wider meaning of that expression. And there is, of course, a particularly noxious type of travelling Briton, who does his best, unconsciously, to deflower his country wherever he goes. Selfish, coarse-fibred, loud-voiced—the sort which thanks God he is a Briton—I suppose because nobody else will do it for him.

We live in times when patriotism is exalted above all other virtues, because there happen to lie before the patriotic tremendous chances for the display of courage and self-sacrifice. Patriotism ever has that advantage, as the world is now constituted; but patriotism and provincialism are sisters under the skin, and they who can only see bloom on the plumage of their own kind, who prefer the bad points of their countrymen to the good points of foreigners, merely write themselves down blind of an eye, and panderers to herd feeling. America is advantaged in this matter. She lives so far away from other nations that she might well be excused for thinking herself the only people in the world; but in the many strains of blood which go to make up America there is as yet a natural corrective to the narrower kind of patriotism. America has vast spaces and many varieties of type and climate, and life to her is still a great adventure. Americans have their own form of self-absorption, but seem free as yet from the special competitive self-centrement which has been forced on Britons through long centuries by countless continental rivalries and wars. Insularity was driven into the very bones of our people by the generation-long wars of Napoleon. A distinguished French writer, André Chevrillon, whose book[B] may be commended to any one who wishes to understand British peculiarities, used these words in a recent letter: "You English are so strange to us French, you are so utterly different from any other people in the world." Yes! We are a lonely race. Deep in our hearts, I think, we feel that only the American people could ever really understand us. And being extraordinarily self-conscious, perverse, and proud, we do our best to hide from Americans that we have any such feeling. It would distress the average Briton to confess that he wanted to be understood, had anything so natural as a craving for fellowship or for being liked. We are a weird people, though we seem so commonplace. In looking at photographs of British types among photographs of other European nationalities, one is struck by something which is in no other of those races—exactly as if we had an extra skin; as if the British animal had been tamed longer than the rest. And so he has. His political, social, legal life was fixed long before that of any other Western country. He was old, though not mouldering, before the Mayflower touched American shores and brought there avatars, grave and civilised as ever founded nation. There is something touching and terrifying about our character, about the depth at which it keeps its real yearnings, about the perversity with which it disguises them, and its inability to show its feelings. We are, deep down, under all our lazy mentality, the most combative and competitive race in the world, with the exception, perhaps, of the American. This is at once a spiritual link with America, and yet one of the great barriers to friendship between the two peoples. We are not sure whether we are better men than Americans. Whether we are really better than French, Germans, Russians, Italians, Chinese, or any other race is, of course, more than a question; but those peoples are all so different from us that we are bound, I suppose, secretly to consider ourselves superior. But between Americans and ourselves, under all differences, there is some mysterious deep kinship which causes us to doubt and makes us irritable, as if we were continually being tickled by that question: Now am I really a better man than he? Exactly what proportion of American blood at this time of day is British, I know not; but enough to make us definitely cousins—always an awkward relationship. We see in Americans a sort of image of ourselves; feel near enough, yet far enough, to criticise and carp at the points of difference. It is as though a man went out and encountered, in the street, what he thought for the moment was himself, and, wounded in his amour propre, instantly began to disparage the appearance of that fellow. Probably community of language rather than of blood accounts for our sense of kinship, for a common means of expression cannot but mould thought and feeling into some kind of unity. One can hardly overrate the intimacy which a common literature brings. The lives of great Americans, Washington and Franklin, Lincoln and Lee and Grant, are unsealed for us, just as to Americans are the lives of Marlborough and Nelson, Pitt and Gladstone and Gordon. Longfellow and Whittier and Whitman can be read by the British child as simply as Burns and Shelley and Keats. Emerson and William James are no more difficult to us than Darwin and Spencer to Americans. Without an effort we rejoice in Hawthorne and Mark Twain, Henry James and Howells, as Americans can in Dickens and Thackeray, Meredith and Thomas Hardy. And, more than all, Americans own with ourselves all literature in the English tongue before the Mayflower sailed; Chaucer and Spenser and Shakespeare, Raleigh, Ben Jonson, and the authors of the English Bible Version are their spiritual ancestors as much as ever they are ours. The tie of language is all-powerful—for language is the food formative of minds. A volume could be written on the formation of character by literary humour alone. The American and Briton, especially the British townsman, have a kind of bone-deep defiance of Fate, a readiness for anything which may turn up, a dry, wry smile under the blackest sky, and an individual way of looking at things which nothing can shake. Americans and Britons both, we must and will think for ourselves, and know why we do a thing before we do it. We have that ingrained respect for the individual conscience which is at the bottom of all free institutions. Some years before the war an intelligent and cultivated Austrian, who had lived long in England, was asked for his opinion of the British. "In many ways," he said, "I think you are inferior to us; but one great thing I have noticed about you which we have not. You think and act and speak for yourselves." If he had passed those years in America instead of in England he must needs have pronounced the same judgment of Americans. Free speech, of course, like every form of freedom, goes in danger of its life in war-time. The other day, in Russia, an Englishman came on a street meeting shortly after the first revolution had begun. An extremist was addressing the gathering and telling them that they were fools to go on fighting, that they ought to refuse and go home, and so forth. The crowd grew angry, and some soldiers were for making a rush at him; but the chairman, a big, burly peasant, stopped them with these words: "Brothers, you know that our country is now a country of free speech. We must listen to this man, we must let him say anything he will. But, brothers, when he's finished, we'll bash his head in!"

I cannot assert that either Britons or Americans are incapable in times like these of a similar interpretation of "free speech." Things have been done in our country, and will be done in America, which should make us blush. But so strong is the free instinct in both countries that some vestiges of it will survive even this war, for democracy is a sham unless it means the preservation and development of this instinct of thinking for oneself throughout a people. "Government of the people by the people for the people" means nothing unless individuals keep their consciences unfettered and think freely. Accustom people to be nose-led and spoon-fed, and democracy is a mere pretence. The measure of democracy is the measure of the freedom and sense of individual responsibility in its humblest citizens. And democracy—I say it with solemnity—has yet to prove itself.

A scientist, Dr. Spurrell, in a recent book, "Man and his Forerunners," diagnoses the growth of civilisations somewhat as follows: A civilisation begins with the enslavement by some hardy race of a tame race living a tame life in more congenial natural surroundings. It is built up on slavery, and attains its maximum vitality in conditions little removed therefrom. Then, as individual freedom gradually grows, disorganisation sets in and the civilisation slowly dissolves away in anarchy. Dr. Spurrell does not dogmatise about our present civilisation, but suggests that it will probably follow the civilisations of the past into dissolution. I am not convinced of that, because of certain factors new to the history of man. Recent discoveries are unifying the world; such old isolated swoops of race on race are not now possible. In our great industrial States, it is true, a new form of slavery has arisen, but not of man by man, rather of man by machines. Moreover, all past civilisations have been more or less Southern, and subject to the sapping influence of the sun. Modern civilisation is essentially Northern. The individualism, however, which, according to Dr. Spurrell, dissolved the Empires of the past, exists already, in a marked degree, in every modern State; and the problem before us is to discover how democracy and liberty of the subject can be made into enduring props rather than dissolvents. It is the problem of making democracy genuine. And certainly, if that cannot be achieved and perpetuated, there is nothing to prevent democracy drifting into anarchism and dissolving modern States, till they are the prey of pouncing dictators, or of States not so far gone in dissolution. What, for instance, will happen to Russia if she does not succeed in making her democracy genuine? A Russia which remains anarchic must very quickly become the prey of her neighbours on West and East.

Ever since the substantial introduction of democracy nearly a century and a half ago with the American War of Independence, Western civilisation has been living on two planes or levels—the autocratic plane, with which is bound up the idea of nationalism, and the democratic, to which has become conjoined the idea of internationalism. Not only little wars, but great wars such as this, come because of inequality in growth, dissimilarity of political institutions between States; because this State or that is basing its life on different principles from its neighbours. The decentralisation, delays, critical temper, and importance of home affairs prevalent in democratic countries make them at once slower, weaker, less apt to strike, and less prepared to strike than countries where bureaucratic brains subject to no real popular check devise world policies which can be thrust, prepared to the last button, on the world at a moment's notice. The free and critical spirit in America, France, and Britain has kept our democracies comparatively unprepared for anything save their own affairs.

We fall into glib usage of words like democracy and make fetiches of them without due understanding. Democracy is inferior to autocracy from the aggressively national point of view; it is not necessarily superior to autocracy as a guarantee of general well-being; it may even turn out to be inferior unless we can improve it. But democracy is the rising tide; it may be dammed or delayed, but cannot be stopped. It seems to be a law in human nature that where, in any corporate society, the idea of self-government sets foot it refuses to take that foot up again. State after State, copying the American example, has adopted the democratic principle; the world's face is that way set. And civilisation is now so of a pattern that the Western world may be looked on as one State and the process of change therein from autocracy to democracy regarded as though it were taking place in a single old-time country such as Greece or Rome. If throughout Western civilisation we can secure the single democratic principle of government, its single level of State morality in thought and action, we shall be well on our way to unanimity throughout the world; for even in China and Japan the democratic virus is at work. It is my belief that only in a world thus uniform, and freed from the danger of pounce by autocracies, have States any chance to develop the individual conscience to a point which shall make democracy proof against anarchy and themselves proof against dissolution; and only in such a world can a League of Nations to enforce peace succeed.

But even if we do secure a single plane for Western civilisation and ultimately for the world, there will be but slow and difficult progress in the lot of mankind. And unless we secure it, there will be only a march backwards.

For this advance to a uniform civilisation the solidarity of the English-speaking races is vital. Without that there will be no bottom on which to build.

The ancestors of the American people sought a new country because they had in them a reverence for the individual conscience; they came from Britain, the first large State in the Christian era to build up the idea of political freedom. The instincts and ideals of our two races have ever been the same. That great and lovable people, the French, with their clear thought and expression, and their quick blood, have expressed those ideals more vividly than either of us. But the phlegmatic and the dry tenacity of our English and American temperaments has ever made our countries the most settled and safe homes of the individual conscience, and of its children—Democracy, Freedom and Internationalism. Whatever their faults—and their offences cry aloud to such poor heaven as remains of chivalry and mercy—the Germans are in many ways a great race, but they possess two qualities dangerous to the individual conscience—unquestioning obedience and exaltation. When they embrace the democratic idea they may surpass us all in its logical development, but the individual conscience will still not be at ease with them. We must look to our two countries to guarantee its strength and activity, and if we English-speaking races quarrel and become disunited, civilisation will split up again and go its way to ruin. We are the ballast of the new order.

I do not believe in formal alliances or in grouping nations to exclude and keep down other nations. Friendships between countries should have the only true reality of common sentiment, and be animated by desire for the general welfare of mankind. We need no formal bonds, but we have a sacred charge in common, to let no petty matters, differences of manner, or divergencies of material interest, destroy our spiritual agreement. Our pasts, our geographical positions, our temperaments make us, beyond all other races, the hope and trustees of mankind's advance along the only line now open—democratic internationalism. It is childish to claim for Americans or Britons virtues beyond those of other nations, or to believe in the superiority of one national culture to another; they are different, that is all. It is by accident that we find ourselves in this position of guardianship to the main line of human development; no need to pat ourselves on the back about it. But we are at a great and critical moment in the world's history—how critical none of us alive will ever realise. The civilisation slowly built since the fall of Rome has either to break up and dissolve into jagged and isolated fragments through a century of wars; or, unified and reanimated by a single idea, to move forward on one plane and attain greater height and breadth.

Under the pressure of this war there is, beneath the lip-service we pay to democracy, a disposition to lose faith in it because of its undoubted weakness and inconvenience in a struggle with States autocratically governed; there is even a sort of secret reaction to autocracy. On those lines there is no way out of a future of bitter rivalries, chicanery and wars, and the probable total failure of our civilisation. The only cure which I can see lies in democratising the whole world and removing the present weaknesses and shams of democracy by education of the individual conscience in every country. Good-bye to that chance if Americans and Britons fall foul of each other, refuse to pool their thoughts and hopes, and to keep the general welfare of mankind in view. They have got to stand together, not in aggressive and jealous policies, but in defence and championship of the self-helpful, self-governing, "live and let live" philosophy of life.

The house of the future is always dark. There are few corner-stones to be discerned in the temple of our fate. But of these few one is the brotherhood and bond of the English-speaking races, not for narrow purposes, but that mankind may yet see faith and good-will enshrined, yet breathe a sweeter air, and know a life where Beauty passes, with the sun on her wings.

We want in the lives of men a "Song of Honour," as in Ralph Hodgson's poem:

"The song of men all sorts and kinds,
As many tempers, moods and minds
As leaves are on a tree,
As many faiths and castes and creeds,
As many human bloods and breeds,
As in the world may be."

In the making of that song the English-speaking races will assuredly unite. What made this world we know not; the principle of life is inscrutable and will for ever be; but we know that Earth is yet on the up-grade of existence, the mountain-top of man's life not reached, that many centuries of growth are yet in front of us before Nature begins to chill this planet till it swims, at last, another moon, in space. In the climb to that mountain-top of a happy life for mankind our two great nations are as guides who go before, roped together in perilous ascent. On their nerve, loyalty, and wisdom the adventure now hangs. What American or British knife will sever the rope?

He who ever gives a thought to the life of man at large, to his miseries and disappointments, to the waste and cruelty of existence, will remember that if American or Briton fail himself, or fail the other, there can but be for us both, and for all other peoples, a hideous slip, a swift and fearful fall into an abyss, whence all shall be to begin over again.

We shall not fail—neither ourselves, nor each other. Our comradeship will endure.

1917.

[B] "England and the War." Hodder & Stoughton.

ANGLO-AMERICAN DRAMA AND ITS FUTURE[C]

There is a maxim particularly suitable to those who follow any art: "Don't talk about what you do!" And yet, once in a way, one must clear the mind and put into words what lies at the back of endeavour.

What, then, is lying at the back of any growth or development there may have been of late in drama?

In my belief, simply an outcrop of sincerity—of fidelity to mood, to impression, to self. A man here and there has turned up who has imagined something true to what he has really seen and felt, and has projected it across the foot-lights in such a way as to make other people feel it. This is all that has happened lately on our stage. And if it be growth, it will not be growth in quantity, since there is nothing like sincerity for closing the doors of theatres. For, just consider what sincerity excludes: All care for balance at the author's bank—even when there is no balance; all habit of consulting the expression on the public's face; all confectioning of French plays; all the convenient practice of adding up your plots on the principle that two and two make five. These it excludes. It includes: Nothing because it pays; nothing because it will make a sensation; no situations faked; no characters falsified; no fireworks; only something imagined and put down in a passion of sincerity. What plays, you may say, are left? Well, that was the development in our drama before this war began. The war arrested it, as it arrested every movement of the day in civil life. But whether in war or peace, the principles which underlie art remain the same and are always worth consideration.

Sincerity in the theatre and commercial success are not necessarily, but they are generally, opposed. It is more or less a happy accident when, they coincide. This grim truth cannot be blinked. Not till the heavens fall will the majority of the public demand sincerity. And all that they who care for sincerity can hope for is that the supply of sincere drama will gradually increase the demand for it—gradually lessen the majority which has no use for that disturbing quality. The burden of this struggle is on the shoulders of the dramatists. It is useless and unworthy for them to complain that the public will not stand sincerity, that they cannot get sincere plays acted, and so forth. If they have not the backbone to produce what they feel they ought to produce, without regard to what the public wants, then good-bye to progress of any kind. If they are of the crew who cannot see any good in a fight unless they know it is going to end in victory; if they expect the millennium with every spring—they will advance nothing. Their job is to set their teeth, do their work in their own way, without thinking much about result, and not at all about reward, except from their own consciences. Those who want sincerity will always be the few, but they may well be more numerous than now; and to increase their number is worth a struggle. That struggle was the much-sneered-at, much-talked-of so-called "new" movement in our British drama.

Now it was the fashion to dub this new drama the "serious" drama; the label was unfortunate, and not particularly true. If Rabelais or Robert Burns appeared again in mortal form and took to writing plays, they would be "new" dramatists with a vengeance—as new as ever Ibsen was, and assuredly they would be sincere. But could they well be called "serious"? Can we call Synge, or St. John Hankin, or Shaw, or Barrie serious? Hardly! Yet they are all of this new movement in their very different ways, because they are sincere. The word "serious," in fact, has too narrow a significance and admits a deal of pompous stuff which is not sincere. While the word "sincere" certainly does not characterise all that is popularly included under the term "new drama," it as certainly does characterise (if taken in its true sense of fidelity to self) all that is really new in it, and excludes no mood, no temperament, no form of expression which can pass the test of ringing true. Look, for example, at the work of those two whom we could so ill spare—Synge and St. John Hankin. They were as far apart as dramatists well could be, except that each had found a special medium—the one a kind of lyric satire, the other a neat, individual sort of comedy—which seemed exactly to express his spirit. Both forms were in a sense artificial, but both were quite sincere; for through them each of these two dramatists, so utterly dissimilar, shaped forth the essence of his broodings and visions of life, with all their flavour and individual limitations. And that is all one means by—all one asks of—sincerity.

Then why make such a fuss about it?

Because it is rare, and an implicit quality of any true work of art, realistic or romantic.

Art is not art unless it is made out of an artist's genuine feeling and vision, not out of what he has been told he ought to feel and see. For art exists not to confirm people in their tastes and prejudices, not to show them what they have seen before, but to present them with a new vision of life. And if drama be an art (which the great public denies daily, but a few of us still believe), it must reasonably be expected to present life as each dramatist sees it, and not to express things because they pander to popular prejudice, or are sensational, or because they pay.

If you want further evidence that the new dramatic movement is marked out by its struggle for sincerity, and by that alone, examine a little the various half-overt oppositions with which it meets.

Why is the commercial manager against it?

Because it is quite naturally his business to cater for the great public; and, as before said, the majority of the public does not, never will, want sincerity; it is too disturbing. The commercial manager will answer: "The great public does not dislike sincerity, it only dislikes dullness." Well! Dullness is not an absolute, but a very relative term—a term likely to have a different meaning for a man who knows something about life and art from that which it has for a man who knows less. And one may remark that if the great public's standard of what is really "amusing" is the true one, it is queer that the plays which tickle the great public hardly ever last a decade, while the plays which do not tickle them occasionally last for centuries. The "dullest" plays, one might say roughly, are those which last the longest. Witness Euripides!

Why are so many actor-managers against the new drama?

Because their hearts are quite naturally set on such insincere distortions of values as are necessary to a constant succession of "big parts" for themselves. Sincerity does not necessarily exclude heroic characters, but it does exclude those mock heroics which actor-managers have been known to prefer—not to real heroics, perhaps, but to simple and sound studies of character.

Why is the Censorship against it?

Because censorship is quite naturally the guardian of the ordinary prejudices of sentiment and taste, and quaintly innocent of knowledge that in any art fidelity of treatment is essential to a theme. Indeed, I am sure that this peculiar office would regard it as fantastic for a poor devil of an artist to want to be faithful or sincere. The demand would appear pedantic and extravagant.

Some say that the critics are against the new drama. That is not in the main true. The inclination of most critics is to welcome anything with a flavour of its own; it would be odd indeed if it were not so—they get so much of the other food! They are, in general, friends to sincerity. But the trouble with the critic is rather the fixed idea. He has to print his opinion of an author's work, while other men have only to think it; and when it comes to receiving a fresh impression of the same author, his already recorded words are liable to act on him rather as the eyes of a snake act on a rabbit. Indeed, it must be very awkward, when you have definitely labelled an author this, or that, to find from his next piece of work that he is the other as well! The critic who can make blank his soul of all that he has said before may indeed exist—in Paradise!

Why is the greater public against the new drama?

By the greater public I in no sense mean the public who don't keep motor cars—the greater public comes from the West-end as much as ever it comes from the East-end. Its opposition to the "new drama" is neither covert, doubtful, nor conscious of itself. The greater public is like an aged friend of mine, who, if you put into his hands anything but Sherlock Holmes, or The Waverley Novels, says: "Oh!

that dreadful book!" His taste is excellent, only he does feel that an operation should be performed on all dramatists and novelists by which they should be rendered incapable of producing anything but what my aged friend is used to. The greater public, in fact, is either a too well-dined organism which wishes to digest its dinner, or a too hard-worked organism longing for a pleasant dream. I sympathise with the greater public!...

A friend once said to me: "Champagne has killed the drama." It was half a truth. Champagne is an excellent thing, and must not be disturbed. Plays should not have anything in them which can excite the mind. They should be of a quality to just remove the fumes by eleven o'clock and make ready the organism for those suppers which were eaten before the war. Another friend once said to me: "It is the rush and hurry and strenuousness of modern life which is scotching the drama." Again, it was half a truth. Why should not the hard-worked man have his pleasant dream, his detective story, his good laugh? The pity is that sincere drama would often provide as agreeable dreams for the hard-worked man as some of those reveries in which he now indulges, if only he would try it once or twice. That is the trouble—to get him to give it a chance.

The greater public will by preference take the lowest article in art offered to it. An awkward remark, and unfortunately true. But if a better article be substituted, the greater public very soon enjoys it every bit as much as the article replaced, and so on—up to a point which we need not fear we shall ever reach. Not that sincere dramatists are consciously trying to supply the public with a better article. A man could not write anything sincere with the elevation of the public as incentive. If he tried, he would be as lost as ever were the Pharisees making broad their phylacteries. He can only express himself sincerely by not considering the public at all. People often say that this is "cant," but it really isn't. There does exist a type of mind which cannot express itself in accordance with what it imagines is required; can only express itself for itself, and take the usually unpleasant consequences. This is, indeed, but an elementary truth, which since the beginning of the world has lain at the bottom of all real artistic achievement. It is not cant to say that the only things vital in drama, as in every art, are achieved when the maker has fixed his soul on the making of a thing which shall seem fine to himself. It is the only standard; all the others—success, money, even the pleasure and benefit of other people—lead to confusion in the artist's spirit, and to the making of dust castles. To please your best self is the only way of being sincere. Most weavers of drama, of course, are perfectly sincere when they start out to ply their shuttles; but how many persevere in that mood to the end of their plays, in defiance of outside consideration? Here—says one to himself—it will be too strong meat; there it will not be sufficiently convincing; this natural length will be too short, that end too appalling; in such and such a shape I shall never get my play taken; I must write that part up and tone this character down. And when it is all done, effectively, falsely—what is there? A prodigious run, perhaps. But—the grave of all which makes the life of an artist worth the living. Well! well! We who believe this will never get too many others to believe it! Those heavens will not fall; theatre doors will remain open; the heavy diners will digest, and the over-driven man will dream. And yet, with each sincere thing made—even if only fit for reposing within a drawer—its maker is stronger, and will some day, perhaps, make that which need not lie covered away, but reach out from him to other men.

It is a wide word—sincerity. "A Midsummer Night's Dream" is no less sincere than "Hamlet," "The Mikado" as faithful to its mood of satiric frolicking as Ibsen's "Ghosts" to its mood of moral horror. Sincerity bars out no themes; it only demands that the dramatist's moods and visions should be intense enough to keep him absorbed; that he should have something to say so engrossing to himself that he has no need to stray here and there and gather purple plums to eke out what was intended to be an apple tart. Here is the heart of the matter: You cannot get sincere drama out of those who do not see and feel with sufficient fervour; and you cannot get good sincere drama out of those who will not hoe their rows to the very end. There is no faking and no scamping to the good in art. You may turn out the machine-made article very natty, but for the real hand-made thing you must have toiled in the sweat of your brow. In Britain it is a little difficult to persuade people that the writing of plays and novels is work. To many it remains one of those inventions of a certain potentate for idle hands to do. To some persons in high life, and addicted to field sports, it is still a species of licensed buffoonery, to be regulated by a sort of circus-master with a whip in one hand and a gingerbread nut in the other. By the truly simple soul it is thus summed up: "Work! Why, 'e sits writin' all day." To some, both green and young, it shines as a vocation entirely glorious and exhilarating. If one may humbly believe the evidence of his own senses, it is not any of these, but a patient calling, glamorous now and then, but with fifty minutes of hard labour and yearning to every ten of satisfaction. Not a pursuit, maybe, which one would change, but then, what man with a profession flies to others that he knows not of?

Novelists, it is true, even if they have not been taken too seriously by the people of these islands, have for a long time past respected themselves, but the calling of a dramatist till quite of late has been but an invertebrate and spiritless concern. Pruned and prismed by the censor, exploited by the actor, dragooned and slashed by the manager, ignored by the public, who never even bothered to inquire the names of those who supplied it with digestives—it was a slave's job. Thanks to a little sincerity it is not now a slave's job, and will not again, I think, become one.

From time to time in that vehicle of improvisation, that modern fairy tale—our daily paper—we read words such as these: "What has become of the boasted renascence of our stage?" or: "So much for all the trumpeting about the new drama!" When we come across such words, we remember that it is only natural for journals to say to-day the opposite of what they said yesterday. For they have to suit all tastes and preserve a decent equilibrium!

There is a new safeguard of the self-respecting dramatist which no amount of improvising for or against will explain away. Plays are now not merely acted, they are published and read, and will be read more and more. This does not mean, as some say, that they are being written for the study—they were never being written more deliberately, more carefully, for the stage. It does mean that they are tending more and more to comply with fidelity to theme, fidelity to self; and therefore are more and more able to bear the scrutiny of cold daylight. And for the first time, perhaps, since the days of Shakespeare there are dramatists in this country, not a few, faithful to themselves.

Now, all this is not merely fortuitous. For, however abhorrent such a notion may be to those yet wedded to Victorian ideals, we were, even before the war, undoubtedly passing through great changes in our philosophy of life. Just as a plant keeps on conforming to its environment, so our beliefs and ideals are conforming to our new social conditions and discoveries. There is in the air a revolt against prejudice, and a feeling that things must be re-tested. The spirit which, dwelling in pleasant places, would never re-test anything is now looked on askance. Even on our stage we are not enamoured of it. It is not the artist's business (be he dramatist or other) to preach. Admitted! His business is to portray; but portray truly he cannot if he has any of that glib doctrinaire spirit, devoid of the insight which comes from instinctive sympathy. He must look at life, not at a mirage of life compounded of authority, tradition, comfort, habit. The sincere artist, by the very nature of him, is bound to be curious and perceptive, with an instinctive craving to identify himself with the experience of others. This is his value, whether he express it in comedy, epic, satire, or tragedy. Sincerity distrusts tradition, authority, comfort, habit; cannot breathe the air of prejudice, and cannot stand the cruelties which arise from it. So it comes about that the new drama's spirit is essentially, inevitably human and—humane, essentially distasteful to many professing followers of the Great Humanitarian, who, if they were but sincere, would see that they secretly abhor His teachings and in practice continually invert them.

It is a fine age we live in—this age of a developing social conscience, and worthy of a fine and great art. But, though no art is fine unless it has sincerity, no amount of sincere intention will serve unless the expression of it be well-nigh perfect. An author is judged, not by intention but by achievement; and criticism is innately inclined to remark first on the peccadillo points of a person, a poem, or a play. If there be a scar on the forehead, a few false quantities, or weak endings, if there is an absence in the third act of some one who appeared in the first—it is always much simpler to complain of this than to feel or describe the essence of the whole. But this very pettiness in our criticism is, fortunately, a sort of safeguard. The French writer Buffon said: "Bien écrire, c'est tout; car bien écrire c'est bien sentir, bien penser, et bien dire." ... Let the artist then, by all means, make his work impeccable, clothe his ideas, feelings, visions, in just such garments as can withstand the winds of criticism. He himself must be his cruellest critic. Before cutting his cloth let him very carefully determine the precise thickness, shape, and colour best suited to the condition of his temperature. For there are still playwrights who, working in the full blast of an affaire between a poet and the wife of a stockbroker, will murmur to themselves: "Now for a little lyricism!" and drop into it. Or when the strong, silent stockbroker has brought his wife once more to heel: "Now for the moral!" and gives it us. Or when things are getting a little too intense: "Now for humour and variety!" and bring in the curate. This kind of tartan kilt is very pleasant on its native heath of London; but—hardly the garment of good writing. Good writing is only the perfect clothing of mood—the just right form. Shakespeare's form, you will say, was extraordinarily loose, wide, plastic; but then his spirit was ever changing its mood—a true chameleon. And as to the form of Mr. Shaw—who was once compared with Shakespeare—why! there is none. And yet, what form could so perfectly express Mr. Shaw's glorious crusade against stupidity, his wonderfully sincere and lifelong mood of sticking pins into a pig!

We are told, ad nauseam, that the stage has laws of its own, to which all dramatists must bow. Quite true! The stage has the highly technical laws of its physical conditions, which cannot be neglected. But even when they are all properly attended to, it is only behind the elbow of one who feels strongly and tries to express sincerely that right expression stands. The imaginative mood, coming who knows when, staying none too long, is a mistress who deserves, and certainly expects, fidelity. True to her while she is there, do not, when she is not there, insult her by looking in every face and thinking it will serve! These are laws of sincerity which not even a past-master in the laws of the stage can afford to neglect. Anything is better than resorting to moral sentiments and solutions because they are current coin, or to decoration because it is "the thing." And—as to humour: though nothing is more precious than the genuine topsy-turvy feeling, nothing is more pitifully unhumorous than the dragged-in epigram or dismal knockabout, which has no connection with the persons or philosophy of the play.

I suppose it is easy to think oneself sincere; it is certainly difficult to be that same. Imagine the smile, and the blue pencil, of the Spirit of Sincerity if we could appoint him Censor. I would not lift my pen against that Censorship though he excised—as perhaps he might—the half of my work. Sometimes one has a glimpse of his ironic face and his swift fingers, busy with those darkening pages. Once I dreamed about him. It was while a certain Commission was sitting on the British Censorship, which still so admirably guards Insincerity, and he was giving evidence before them. This, I remember, was what he said:

"You wish to learn of me what is sincerity? Look into yourselves, for what lies deepest within you. Each living thing varies from every other living thing, and never twice are there quite the same set of premises from which to draw conclusion. Give up asking of any but yourselves for the whereabouts of truth; and if some one says that he can tell you where it is, don't believe him; he might as well lay a trail of sand and think it will stay there for ever." He stopped, and I could see him looking to judge what impression he had made upon the Commission. But those gentlemen behaved as if they had not heard him. The Spirit of Sincerity coughed. "By Jove, gentlemen," he said, "it's clear you don't care what impression you make on me. Evidently it is for me to learn sincerity from you!"

There was once a gentleman, lately appointed to assist in the control of the exuberance of plays, who stated in public print that there had been no plays of any value written since 1885, entirely denying that this new drama was any better than the old drama, cut to the pattern of Scribe and Sardou. Certainly, novelty is not necessarily improvement. Comparison must be left to history. But it is just as well to remember that we are not born connoisseurs of plays. Without trying the new we shall not know if it is better than the old. To appreciate even drama at its true value, a man must be educated just a little. When I first went to the National Gallery in London I was struck dumb with love of Landseer's stags and a Greuze damsel with her cheek glued to her own shoulder, and became voluble from admiration of the large Turner and the large Claude hung together in that perpetual prize-fight! At a second visit I discovered Sir Joshua's "Countess of Albemarle" and old Crome's "Mousehold Heath," and did not care quite so much for Landseer's stags. And again and again I went, and each time saw a little differently, a little clearer, until at last my time was spent before Titian's "Bacchus and Ariadne," Botticelli's "Portrait of a Young Man," the Francescas, Da Messina's little "Crucifixion," the Uccello battle picture (that great test of education), the Velasquez (?) "Admiral," Hogarth's "Five Servants," and the immortal "Death of Procris." Admiration for stags and maidens—where was it?

This analogy of pictures does not pretend that our "new drama" is as far in front of the old as the "Death of Procris" is in front of Landseer's stags. Alas, no! It merely suggests that taste is encouraged by an open mind, and is a matter of gradual education.

To every man his sincere opinion! But before we form opinions, let us all walk a little through our National Gallery of drama, with inquiring eye and open mind, to see and know for ourselves. For, to know, a man cannot begin too young, cannot leave off too old. And always he must have a mind which feels it will never know enough. In this way alone he will, perhaps, know something before he dies.

And even if he require of the drama only buffoonery, or a digestive for his dinner, why not be able to discern good buffoonery from bad, and the pure digestive from the drug?

One is, I suppose, prejudiced in favour of this "new drama" of sincerity, of these poor productions of the last fifteen years, or so. It may be, indeed, that many of them will perish and fade away. But they are, at all events, the expression of the sincere moods of men who ask no more than to serve an art, which, heaven knows, has need of a little serving.

So much for the principles underlying the advance of the drama. But what about the chances of drama itself under the new conditions which will obtain when the war ends?

For the moment our world is still convulsed, and art of every kind trails a lame foot before a public whose eyes are fixed on the vast and bloody stage of the war. When the last curtain falls, and rises again on the scenery of Peace, shall we have to revalue everything? Surely not the fundamental truths; these reflections on the spirit which underlie all true effort in dramatic art may stand much as they were framed, now five years ago. Fidelity to mood, to impression, to self will remain what it was—the very kernel of good dramatic art; whether that fidelity will find a more or less favourable environment remains the interesting speculation. When we come to after-war conditions a sharp distinction will have to be drawn between the chances of sincere drama in America and Britain. It is my strong impression that sincere dramatists in America are going to have an easier time than they had before the war, but that with us they are going to have a harder. My reasons are threefold. The first and chief reason is economic. However much America may now have to spend, with her late arrival, vaster resources, and incomparably greater recuperative power, she will feel the economic strain but little in comparison with Britain. Britain, not at once, but certainly within five years of the war's close, will find that she has very much less money to spend on pleasure. Now, under present conditions of education, when the average man has little to spend on pleasure, he spends it first in gratifying his coarser tastes. And the average Briton is going to spend his little on having his broad laughs and his crude thrills. By the time he has gratified that side of himself he will have no money left. Those artists in Britain who respect æsthetic truths and practise sincerity will lose even the little support they ever had from the great public there; they will have to rely entirely on that small public which always wanted truth and beauty, and will want it even more passionately after the war. But that little public will be poorer also, and, I think, not more numerous than it was. The British public is going to be split more definitely into two camps—a very big and a very little camp. What this will mean to the drama of sincerity only those who have watched its struggle in the past will be able to understand. The trouble in Britain—and I daresay in every country—is that the percentage of people who take art of any kind seriously is ludicrously small. And our impoverishment will surely make that percentage smaller by cutting off the recruiting which was always going on from the ranks of the great public. How long it will take Britain to recover even pre-war conditions I do not venture to suggest. But I am pretty certain that there is no chance for a drama of truth and beauty there for many years to come, unless we can get it endowed in such a substantial way as shall tide it over—say—the next two decades. What we require is a London theatre undeviatingly devoted to the production of nothing but the real thing, which will go its own way, year in, year out, quite without regard to the great public; and we shall never get it unless we can find some benevolent, public-spirited person or persons who will place it in a position of absolute security. If we could secure this endowment, that theatre would become in a very few years the most fashionable, if not the most popular, in London, and even the great public would go to it. Nor need such a theatre be expensive—as theatres go—for it is to the mind and not to the eye that it must appeal. A sufficient audience is there ready; what is lacking is the point of focus, a single-hearted and coherent devotion to the best, and the means to pursue that ideal without extravagance but without halting. Alas! in England, though people will endow or back almost anything else, they will not endow or back an art theatre.

So much for the economic difficulty in Britain; what about America? The same cleavage obtains in public taste, of course, but numbers are so much larger, wealth will be so much greater, the spirit is so much more inquiring, the divisions so much less fast set, that I do not anticipate for America any block on the line. There will still be plenty of money to indulge every taste.

Art, and especially, perhaps, dramatic art, which of all is most dependent on a favourable economic condition, will gravitate towards America, which may well become in the next ten years not only the mother, but the foster-mother, of the best Anglo-Saxon drama.

My next reason for thinking that sincerity in art will have a better chance with Americans than in Britain in the coming years is psychological. They are so young a nation, we are so old; world-quakes to them are such an adventure, to us a nerve-racking, if not a health-shattering event. They will take this war in their stride, we have had to climb laboriously over it. They will be left buoyant; we, with the rest of Europe, are bound to lie for long years after in the trough of disillusionment. The national mood with them will be more than ever that of inquiry and exploit. With us, unless I make a mistake, after a spurt of hedonism—a going on the spree—there will be lassitude. Every European country has been overtried in this hideous struggle, and Nature, with her principle of balance, is bound to take redress. For Americans the war, nationally speaking, will have been but a bracing of the muscles and nerves, a clearing of the skin and eyes. Such a mental and moral condition will promote in them a deeper philosophy and a more resolute facing of truth.

And that brings me to my third reason. The American outlook will be permanently enlarged by this tremendous experience. Materially and spiritually she will have been forced to witness and partake of the life, thought, culture, and troubles of the old world. She will have, unconsciously, assimilated much, been diverted from the beer and skittles of her isolated development in a great new country. Americans will find themselves suddenly grown up. Not till a man is grown up does he see and feel things deeply enough to venture into the dark well of sincerity.

America is an eager nation. She has always been in a hurry. If I had to point out the capital defect in the attractive temperament of the American people, I should say it was a passion for short cuts. That has been, in my indifferent judgment, the very natural, the inevitable weakness in America's spiritual development. The material possibilities, the opportunities for growth and change, the vast spaces, the climate, the continual influxions of new blood and new habits, the endless shifts of life and environment, all these factors have been against that deep brooding over things, that close and long scrutiny into the deeper springs of life, out of which the sincerest and most lasting forms of art emerge; nearly all the conditions of American existence during the last fifty years have been against the settled life and atmosphere which influence men to the re-creation in art form of that which has sunk deep into their souls. Those who have seen the paintings of the Italian artist Segantini will understand what I mean. There have been many painters of mountains, but none whom I know of save he who has reproduced the very spirit of those great snowy spaces. He spent his life among them till they soaked into his nerves, into the very blood of him. All else he gave up, to see and feel them so that he might reproduce them in his art. Or let me take an instance from America. That enchanting work of art "Tom Sawyer and Huckleberry Finn," by the great Mark Twain. What reproduction of atmosphere and life; what scent of the river, and old-time country life, it gives off! How the author must have been soaked in it to have produced those books!

The whole tendency of our age has been away from hand-made goods, away from the sort of life which produced the great art of the past. That is too big a subject to treat of here. But certainly a sort of feverish impatience has possessed us all, America not least. It may be said that this will be increased by the war. I think the opposite. Hard spiritual experience and contact with the old world will deepen the American character and cool its fevers, and Americans will be more thorough, less impatient, will give themselves to art and to the sort of life which fosters art, more than they have ever yet given themselves. Great artists, like Whistler and Henry James, will no longer seek their quiet environments in Europe. I believe that this war will be for America the beginning of a great art age; I hope so with all my heart. For art will need a kind home and a new lease of life.

A certain humble and yet patient and enduring belief in himself and his own vision is necessary to the artist. I think that Americans have only just begun to believe in themselves as artists, but that this belief is now destined to grow quickly. America has a tremendous atmosphere of her own, a wonderful life, a wonderful country, but so far she has been skating over its surface. The time has come when she will strike down, think less in terms of material success and machine-made perfections. The time has come when she will brood, and interpret more and more the underlying truths, and body forth an art which shall be a spiritual guide, shed light, and show the meaning of her multiple existence. It will reveal dark things, but also those quiet heights to which man's spirit turns for rest and faith in this bewildering maze of a world. And to this art about to come—art inevitably moves slowly—into its own, to American drama, poetry, fiction, music, painting, sculpture—sincerity, an unswerving fidelity to self, alone will bring the dignity worthy of a great and free people.

1913-1917.

[C] The first part of this paper was published in the Hibbert Journal in 1910.

SPECULATIONS[D]

"When we survey the world around, the wondrous things which there abound"—especially the developments of these last years—there must come to some of us a doubt whether this civilisation of ours is to have a future. Mr. Lowes Dickenson, in an able book, "The Choice Before Us," has outlined the alternate paths which the world may tread after the war—"National Militarism" or "International Pacifism." He has pointed out with force the terrible dangers on the first of these two paths, the ruinous strain and ultimate destruction which a journey down it will inflict on every nation. But, holding a brief for International Pacifism, he was not, in that book, at all events, concerned to point out the dangers which beset Peace. When, in the words of President Wilson, we have made the world safe for democracy, it will be high time to set about making it safe against civilisation itself.

The first thing, naturally, is to ensure a good long spell of peace. If we do not, we need not trouble ourselves for a moment over the future of civilisation—there will be none. But a long spell of peace is probable; for, though human nature is never uniform, and never as one man shall we get salvation; sheer exhaustion, and disgust with its present bed-fellows—suffering, sacrifice, and sudden death—will almost surely force the world into international quietude. For the first time in history organised justice, such as for many centuries has ruled the relations between individuals, may begin to rule those between States, and free us from menace of war for a period which may be almost indefinitely prolonged. To perpetuate this great change in the life of nations is very much an affair of getting men used to that change; of setting up a Tribunal which they can see and pin their faith to, which works, and proves its utility, which they would miss if it were dissolved. States are proverbially cynical, but if an International Court of Justice, backed by international force, made good in the settlement of two or three serious disputes, allayed two or three crises, it would with each success gain prestige, be firmer and more difficult to uproot, till it might at last become as much a matter of course in the eyes of the cynical States as our Law Courts are in the eyes of our enlightened selves.

Making, then, the large but by no means hopeless assumption that such a change may come, how is our present civilisation going to "pan out"?

In Samuel Butler's imagined country, "Erewhon," the inhabitants had broken up all machinery, abandoned the use of money, and lived in a strange elysium of health and beauty. I often wonder how, without something of the sort, modern man is to be prevented from falling into the trombone he blows so loudly, from being destroyed by the very machines he has devised for his benefit. The problem before modern man is clearly that of becoming master, instead of slave, of his own civilisation. The history of the last hundred and fifty years, especially in England, is surely one long story of ceaseless banquet and acute indigestion. Certain Roman Emperors are popularly supposed to have taken drastic measures during their feasts to regain their appetites; we have not their "slim" wisdom; we do not mind going on eating when we have had too much.

I do not question the intentions of civilisation—they are most honourable. To be clean, warm, well nourished, healthy, decently leisured, and free to move quickly about the world, are certainly pure benefits. And these are presumably the prime objects of our toil and ingenuity, the ideals to be served, by the discovery of steam, electricity, modern industrial machinery, telephony, flying. If we attained those ideals, and stopped there—well and good. Alas! the amazing mechanical conquests of the age have crowded one on another so fast that we have never had time to digest their effects. Each as it came we hailed as an incalculable benefit to mankind, and so it was, or would have been, if we had not the appetites of cormorants and the digestive powers of elderly gentlemen. Our civilisation reminds one of the corpse in the Mark Twain story which, at its own funeral, got up and rode with the driver. It is watching itself being buried. We discover, and scatter discovery broadcast among a society uninstructed in the proper use of it. Consider the town-ridden, parasitic condition of Great Britain—the country which cannot feed itself. If we are beaten in this war, it will be because we have let our industrial system run away with us; because we became so sunk in machines and money-getting that we forgot our self-respect. No self-respecting nation would have let its food-growing capacity and its country life down to the extent that we have. If we are beaten—which God forbid—we shall deserve our fate. And why did our industrial system get such a mad grip on us? Because we did not master the riot of our inventions and discoveries. Remember the spinning jenny—whence came the whole system of Lancashire cotton factories which drained a countryside of peasants and caused a deterioration of physique from which as yet there has been no recovery. Here was an invention which was to effect a tremendous saving of labour and be of sweeping benefit to mankind. Exploited without knowledge, scruple, or humanity, it also caused untold misery and grievous national harm. Read, mark, and learn Mr. and Mrs. Hammond's book, "The Town Labourer." The spinning jenny and similar inventions have been the forces which have dotted beautiful counties of England with the blackest and most ill-looking towns in the world, have changed the proportion of country- to town-dwellers from about 3 as against 2 in 1761 to 2 as against 7 in 1911; have strangled our powers to feed ourselves, and so made us a temptation to our enemies and a danger to the whole world. We have made money by it; our standard of wealth has gone up. I remember having a long talk with a very old shepherd on the South Downs, whose youth and early married life were lived on eight shillings a week; and he was no exception. Nowadays our agricultural wage averages over thirty shillings, though it buys but little more than the eight. Still, the standard of wealth has superficially advanced, if that be any satisfaction. But have health, beauty, happiness among the great bulk of the population?

Consider the mastery of the air. To what use has it been put, so far? To practically none, save the destruction of life. About five years before the war some of us in England tried to initiate an international movement to ban the use of flying for military purposes. The effort was entirely abortive. The fact is, man never goes in front of events, always insists on disastrously buying his experience. And I am inclined to think we shall continue to advance backwards unless we intern our inventors till we have learned to run the inventions of the last century instead of letting them run us. Counsels of perfection, however, are never pursued. But what can we do? We can try to ban certain outside dangers internationally, such as submarines and air-craft, in war; and, inside, we might establish a Board of Scientific Control to ensure that no inventions are exploited under conditions obviously harmful.

Suppose, for instance, that the spinning jenny had come before such a Board, one imagines they might have said: "If you want to use this peculiar novelty, you must first satisfy us that your employees are going to work under conditions favourable to health"—in other words, the Factory Acts, Town Planning, and no Child Labour, from the start. Or, when rubber was first introduced: "You are bringing in this new and, we dare say, quite useful article. We shall, however, first send out and see the conditions under which you obtain it." Having seen, they would have added: "You will alter those conditions, and treat your native labour humanely, or we will ban your use of this article," to the grief and anger of those periwig-pated persons who write to the papers about grandmotherly legislation and sickly sentimentalism.

Seriously, the history of modern civilisation shows that, while we can only trust individualism to make discoveries, we cannot at all trust it to apply discovery without some sort of State check in the interests of health, beauty, and happiness. Officialdom is on all our nerves. But this is a very vital matter, and the suggestion of a Board of Scientific Control is not so fantastic as it seems. Certain results of inventions and discoveries cannot, of course, be foreseen, but able and impartial brains could foresee a good many and save mankind from the most rampant results of raw and unconsidered exploitation. The public is a child; and the child who suddenly discovers that there is such a thing as candy, if left alone, can only be relied on to make itself sick.

Let us stray for a frivolous moment into the realms of art, since the word art is claimed for what we know as the "film." This discovery went as it pleased for a few years in the hands of inventors and commercial agents. In these few years such a raging taste for cowboy, crime, and Chaplin films has been developed, that a Commission which has just been sitting on the matter finds that the public will not put up with more than a ten per cent. proportion of educational film in the course of an evening's entertainment. Now, the film as a means of transcribing actual life is admittedly of absorbing interest and great educational value; but, owing to this false start, we cannot get it swallowed in more than extremely small doses as a food and stimulant, while it is being gulped down to the dregs as a drug or irritant. Of the film's claim to the word art I am frankly sceptical. My mind is open—and when one says that, one generally means it is shut. But art is long: the Cro-Magnon men of Europe decorated the walls of their caves quite beautifully, some say twenty-five, some say seventy, thousand years ago; so it may well require a generation to tell us what is art and what is not among the new experiments continually being made. Still, the film is a restless thing, and I cannot think of any form of art, as hitherto we have understood the word, to which that description could be applied, unless it be those Wagner operas which I have disliked not merely since the war began, but from childhood up. During the filming of the play "Justice" I attended at rehearsal to see Mr. Gerald du Maurier play the cell scene. Since in that scene there is not a word spoken in the play itself, there is no difference in kind between the appeal of play or film. But the live rehearsal for the filming was at least twice as affecting as the dead result of that rehearsal on the screen. The film, of course, is in its first youth, but I see no signs as yet that it will ever overcome the handicap of its physical conditions, and attain the real emotionalising powers of art. The film sweeps up into itself, of course, a far wider surface of life in a far shorter space of time; but the medium is flat, has no blood in it; and experience tells one that no amount of surface and quantity in art ever make up for lack of depth and quality. Who would not cheerfully give the Albert Memorial for a little figure by Donatello! Since, however, the film takes the line of least resistance, and makes a rapid, lazy, superficial appeal, it may very well oust the drama. And, to my thinking, of course, that will be all to the bad, and intensely characteristic of machine-made civilisation, whose motto seems to be: "Down with Shakespeare and Euripides—up with the Movies!" The film is a very good illustration of the whole tendency of modern life under the too-rapid development of machines; roughly speaking, we seem to be turning up yearly more and more ground to less and less depth. We are getting to know life as superficially as the Egyptian interpreter knew language, who, [as we read in the Manchester Guardian,] when the authorities complained that he was overstaying his leave, wrote back: "My absence is impossible. Some one has removed my wife. My God, I am annoyed."

There is an expression—"high-brow"—maybe complimentary in origin, but become in some sort a term of contempt. A doubter of our general divinity is labelled "high-brow" at once, and his doubts drop like water off the public's back. Any one who questions our triumphant progress is tabooed for a pedant. That will not alter the fact, I fear, that we are growing feverish, rushed, and complicated, and have multiplied conveniences to such an extent that we do nothing with them but scrape the surface of life. We were rattling into a new species of barbarism when the war came, and unless we take a pull, shall continue to rattle after it is over. The underlying cause in every country is the increase of herd-life, based on machines, money-getting, and the dread of being dull. Every one knows how fearfully strong that dread is. But to be capable of being dull is in itself a disease.

And most of modern life seems to be a process of creating disease, then finding a remedy which in its turn creates another disease, demanding fresh remedy, and so on. We pride ourselves, for example, on scientific sanitation; well, what is scientific sanitation if not one huge palliative of evils, which have arisen from herd-life, enabling herd-life to be intensified, so that we shall presently need even more scientific sanitation? The old shepherd on the South Downs had never come in contact with it, yet he was very old, very healthy, hardy, and contented. He had a sort of simple dignity, too, that we have most of us lost. The true elixirs vitæ—for there be two, I think—are open-air life and a proud pleasure in one's work; we have evolved a mode of existence in which it is comparatively rare to find these two conjoined. In old countries, such as Britain, the evils of herd-life are at present vastly more acute than in a new country such as America. On the other hand, the further one is from hell the faster one drives towards it, and machines are beginning to run along with America even more violently than with Europe.

When our Tanks first appeared they were described as snouting monsters creeping at their own sweet will. I confess that this is how my inflamed eye sees all our modern machines—monsters running on their own, dragging us along, and very often squashing us.

We are, I believe, awakening to the dangers of this "Gadarening," this rushing down the high cliff into the sea, possessed and pursued by the devils of—machinery. But if any man would see how little alarmed he really is—let him ask himself how much of his present mode of existence he is prepared to alter. Altering the modes of other people is delightful; one would have great hope of the future if we had nothing before us but that. The medieval Irishman, in Froude, indicted for burning down the cathedral at Armagh, together with the Archbishop, defended himself thus: "As for the cathedral, 'tis true I burned it; but indeed an' I wouldn't have, only they told me himself was inside." We are all ready to alter our opponents, if not to burn them. But even if we were as ardent reformers as that Irishman we could hardly force men to live in the open, or take a proud pleasure in their work, or enjoy beauty, or not concentrate themselves on making money. No amount of legislation will make us "lilies of the field" or "birds of the air," or prevent us from worshipping false gods, or neglecting to reform ourselves.

I once wrote the unpopular sentence, "Democracy at present offers the spectacle of a man running down a road followed at a more and more respectful distance by his own soul." I am a democrat, or I should never have dared. For democracy, substitute "Modern Civilisation," which prides itself on redress after the event, agility in getting out of the holes into which it has snouted, and eagerness to snout into fresh ones. It foresees nothing, and avoids less. It is purely empirical, if one may use such a "high-brow" word.

Politics are popularly supposed to govern the direction, and statesmen to be the guardian angels, of Civilisation. It seems to me that they have little or no power over its growth. They are of it, and move with it. Their concern is rather with the body than with the mind or soul of a nation. One needs not to be an engineer to know that to pull a man up a wall one must be higher than he; that to raise general taste one must have better taste than that of those whose taste he is raising.

Now, to my indifferent mind, education in the large sense—not politics at all—is the only agent really capable of improving the trend of civilisation, the only lever we can use. Believing this, I think it a thousand pities that neither Britain nor America, nor, so far as I know, any other country, has as yet evolved machinery through which there might be elected a supreme Director, or, say, a little Board of three Directors, of the nation's spirit, an Educational President, as it were, with power over the nation's spirit analogous to that which America's elected political President has over America's body. Our Minister of Education is as a rule an ordinary Member of the Government, an ordinary man of affairs—though at the moment an angel happens to have strayed in. Why cannot education be regarded, like religion in the past, as something sacred, not merely a department of political administration? Ought we not for this most vital business of education to be ever on the watch for the highest mind and the finest spirit of the day to guide us? To secure the appointment of such a man, or triumvirate, by democratic means, would need a special sifting process of election, which could never be too close and careful. One might use for the purpose the actual body of teachers in the country to elect delegates to select a jury to choose finally the flower of the national flock. It would be worth any amount of trouble to ensure that we always had the best man or men. And when we had them we should give them a mandate as real and substantial as America now gives to her political President. We should intend them not for mere lay administrators and continuers of custom, but for true fountain-heads and initiators of higher ideals of conduct, learning, manners, and taste; nor stint them of the means necessary to carry those ideals into effect. Hitherto, the supposed direction of ideals—in practice almost none—has been left to religion. But religion as a motive force is at once too personal, too lacking in unanimity, and too specialised to control the educational needs of a modern State; religion, as I understand it, is essentially emotional and individual; when it becomes practical and worldly it strays outside its true province and loses beneficence. Education as I want to see it would take over the control of social ethics, and learning, but make no attempt to usurp the emotional functions of religion. Let me give you an example: Those elixirs vitæ—open-air life and a proud pleasure in one's work—imagine those two principles drummed into the heads and hearts of all the little scholars of the age, by men and women who had been taught to believe them the truth. Would this not gradually have an incalculable effect on the trend of our civilisation? Would it not tend to create a demand for a simple and sane life; help to get us back to the land; produce reluctance to work at jobs in which no one can feel pride and pleasure, and so diminish the power of machines and of commercial exploitation? But teachers could only be inspired with such ideals by master spirits. And my plea is that we should give ourselves the chance of electing and making use of such master spirits. We all know from everyday life and business that the real, the only problem is to get the best men to run the show; when we get them the show runs well, when we don't there is nothing left but to pay the devil. The chief defect of modern civilisation based on democracy is the difficulty of getting best men quickly enough. Unless Democracy—government by the people—makes of itself Aristocracy—government by the best people—it is running steadily to seed. Democracy to be sound must utilise not only the ablest men of affairs, but the aristocracy of spirit. The really vital concern of such an elected Head of Education, himself the best man of all, would be the discovery and employment of other best men, best Heads of Schools and Colleges, whose chief concern in turn would be the discovery and employment of best subordinates. The better the teacher the better the ideals; quite obviously, the only hope of raising ideals is to raise the standard of those who teach, from top to toe of the educational machine. What we want, in short, is a sort of endless band—throwing up the finest spirit of the day till he forms a head or apex whence virtue runs swiftly down again into the people who elected him. This is the principle, as it seems to me, of the universe itself, whose symbol is neither circle nor spire, but circle and spire mysteriously combined.

America has given us an example of this in her political system; perhaps she will now oblige in her educational. I confess that I look very eagerly and watchfully towards America in many ways. After the war she will be more emphatically than ever, in material things, the most important and powerful nation of the earth. We British have a legitimate and somewhat breathless interest in the use she will make of her strength, and in the course of her national life, for this will greatly influence the course of our own. But power for real light and leading in America will depend, not so much on her material wealth, or her armed force, as on what the attitude towards life and the ideals of her citizens are going to be. Americans have a certain eagerness for knowledge; they have also, for all their absorption in success, the aspiring eye. They do want the good thing. They don't always know it when they see it, but they want it. These qualities, in combination with material strength, give America her chance. Yet, if she does not set her face against "Gadarening," we are all bound for downhill. If she goes in for spreadeagleism, if her aspirations are towards quantity not quality, we shall all go on being commonised. If she should get that purse-and-power-proud fever which comes from national success, we are all bound for another world flare-up. The burden of proving that democracy can be real and yet live up to an ideal of health and beauty will be on America's shoulders, and on ours. What are we and Americans going to make of our inner life, of our individual habits of thought? What are we going to reverence, and what despise? Do we mean to lead in spirit and in truth, not in mere money and guns? Britain is an old country, still in her prime, I hope; but America is as yet on the threshold. Is she to step out into the sight of the world as a great leader? That is for America the long decision, to be worked out, not so much in her Senate and her Congress, as in her homes and schools. On America, after the war, the destiny of civilisation may hang for the next century. If she mislays, indeed, if she does not improve the power of self-criticism—that special dry American humour which the great Lincoln had—she might soon develop the intolerant provincialism which has so often been the bane of the earth and the undoing of nations. If she gets swelled-head the world will get cold-feet. Above all, if she does not solve the problems of town life, of Capital and Labour, of the distribution of wealth, of national health, and attain to a mastery over inventions and machinery—she is in for a cycle of mere anarchy, disruption, and dictatorships, into which we shall all follow. The motto "noblesse oblige" applies as much to democracy as ever it did to the old-time aristocrat. It applies with terrific vividness to America. Ancestry and Nature have bestowed on her great gifts. Behind her stand Conscience, Enterprise, Independence, and Ability—such were the companions of the first Americans, and are the comrades of American citizens to this day. She has abounding energy, an unequalled spirit of discovery; a vast territory not half developed, and great natural beauty. I remember sitting on a bench overlooking the Grand Canyon of Arizona; the sun was shining into it, and a snow-storm was whirling down there. All that most marvellous work of Nature was flooded to the brim with rose and tawny-gold, with white, and wine-dark shadows; the colossal carvings as of huge rock-gods and sacrificial altars, and great beasts, along its sides, were made living by the very mystery of light and darkness, on that violent day of spring—I remember sitting there, and an old gentleman passing close behind, leaning towards me and saying in a sly, gentle voice: "How are you going to tell it to the folks at home?" America has so much that one despairs of telling to the folks at home, so much grand beauty to be to her an inspiration and uplift towards high and free thought and vision. Great poems of Nature she has, wrought in the large, to make of her and keep her a noble people. In our beloved Britain—all told, not half the size of Texas—there is a quiet beauty of a sort which America has not. I walked not long ago from Worthing to the little village of Steyning, in the South

Downs. It was such a day as one too seldom gets in England; when the sun was dipping and there came on the cool chalky hills the smile of late afternoon, and across a smooth valley on the rim of the Down one saw a tiny group of trees, one little building, and a stack, against the clear-blue, pale sky—it was like a glimpse of Heaven, so utterly pure in line and colour, so removed, and touching. The tale of loveliness in our land is varied and unending, but it is not in the grand manner. America has the grand manner in her scenery and in her blood, for over there all are the children of adventure and daring, every single white man an emigrant himself or a descendant of one who had the pluck to emigrate. She has already had past-masters in dignity, but she has still to reach as a nation the grand manner in achievement. She knows her own dangers and failings, her qualities and powers; but she cannot realise the intense concern and interest, deep down behind our provoking stolidities, with which we of the old country watch her, feeling that what she does reacts on us above all nations, and will ever react more and more. Underneath surface differences and irritations we English-speaking peoples are fast bound together. May it not be in misery and iron! If America walks upright, so shall we; if she goes bowed under the weight of machines, money, and materialism, we, too, shall creep our ways. We run a long race, we nations; a generation is but a day. But in a day a man may leave the track, and never again recover it!

Democracies must not be content to leave the ideals of health and beauty to artists and a leisured class; that is the way into a treeless, waterless desert. It has struck me forcibly that we English-speaking democracies are all right underneath, and all wrong on the surface; our hearts are sound, but our skin is in a deplorable condition. Our taste, take it all round, is dreadful. For a petty illustration: Ragtime music. Judging by its popularity, one would think it must be a splendid discovery; yet it suggests little or nothing but the comic love-making of two darkies. We ride it to death; but its jigging, jogging, jumpy jingle refuses to die on us, and America's young and ours grow up in the tradition of its soul-forsaken sounds. Take another tiny illustration: The new dancing. Developed from cake-walk, to fox-trot, by way of tango. Precisely the same spiritual origin! And not exactly in the grand manner to one who, like myself, loves and believes in dancing. Take the "snappy" side of journalism. In San Francisco a few years ago the Press snapped a certain writer and his wife, in their hotel, and next day there appeared a photograph of two intensely wretched-looking beings stricken by limelight, under the headline: "Blank and wife enjoy freedom and gaiety in the air." Another writer told me that as he set foot on a car leaving a great city a young lady grabbed him by the coat-tail and cried: "Say, Mr. Asterisk, what are your views on a future life?" Not in the grand manner, all this; but, if you like, a sign of vitality and interest; a mere excrescence. But are not these excrescences symptoms of a fever lying within our modern civilisation, a febrility which is going to make achievement of great ends and great work more difficult? We Britons, as a breed, are admittedly stolid; we err as much on that score as Americans on the score of restlessness; yet we are both subject to these excrescences. There is something terribly infectious about vulgarity; and taste is on the down-grade following the tendencies of herd-life. It is not a process to be proud of.

Enough of Jeremiads, there is a bright side to our civilisation.

This modern febrility does not seem able to attack the real inner man. If there is a lamentable increase of vulgarity, superficiality, and restlessness in our epoch, there is also an inspiring development of certain qualities. Those who were watching human nature before the war were pretty well aware of how, under the surface, unselfishness, ironic stoicism, and a warm humanity were growing. These are the great Town Virtues; the fine flowers of herd-life. A big price is being paid for them, but they are almost beyond price. The war has revealed them in full bloom. Revealed them, not produced them! Who, in the future, with this amazing show before him, will dare to talk about the need for war to preserve courage and unselfishness? From the first shot these wonders of endurance, bravery, and sacrifice were shown by the untrained citizens of countries nearly fifty years deep in peace! Never, I suppose, in the world's history, has there been so marvellous a display, in war, of the bedrock virtues. The soundness at core of the modern man has had one long triumphant demonstration. Out of a million instances, take that little story of a Mr. Lindsay, superintendent of a pumping station at some oil-wells in Mesopotamia. A valve in the oil-pipe had split, and a fountain of oil was being thrown up on all sides, while, thirty yards off, and nothing between, the furnaces were in full blast. To prevent a terrible conflagration and great loss of life, and to save the wells, it was necessary to shut off those furnaces. That meant dashing through the oil-stream and arriving saturated at the flames. The superintendent did not hesitate a moment, and was burnt to death. Such deeds as this men and women have been doing all through the war.

When you come to think, this modern man is a very new and marvellous creature. Without quite realising it, we have evolved a fresh species of stoic, even more stoical, I suspect, than were the old Stoics. Modern man has cut loose from leading-strings; he stands on his own feet. His religion is to take what comes without flinching or complaint, as part of the day's work, which an unknowable God, Providence, Creative Principle, or whatever it shall be called, has appointed. Observation tells me that modern man at large, far from inclining towards the new, personal, elder-brotherly God of Mr. Wells, has turned his face the other way. He confronts life and death alone. By courage and kindness modern man exists, warmed by the glow of the great human fellowship. He has re-discovered the old Greek saying: "God is the helping of man by man"; has found out in his unselfconscious way that if he does not help himself, and help his fellows, he cannot reach that inner peace which satisfies. To do his bit, and to be kind! It is by that creed, rather than by any mysticism, that he finds the salvation of his soul. His religion is to be a common-or-garden hero, without thinking anything of it; for, of a truth, this is the age of conduct.

After all, does not the only real spiritual warmth, not tinged by Pharisaism, egotism, or cowardice, come from the feeling of doing your work well and helping others; is not all the rest embroidery, luxury, pastime, pleasant sound and incense? Modern man, take him in the large, does not believe in salvation to beat of drum; or that, by leaning up against another person, however idolised and mystical, he can gain support. He is a realist with too romantic a sense, perhaps, of the mystery which surrounds existence to pry into it. And, like modern civilisation itself, he is the creature of West and North, of atmospheres, climates, manners of life which foster neither inertia, reverence, nor mystic meditation. Essentially man of action, in ideal action he finds his only true comfort; and no attempts to discover for him new gods and symbols will divert him from the path made for him by the whole trend of his existence. I am sure that padres at the front see that the men whose souls they have gone out to tend are living the highest form of religion; that in their comic courage, unselfish humanity, their endurance without whimper of things worse than death, they have gone beyond all pulpit-and-death-bed teaching. And who are these men? Just the early manhood of the race, just modern man as he was before the war began and will be when the war is over.

This modern world, of which we English and Americans are perhaps the truest types, stands revealed, from beneath its froth, frippery, and vulgar excrescences, sound at core—a world whose implicit motto is: "The good of all humanity." But the herd-life, which is its characteristic, brings many evils, has many dangers; and to preserve a sane mind in a healthy body is the riddle before us. Somehow we must free ourselves from the driving domination of machines and money-getting, not only for our own sakes but for that of all mankind.

And there is another thing of the most solemn importance: We English-speaking nations are by chance as it were the ballast of the future. It is absolutely necessary that we should remain united. The comradeship we now feel must and surely shall abide. For unless we work together, and in no selfish or exclusive spirit—good-bye to Civilisation! It will vanish like the dew off grass. The betterment not only of the British nations and America, but of all mankind, is and must be our object.

When from all our hearts this great weight is lifted; when no longer in those fields death sweeps his scythe, and our ears at last are free from the rustling thereof—then will come the test of magnanimity in all countries. Will modern man rise to the ordering of a sane, a free, a generous life? Each of us loves his own country best, be it a little land or the greatest on earth; but jealousy is the dark thing, the creeping poison. Where there is true greatness, let us acclaim it; where there is true worth, let us prize it—as if it were our own.

This earth is made too subtly, of too multiple warp and woof, for prophecy. When he surveys the world around, the wondrous things which there abound, the prophet closes foolish lips. Besides, as the historian tells us: "Writers have that undeterminateness of spirit which commonly makes literary men of no use in the world." So I, for one, prophesy not. Still, we do know this: All English-speaking peoples will go to the adventure of peace with something of big purpose and spirit in their hearts, with something of free outlook. The world is wide and Nature bountiful enough for all, if we keep sane minds. The earth is fair and meant to be enjoyed, if we keep sane bodies. Who dare affront this world of beauty with mean views? There is no darkness but what the ape in us still makes, and in spite of all his monkey-tricks modern man is at heart further from the ape than man has yet been.

To do our jobs really well and to be brotherly! To seek health, and ensue beauty! If, in Britain and America, in all the English-speaking nations, we can put that simple faith into real and thorough practice, what may not this century yet bring forth? Shall man, the highest product of creation, be content to pass his little day in a house, like unto Bedlam?

When the present great task in which we have joined hands is ended; when once more from the shuttered mad-house the figure of Peace steps forth and stands in the sun, and we may go our ways again in the beauty and wonder of a new morning—let it be with this vow in our hearts: "No more of Madness—in War, in Peace!"

1917-18.

[D] A paper read on March 21st, 1918.

THE LAND, 1917

I

If once more through ingenuity, courage, and good luck we find the submarine menace "well in hand," and go to sleep again—if we reach the end of the war without having experienced any sharp starvation, and go our ways to trade, to eat, and forget—What then? It is about twenty years since the first submarine could navigate—and about seventeen since flying became practicable. There are a good many years yet before the world, and numberless developments in front of these new accomplishments. Hundreds of miles are going to be what tens are now; thousands of machines will take the place of hundreds.

We have ceased to live on an island in any save a technically geographical sense, and the sooner we make up our minds to the fact, the better. If in the future we act as we have in the past—rather the habit of this country—I can imagine that in fifteen years' time or so we shall be well enough prepared against war of the same magnitude and nature as this war, and that the country which attacks us will launch an assault against defences as many years out of date.

I can imagine a war starting and well-nigh ending at once, by a quiet and simultaneous sinking, from under water and from the air, of most British ships, in port or at sea. I can imagine little standardised submarines surreptitiously prepared by the thousand, and tens of thousands of the enemy population equipped with flying machines, instructed in flying as part of their ordinary civil life, and ready to serve their country at a moment's notice, by taking a little flight and dropping a little charge of an explosive many times more destructive than any in use now. The agility of submarines and flying machines will grow almost indefinitely. And even if we carry our commerce under the sea instead of on the surface, we shall not be guaranteed against attack by air. The air menace is, in fact, infinitely greater than that from under water. I can imagine all shipping in port, the Houses of Parliament, the Bank of England, most commercial buildings of importance, and every national granary wrecked or fired in a single night, on a declaration of war springing out of the blue. The only things I cannot imagine wrecked or fired are the British character and the good soil of Britain.

These are sinister suggestions, but there is really no end to what might now be done to us by any country which deliberately set its own interests and safety above all considerations of international right, especially if such country were moved to the soul by longing for revenge, and believed success certain. After this world-tragedy let us hope nations may have a little sense, less of that ghastly provincialism whence this war sprang; that no nation may teach in its schools that it is God's own people, entitled to hack through, without consideration of others; that professors may be no longer blind to all sense of proportion; Emperors things of the past; diplomacy open and responsible; a real Court of Nations at work; Military Chiefs unable to stampede a situation; journalists obliged to sign their names and held accountable for inflammatory writings. Let us hope, and let us by every means endeavour to bring about this better state of the world. But there is many a slip between cup and lip; there is also such a thing as hatred. And to rely blindly on a peace which, at the best, must take a long time to prove its reality, is to put our heads again under our wings. Once bit, twice shy. We shall make a better world the quicker if we try realism for a little.

Britain's situation is now absurdly weak, without and within. And its weakness is due to one main cause—the fact that we do not grow our own food. To get the better of submarines in this war will make no difference to our future situation. A little peaceful study and development of submarines and aircraft will antiquate our present antidotes. You cannot chain air and the deeps to war uses and think you have done with their devilish possibilities a score of years afterwards because for the moment the submarine menace or the air menace is "well in hand."

At the end of the war I suppose the Channel Tunnel will be made. And quite time too! But even that will not help us. We get no food from Europe, and never shall again. Not even by linking ourselves to Europe can we place ourselves in security from Europe. Faith may remove mountains, but it will not remove Britain to the centre of the Atlantic. Here we shall remain, every year nearer and more accessible to secret and deadly attack.

The next war, if there be one—which Man forbid—may be fought without the use of a single big ship or a single infantryman. It may begin, instead of ending, by being a war of starvation; it may start, as it were, where it leaves off this time. And the only way of making even reasonably safe is to grow our own food. If for years to come we have to supplement by State granaries, they must be placed underground; not even there will they be too secure. Unless we grow our own food after this war we shall be the only great country which does not, and a constant temptation to any foe. To be self-sufficing will be the first precaution taken by our present enemies, in order that blockade may no longer be a weapon in our hands, so far as their necessary food is concerned.

Whatever arrangements the world makes after the war to control the conduct of nations in the future, the internal activities of those nations will remain unfettered, capable of deadly shaping and plausible disguise in the hands of able and damnable schemers.

The submarine menace of the present is merely awkward, and no doubt surmountable—it is nothing to the submarine-cum-air menace of peace time a few years hence. It will be impossible to guard against surprise under the new conditions. If we do not grow our own food, we could be knocked out of time in the first round.

But besides the danger from overseas, we have an inland danger to our future just as formidable—the desertion of our countryside and the town-blight which is its corollary.

Despair seizes on one reading that we should cope with the danger of the future by new cottages, better instruction to farmers, better kinds of manure and seed, encouragement to co-operative societies, a cheerful spirit, and the storage of two to three years' supply of grain. Excellent and necessary, in their small ways—they are a mere stone to the bread we need.

In that programme and the speech which put it forward I see insufficient grasp of the outer peril and hardly any of the gradual destruction with which our overwhelming town life threatens us; not one allusion to the physical and moral welfare of our race, except this: "That boys should be in touch with country life and country tastes is of first importance, and that their elementary education should be given in terms of country things is also of enormous importance." That is all, and it shows how far we have got from reality, and how difficult it will be to get back; for the speaker was once Minister for Agriculture.

Our justifications for not continuing to feed ourselves were: Pursuit of wealth, command of the sea, island position. Whatever happens in this war, we have lost the last two in all but a superficial sense. Let us see whether the first is sufficient justification for perseverance in a mode of life which has brought us to an ugly pass.

Our wonderful industrialism began about 1766, and changed us from exporting between the years 1732 and 1766 11,250,000 quarters of wheat to importing 7,500,000 quarters between the years 1767 and 1801. In one hundred and fifty years it has brought us to the state of importing more than three-quarters of our wheat, and more than half our total food. Whereas in 1688 (figures of Gregory and Davenant) about four-fifths of the population of England was rural, in 1911 only about two-ninths was rural. This transformation has given us great wealth, extremely ill-distributed; plastered our country with scores of busy, populous, and hideous towns; given us a merchant fleet which before the war had a gross tonnage of over 20,000,000, or not far short of half the world's shipping. It has, or had, fixed in us the genteel habit of eating very doubtfully nutritious white bread made of the huskless flour of wheat;

reduced the acreage of arable land in the United Kingdom from its already insufficient maximum of 23,000,000 acres to its 1914 figure of 19,000,000 acres; made England, all but its towns, look very like a pleasure garden; and driven two shibboleths deep into our minds, "All for wealth" and "Hands off the food of the people."

All these "good" results have had certain complementary disadvantages, some of which we have just seen, some of which have long been seen.

Of these last, let me first take a small sentimental disadvantage. We have become more parasitic by far than any other nation. To eat we have to buy with our manufactures an overwhelming proportion of our vital foods. The blood in our veins is sucked from foreign bodies, in return for the clothing we give them—not a very self-respecting thought. We have a green and fertile country, and round it a prolific sea. Our country, if we will, can produce, with its seas, all the food we need to eat. We know that quite well, but we elect to be nourished on foreign stuff, because we are a practical people and prefer shekels to sentiment. We do not mind being parasitic. Taking no interest nationally in the growth of food, we take no interest nationally in the cooking of it; the two accomplishments subtly hang together. Pride in the food capacity, the corn and wine and oil, of their country has made the cooking of the French the most appetising and nourishing in the world. The French do cook: we open tins. The French preserve the juices of their home-grown food: we have no juices to preserve. The life of our poorer classes is miserably stunted of essential salts and savours. They throw away skins, refuse husks, make no soups, prefer pickle to genuine flavour. But home-grown produce really is more nourishing than tinned and pickled and frozen foods. If we honestly feed ourselves we shall not again demand the old genteel flavourless white bread without husk or body in it; we shall eat wholemeal bread, and take to that salutary substance, oatmeal, which, if I mistake not, has much to say in making the Scots the tallest and boniest race in Europe.

Now for a far more poignant disadvantage. We have become tied up in teeming congeries, to which we have grown so used that we are no longer able to see the blight they have brought on us. Our great industrial towns, sixty odd in England alone, with a population of 15,000,000 to 16,000,000, are our glory, our pride, and the main source of our wealth. They are the growth, roughly speaking, of five generations. They began at a time when social science was unknown, spread and grew in unchecked riot of individual moneymaking, till they are the nightmare of social reformers, and the despair of all lovers of beauty. They have mastered us so utterly, morally and physically, that we regard them and their results as matter of course. They are public opinion, so that for the battle against town-blight there is no driving force. They paralyse the imaginations of our politicians because their voting power is so enormous, their commercial interests are so huge, and the food necessities of their populations seem so paramount.

I once bewailed the physique of our towns to one of our most cultivated and prominent Conservative statesmen. He did not agree. He thought that probably physique was on the up-grade. This commonly held belief is based on statistics of longevity and sanitation. But the same superior sanitation and science applied to a rural population would have lengthened the lives of a much finer and better-looking stock. Here are some figures: Out of 1,650 passers-by, women and men, observed in perhaps the "best" district of London—St. James's Park, Trafalgar Square, Westminster Bridge, and Piccadilly—in May of this year, only 310 had any pretensions to not being very plain or definitely ugly-not one in five. And out of that 310 only eleven had what might be called real beauty. Out of 120 British soldiers observed round Charing Cross, sixty—just one-half—passed the same standard. But out of seventy-two Australian soldiers, fifty-four, or three-quarters, passed, and several had real beauty. Out of 120 men, women, and children taken at random in a remote country village (five miles from any town, and eleven miles from any town of 10,000 inhabitants) ninety—or just three-quarters also—pass this same standard of looks. It is significant that the average here is the same as the average among Australian soldiers, who, though of British stock, come from a country as yet unaffected by town life. You ask, of course, what standard is this? A standard which covers just the very rudiments of proportion and comeliness. People in small country towns, I admit, have little or no more beauty than people in large towns. This is curious, but may be due to too much inbreeding.

The first counter to conclusions drawn from such figures is obviously: "The English are an ugly people." I said that to a learned and æsthetic friend when I came back from France last spring. He started, and then remarked: "Oh, well; not as ugly as the French, anyway." A great error; much plainer if you take the bulk, and not the pick, of the population in both countries. It may not be fair to attribute French superiority in looks entirely to the facts that they grow nearly all their own food (and cook it well), and had in 1906 four-sevenths of their population in the country as against our own two-ninths in 1911, because there is the considerable matter of climate. But when you get so high a proportion of comeliness in remote country districts in England, it is fair to assume that climate does not account for anything like all the difference. I do not believe that the English are naturally an ugly people. The best English type is perhaps the handsomest in the world. The physique and looks of the richer classes are as notoriously better than those of the poorer classes as the physique and looks of the remote country are superior to those of crowded towns. Where conditions are free from cramp, poor air, poor food, and herd-life, English physique quite holds its own with that of other nations.

We do not realise the great deterioration of our stock, the squashed-in, stunted, disproportionate, commonised look of the bulk of our people, because, as we take our walks abroad, we note only faces and figures which strike us as good-looking; the rest pass unremarked. Ugliness has become a matter of course. There is no reason, save town life, why this should be so. But what does it matter if we have become ugly? We work well, make money, and have lots of moral qualities. A fair inside is better than a fair outside. I do think that we are in many ways a very wonderful people; and our townsfolk not the least wonderful. But that is all the more reason for trying to preserve our physique.

Granted that an expressive face, with interest in life stamped on it, is better than "chocolate box" or "barber's block" good looks, that agility and strength are better than symmetry without agility and strength; the trouble is that there is no interest stamped on so many of our faces, no agility or strength in so many of our limbs. If there were, those faces and limbs would pass my standard. The old Greek cult of the body was not to be despised. I defy even the most rigid Puritans to prove that a satisfactory moral condition can go on within an exterior which exhibits no signs of a live, able, and serene existence. By living on its nerves, overworking its body, starving its normal aspirations for fresh air, good food, sunlight, and a modicum of solitude, a country can get a great deal out of itself, a terrific lot of wealth, in three or four generations; but it is living on its capital, physically speaking. This is precisely what we show every sign of doing; and partly what I mean by "town-blight."

II

The impression I get, in our big towns, is most peculiar—considering that we are a free people. The faces and forms have a look of being possessed. To express my meaning exactly is difficult. There is a dulled and driven look, and yet a general expression of "Keep smiling—Are we down-hearted? No." It is as if people were all being forced along by a huge invisible hand at the back of their necks, whose pressure they resent yet are trying to make the best of, because they cannot tell whence it comes. To understand, you must watch the grip from its very beginnings. The small children who swarm in the little grey playground streets of our big towns pass their years in utter abandonment. They roll and play and chatter in conditions of amazing unrestraint and devil-may-care-dom in the midst of amazing dirt and ugliness. The younger they are, as a rule, the chubbier and prettier they are. Gradually you can see herd-life getting hold of them, the impact of ugly sights and sounds commonising the essential grace and individuality of their little features. On the lack of any standard or restraint, any real glimpse of Nature, any knowledge of a future worth striving for, or indeed of any future at all, they thrive forward into that hand-to-mouth mood from which they are mostly destined never to emerge. Quick and scattery as monkeys, and never alone, they become, at a rake's progress, little fragments of the herd. On poor food, poor air, and habits of least resistance, they wilt and grow distorted, acquiring withal the sort of pathetic hardihood which a Dartmoor pony will draw out of moor life in a frozen winter. All round them, by day, by night, stretches the huge, grey, grimy waste of streets, factory walls, chimneys, murky canals, chapels, public-houses, hoardings, posters, butchers' shops—a waste where nothing beautiful exists save a pretty cat or pigeon, a blue sky, perhaps, and a few trees and open spaces. The children of the class above, too, of the small shop-people, the artisans—do they escape? Not really. The same herd-life and the same sights and sounds pursue them from birth; they also are soon divested of the grace and free look which you see in country children walking to and from school or roaming the hedges. Whether true slum children, or from streets a little better off, quickly they all pass out of youth into the iron drive of commerce and manufacture, into the clang and clatter, the swish and whirr of wheels, the strange, dragging, saw-like hubbub of industry, or the clicking and pigeon-holes of commerce; perch on a devil's see-saw from monotonous work to cheap sensation and back. Considering the conditions it is wonderful that they stand it as well as they do; and I should be the last to deny that they possess remarkable qualities. But the modern industrial English town is a sort of inferno where people dwell with a marvellous philosophy. What would you have? They have never seen any way out of it. And this, perhaps, would not be so pitiful if for each bond-servant of our town-tyranny there was in store a prize—some portion of that national wealth in pursuit of which the tyrant drives us; if each worker had before him the chance of emergence at, say, fifty. But, Lord God! for five that emerge, ninety-and-five stay bound, less free and wealthy at the end of the chapter than they were at the beginning. And the quaint thing is—they know it; know that they will spend their lives in smoky, noisy, crowded drudgery, and in crowded drudgery die. Wealth goes to wealth, and all they can hope for is a few extra shillings a week, with a corresponding rise in prices. They know it, but it does not disturb them, for they were born of the towns, have never glimpsed at other possibilities. Imprisoned in town life from birth, they contentedly perpetuate the species of a folk with an ebbing future. Yes, ebbing! For if it be not, why is there now so much conscious effort to arrest the decay of town workers' nerves and sinews? Why do we bother to impede a process which is denied? If there be no town-blight on us, why a million indications of uneasiness and a thousand little fights against the march of a degeneration so natural, vast, and methodical, that it brings them all to naught? Our physique is slowly rotting, and that is the plain truth of it.

But it does not stop with deteriorated physique. Students of faces in the remoter country are struck by the absence of what, for want of a better word, we may call vulgarity. That insidious defacement is seen to be a thing of towns, and not at all a matter of "class." The simplest country cottager, shepherd, fisherman, has as much, often a deal more, dignity than numbers of our upper classes, who, in spite of the desire to keep themselves unspotted, are still, from the nature of their existence, touched by the herd-life of modern times. For vulgarity is the natural product of herd-life; an amalgam of second-hand thought, cheap and rapid sensation, defensive and offensive self-consciousness, gradually plastered over the faces, manners, voices, whole beings, of those whose elbows are too tightly squeezed to their sides by the pressure of their fellows, whose natures are cut off from Nature, whose senses are rendered imitative by the too insistent impact of certain sights and sounds. Without doubt the rapid increase of town-life is responsible for our acknowledged vulgarity. The same process is going on in America and in Northern Germany; but we unfortunately had the lead, and seem to be doing our best to keep it. Cheap newspapers, on the sensational tip-and-run system, perpetual shows of some kind or other, work in association, every kind of thing in association, at a speed too great for individual digestion, and in the presence of every device for removing the need for individual thought; the thronged streets, the football match with its crowd emotions; beyond all, the cinema—a compendium of all these other influences—make town-life a veritable forcing-pit of vulgarity. We are all so deeply in it that we do not see the process going on; or, if we admit it, hasten to add: "But what does it matter?—there's no harm in vulgarity; besides, it's inevitable, you can't set the tide back." Obviously, the vulgarity of town-life cannot be exorcised by Act of Parliament; there is not indeed the faintest chance that Parliament will recognise such a side to the question at all, since there is naturally no public opinion on this matter.

Everybody must recognise and admire certain qualities specially fostered by town-life; the extraordinary patience, cheerful courage, philosophic irony, and unselfishness of our towns-people—qualities which in this war, both at the front and at home, have been of the greatest value. They are worth much of the price paid. But in this life all is a question of balance; and my contention is, not so much that town-life in itself is bad, as that we have pushed it to a point of excess terribly dangerous to our physique, to our dignity, and to our sense of beauty. Must our future have no serene and simple quality, not even a spice of the influence of Nature, with her air, her trees, her fields, and wide skies? Say what you like, it is elbow-room for limbs and mind and lungs which keeps the countryman free from that dulled and driven look, and gives him individuality. I know all about the "dullness" and "monotony" of rural life, bad housing and the rest of it. All true enough, but the cure is not exodus, it is improvement in rural-life conditions, more co-operation, better cottages, a fuller, freer social life. What we in England now want more than anything is air—for lungs and mind. We have overdone herd-life. We are dimly conscious of this, feel vaguely that there is something "rattling" and wrong about our progress, for we have had many little spasmodic "movements" back to the land these last few years. But what do they amount to? Whereas in 1901 the proportion of town to country population in England and Wales was 3 10/37—1, in 1911 it was 3 17/20—1; very distinctly greater! At this crab's march we shall be some time getting "back to the land." Our effort, so far, has been something like our revival of Morris dancing, very pleasant and æsthetic, but without real economic basis or strength to stand up against the lure of the towns. And how queer, ironical, and pitiful is that lure, when you consider that in towns one-third of the population are just on or a little below the line of bare subsistence; that the great majority of town workers have hopelessly monotonous work, stuffy housing, poor air, and little leisure. But there it is—the charm of the lighted-up unknown, of company, and the streets at night! The countryman goes to the town in search of adventure. Honestly—does he really find it? He thinks he is going to improve his prospects and his mind. His prospects seldom brighten. He sharpens his mind, only to lose it and acquire instead that of the herd.

To compete with this lure of the towns, there must first be national consciousness of its danger; then coherent national effort to fight it. We must destroy the shibboleth: "All for wealth!" and re-write it: "All for health!"—the only wealth worth having. Wealth is not an end, surely. Then, to what is it the means, if not to health? Once we admit that in spite of our wealth our national health is going downhill through town-blight, we assert the failure of our country's ideals and life. And if, having got into a vicious state of congested town existence, we refuse to make an effort to get out again, because it is necessary to "hold our own commercially," and feed "the people" cheaply, we are in effect saying: "We certainly are going to hell, but look—how successfully!" I suggest rather that we try to pull ourselves up again out of the pit of destruction, even if to do so involves us in a certain amount of monetary loss and inconvenience. Yielding to no one in desire that "the people" should be well, nay better, fed, I decline utterly to accept the doctrine that there is no way of doing this compatible with an increased country population and the growth of our own food. In national matters, where there is a general and not a mere Party will, there is a way, and the way is not to be recoiled from because the first years of the change may necessitate Governmental regulation. Many people hold that our salvation will come through education. Education on right lines underlies everything, of course; but unless education includes the growth of our own food and return to the land in substantial measure, education cannot save us.

It may be natural to want to go to hell; it is certainly easy; we have gone so far in that direction that we cannot hope to be haloed in our time. For good or evil, the great towns are here, and we can but mitigate. The indicated policy of mitigation is fivefold:—

(1) Such solid economic basis to the growth of our food as will give us again national security, more arable land than we have ever had, and on it a full complement of well-paid workers, with better cottages, and a livened village life.

(2) A vast number of small holdings, State-created, with co-operative working.

(3) A wide belt-system of garden allotments round every town, industrial or not.

(4) Drastic improvements in housing, feeding, and sanitation in the towns themselves.

(5) Education that shall raise not only the standard of knowledge but the standard of taste in town and country.

All these ideals are already well in the public eye—on paper. But they are incoherently viewed and urged; they do not as yet form a national creed. Until welded and supported by all parties in the State, they will not have driving power enough to counteract the terrific momentum with which towns are drawing us down into the pit. One section pins its faith to town improvement; another to the development of small holdings; a third to cottage building; a fourth to education; a fifth to support of the price of wheat; a sixth to the destruction of landlords. Comprehensive vision of the danger is still lacking, and comprehensive grasp of the means to fight against it.

We are by a long way the most town-ridden country in the world; our towns by a long way the smokiest and worst built, with the most inbred town populations. We have practically come to an end of our country-stock reserves. Unless we are prepared to say: "This is a desirable state of things; let the inbreeding of town stocks go on—we shall evolve in time a new type immune to town life; a little ratty fellow all nerves and assurance, much better than any country clod!"—which, by the way, is exactly what some of us do say! Unless we mean as a nation to adopt this view and rattle on, light-heartedly, careless of menace from without and within, assuring ourselves that health and beauty, freedom and independence, as hitherto understood, have always been misnomers, and that nothing whatever matters so long as we are rich—unless all this, we must give check to the present state of things, restore a decent balance between town and country stock, grow our own food, and establish a permanent tendency away from towns.

All this fearfully unorthodox and provocative of sneers, and—goodness knows—I do not enjoy saying it. But needs must when the devil drives. It may be foolish to rave against the past and those factors and conditions which have put us so utterly in bond to towns—especially since this past and these towns have brought us such great wealth and so dominating a position in the world. It cannot be foolish, now that we have the wealth and the position, to resolve with all our might to free ourselves from bondage, to be masters, not servants, of our fate, to get back to firm ground, and make Health and Safety what they ever should be—the true keystones of our policy.

III

In the midst of a war like this the first efforts of any Government have to be directed to immediate ends. But under the pressure of the war the Government has a unique chance to initiate the comprehensive, far-reaching policy which alone can save us. Foundations to safety will only be laid if our representatives can be induced now to see this question of the land as the question of the future, no matter what happens in the war; to see that, whatever success we attain, we cannot remove the two real dangers of the future, sudden strangulation through swift attack by air and under sea—unless we grow our own food; and slow strangulation by town-life—unless we restore the land. Our imaginations are stirred, the driving force is here, swift action possible, and certain extraordinary opportunities are open which presently must close again.

On demobilisation we have the chance of our lives to put men on the land. Because this is still a Party question, to be sagaciously debated up hill and down dale three or four years hence, we shall very likely grasp the mere shadow and miss the substance of that opportunity. If the Government had a mandate "Full steam ahead" we could add at the end of the war perhaps a million men (potentially four million people) to our food-growing country population; as it is, we may add thereto a few thousands, lose half a million to the Colonies, and discourage the rest—patting our own backs the while. To put men on the land we must have the land ready in terms of earth, not of paper; and have it in the right places, within easy reach of town or village. Things can be done just now. We know, for instance, that in a few months half a million allotment-gardens have been created in urban areas and more progress made with small holdings than in previous years. I repeat, we have a chance which will not recur to scotch the food danger, and to restore a healthier balance between town and country stocks. Shall we be penny-wise and lose this chance for the luxury of "free and full discussion of a controversial matter at a time when men's minds are not full of the country's danger"? This is the country's danger—there is no other. And this is the moment for full and free discussion of it, for full and free action too. Who doubts that a Government which brought this question of the land in its widest aspects to the touch-stone of full debate at once, would get its mandate, would get the power it wanted—not to gerrymander, but to build?

Consider the Corn Production Bill. I will quote Mr. Prothero: "National security is not an impracticable dream. It is within our reach, within the course of a few years, and it involves no great dislocation of other industries." (Note that.) "For all practical purposes, if we could grow at home here 82 per cent, of all the food that we require for five years, we should be safe, and that amount of independence of sea-borne supplies we can secure, and secure within a few years.... We could obtain that result if we could add 8,000,000 acres of arable land to our existing area—that is to say, if we increased it from 19,000,000 acres to 27,000,000 acres. If you once got that extension of your arable area, the nation would be safe from the nightmare of a submarine menace, and the number of additional men who would be required on the land would be something about a quarter of a million." (Note that.) "The present Bill is much less ambitious." It is. And it is introduced by one who knows and dreads, as much as any of us, the dangerous and unballasted condition into which we have drifted; introduced with, as it were, apology, as if he feared that, unambitious though, it be, it will startle the nerves of Parliament. On a question so vast and vital you are bound to startle by any little measure. Nothing but an heroic measure would arouse debate on a scale adequate to reach and stir the depths of our national condition, and wake us all, politicians and public, to appreciate the fact that our whole future is in this matter, and that it must be tackled.

If we are not capable now of grasping the vital nature of this issue we assuredly never shall be. Only five generations have brought us to the parasitic, town-ridden condition we are in. The rate of progress in deterioration will increase rapidly with each coming generation. We have, as it were, turned seven-ninths of our population out into poor paddocks, to breed promiscuously among themselves. We have the chance to make our English and Welsh figures read: Twenty-four millions of town-dwellers to twelve of country, instead of, as now, twenty-eight millions to eight. Consider what that would mean to the breeding of the next generation. In such extra millions of country stock our national hope lies. What we should never dream of permitting with our domestic animals, we are not only permitting but encouraging among ourselves; we are doing all we can to perpetuate and increase poor stock; stock without either quality or bone, run-down, and ill-shaped. And, just as the progress in the "stock" danger is accelerated with each generation, so does the danger from outside increase with every year which sees flying and submarining improve, and our food capacity standing still.

The great argument against a united effort to regain our ballast is: We must not take away too many from our vital industries. Why, even the Minister of Agriculture, who really knows and dreads the danger, almost apologises for taking two hundred and fifty thousand from those vital industries, to carry out, not his immediate, but his ideal, programme. Vital industries! Ah! vital to Britain's destruction within the next few generations unless we mend our ways! The great impediment is the force of things as they are, the huge vested interests, the iron network of vast enterprises frightened of losing profit. If we pass this moment, when men of every class and occupation, even those who most thrive on our town-ridden state, are a little frightened; if we let slip this chance for a real reversal—can we hope that anything considerable will be done, with the dice loaded as they are, the scales weighted so hopelessly in favour of the towns? Representatives of seven-ninths will always see that representatives of two-ninths do not outvote them. This is a crude way of putting it, but it serves; because, after all, an elector is only a little bundle of the immediate needs of his locality and mode of life, outside of which he cannot see, and which he does not want prejudiced. He is not a fool, like me, looking into the future. And his representatives have got to serve him. The only chance, in a question so huge, vital, and long as this, is that greatly distrusted agent—Panic Legislation. When panic makes men, for a brief space, open their eyes and see truth, then it is valuable. Before our eyes close again and see nothing but the darkness of the daily struggle for existence, let us take advantage, and lay foundations which will be difficult, at least, to overturn.

What has been done so far, and what more can be done? A bounty on corn has been introduced. I suppose nobody, certainly not its promoter, is enamoured of this. But it does not seem to have occurred to every one that you cannot eat nuts without breaking their shells, or get out of evil courses without a transition period of extreme annoyance to yourself. "Bounty" is, in many quarters, looked on as a piece of petting to an interest already pampered. Well—while we look on the land as an "interest" in competition with other "interests" and not as the vital interest of the country, underlying every other, so long shall we continue to be "in the soup." The land needs fostering, and again fostering, because the whole vicious tendency of the country's life has brought farming to its present pass and farmers to their attitude of mistrust. Doctrinaire objections are now ridiculous. An economic basis must be re-established, or we may as well cry "Kamerad" at once and hold up our hands to Fate. The greater the arable acreage in this country, the less will be the necessity for a bounty on corn. Unlike most stimulants, it is one which gradually stimulates away the need for it. With every year and every million acres broken up, not only will the need for bounty diminish, but the present mistrustful breed of farmer will be a step nearer to extinction. Shrewd, naturally conservative, and somewhat intolerant of anything so dreamy as a national point of view, they will not live for ever. The up-growing farmer will not be like them, and about the time the need for bounty is vanishing the new farmer will be in possession. But in the meantime land must be broken up until 8,000,000 acres at least are conquered; and bounty is the only lever. It will not be lever enough without constant urging. In Mr. Prothero's history of English farming occur these words: "A Norfolk farmer migrated to Devonshire in 1780, where he drilled and hoed his roots; though his crops were far superior to those of other farmers in the district, yet at the close of the century no neighbour had followed his example."

But even the break-up of 8,000,000 acres, though it may make us safe for food, will only increase our country population by 250,000 labourers and their families (a million souls)—a mere beginning towards the satisfaction of our need. We want in operation, before demobilisation begins, a great national plan for the creation of good small holdings run on co-operative lines. And to this end, why should not the suggestion of tithe redemption, thrown out by Mr. Prothero, on pages 399 and 400 of "English Farming: Past and Present," be adopted? The annual value of tithes is about £5,000,000. Their extinction should provide the Government with about 2,500,000 acres, enough at one stroke to put three or four hundred thousand soldiers on the land. The tithe-holders would get their money, landlords would not be prejudiced; the Government, by virtue of judicious choice and discretionary compulsion, would obtain the sort of land it wanted, and the land would be for ever free of a teasing and vexatious charge. The cost to the Government would be £100,000,000 (perhaps more) on the best security it could have. "Present conditions," I quote from the book, "are favourable to such a transaction. The price of land enables owners to extinguish the rent charge by the surrender of a reasonable acreage, and the low price of Consols enables investors to obtain a larger interest for their money." For those not familiar with this notion, the process, in brief, is this: The Government pays the tithe-holder the capitalised value of his tithe, and takes over from the landlord as much land as produces in net annual rent the amount of the tithe-rent charge, leaving the rest of his land tithe-free for ever. There are doubtless difficulties and objections, but so there must be to any comprehensive plan for obtaining an amount of land at all adequate. Time is of desperate importance in this matter. It is already dangerously late, but if the Government would turn-to now with a will, the situation could still be saved, and this unique chance for re-stocking our countryside would not be thrown away.

I alluded to the formation within a few months of half a million garden-allotments—plots of ground averaging about ten poles each, taken under the Defence of the Realm Act from building and other land in urban areas, and given to cultivators, under a guarantee, for the growth of vegetables. This most valuable effort, for which the Board of Agriculture deserves the thanks of all, is surely capable of very great extension. Every town, no matter how quickly it may be developing, is always surrounded by a belt of dubious land—not quite town and not quite country. When town development mops up plots in cultivation, a hole can be let out in an elastic belt which is capable of almost indefinite expansion. But this most useful and health-giving work has only been possible under powers which will cease when the immediate danger to the State has passed. If a movement, which greatly augments our home-grown food supply and can give quiet, healthy, open-air, interesting work for several hours a week to perhaps a million out of our congested town populations—if such a movement be allowed to collapse at the coming of peace, it will be nothing less than criminal. I plead here that the real danger to the State will not pass but rather begin, with the signing of peace, that the powers to acquire and grant these garden-allotments should be continued, and every effort made to foster and extend the movement. Considering that, whatever we do to re-colonise our land, we must still have in this country a dangerously huge town population, this kitchen-garden movement can be of incalculable value in combating town-blight, in securing just that air to lungs and mind, and just that spice of earth reality which all town-dwellers need so much.

Extension of arable land by at least 8,000,000 acres; creation of hundreds of thousands of small holdings by tithe redemption, or another scheme still in the blue; increase and perpetuation of garden-allotments—besides all these we want, of course, agricultural schools and facilities for training; co-operatively organised finance, transport, and marketing of produce; for without schooling, and co-operation, no system of small holding on a large scale can possibly succeed. We now have the labourer's minimum wage, which, I think, will want increasing; but we want good rural housing on an economically sound basis, an enlivened village life, and all that can be done to give the worker on the land a feeling that he can rise, the sense that he is not a mere herd, at the beck and call of what has been dubbed the "tyranny of the countryside." The land gives work which is varied, alive, and interesting beyond all town industries, save those, perhaps, of art and the highly-skilled crafts and professions. If we can once get land-life back on to a wide and solid basis, it should hold its own.

Dare any say that this whole vast question of the land, with its throbbing importance, yea—seeing that demobilisations do not come every year—its desperately immediate importance, is not fit matter for instant debate and action; dare any say that we ought to relegate it to that limbo "After the war"? In grim reality it takes precedence of every other question. It is infinitely more vital to our safety and our health than consideration of our future commercial arrangements. In our present Parliament—practically, if not sentimentally speaking—all shades of opinion are as well represented as they are likely to be in future Parliaments—even the interests of our women and our soldiers; to put off the good day when this question is threshed out, is to crane at an imagined hedge.

Let us know now at what we are aiming, let us admit and record in the black and white of legislation that we intend to trim our course once more for the port of health and safety. If this Britain of ours is going to pin her whole future to a blind pursuit of wealth, without considering whether that wealth is making us all healthier and happier, many of us, like Sancho, would rather retire at once, and be made "governors of islands." For who can want part or lot on a ship which goes yawing with every sail set into the dark, without rudder, compass, or lighted star?

I, for one, want a Britain who refuses to take the mere immediate line of least resistance, who knows and sets her course, and that a worthy one. So do we all, I believe, at heart—only, the current is so mighty and strong, and we are so used to it!

By the parasitic and town-ridden condition we are in now, and in which without great and immediate effort we are likely to remain, we degrade our patriotism. That we should have to tremble lest we be starved is a miserable, a humiliating thought. To have had so little pride and independence of spirit as to have come to this, to have been such gobblers at wealth—who dare defend it? We have made our bed; let us, now, refuse to lie thereon. Better the floor than this dingy feather couch of suffocation.

Our country is dear to us, and many are dying for her. There can be no consecration of their memory so deep or so true as this regeneration of The Land.

1917

I

INTRODUCTORY

Can one assume that the pinch of this war is really bringing home to us the vital need of growing our own food henceforth? I do not think so. Is there any serious shame felt at our parasitic condition? None. Are we in earnest about the resettlement of the land? Not yet.

All our history shows us to be a practical people with short views. "Tiens! Une montagne!" Never was a better summing up of British character than those words of the French cartoonist during the Boer War, beneath his picture of a certain British General of those days, riding at a hand gallop till his head was butting a cliff. Without seeing a hand's breadth before our noses we have built our Empire, our towns, our law. We are born empiricists, and must have our faces ground by hard facts, before we attempt to wriggle past them. We have thriven so far, but the ruin of England is likely to be the work of practical men who burn the house down to roast the pig, because they cannot see beyond the next meal. Visions are airy; but I propose to see visions for a moment, and Britain as she might be in 1948.

I see our towns, not indeed diminished from their present size, but no larger; much cleaner, and surrounded by wide belts of garden allotments, wherein town workers spend many of their leisure hours. I see in Great Britain fifty millions instead of forty-one; but the town population only thirty-two millions as now, and the rural population eighteen millions instead of the present nine. I see the land farmed in three ways: very large farms growing corn and milk, meat and wool, or sugar beet; small farms co-operatively run growing everything; and large groups of co-operative small holdings, growing vegetables, fruit, pigs, poultry, and dairy produce to some extent. There are no game laws to speak of, and certainly no large areas of ground cut to waste for private whims. I see very decent cottages everywhere, with large plots of ground at economic rents, and decently waged people paying them; no tithes, but a band of extinguished tithe-holders, happy with their compensation. The main waterways of the country seem joined by wide canals, and along these canals factories are spread out on the garden city plan, with allotments for the factory workers. Along better roads run long chains of small holdings, so that the co-operated holders have no difficulty in marketing their produce. I see motor transport; tractor ploughs; improved farm machinery; forestry properly looked after, and foreshores reclaimed; each village owning its recreation hall, with stage and cinema attached; and public-houses run only on the principle of no commission on the drink sold; every school teaching the truth that happiness and health, not mere money and learning, are the prizes of life and the objects of education, and for ever impressing on the scholars that life in the open air and pleasure in their work are the two chief secrets of health and happiness. In every district a model farm radiates scientific knowledge of the art of husbandry, bringing instruction to each individual farmer, and leaving him no excuse for ignorance. The land produces what it ought; not, as now, feeding with each hundred acres only fifty persons, while a German hundred acres, not nearly so favoured by Nature, feeds seventy-five. Every little girl has been taught to cook. Farmers are no longer fearful of bankruptcy, as in the years from 1875 to 1897, but hold their own with all comers, proud of their industry, the spine and marrow of a country which respects itself once more. There seems no longer jealousy or division between town and country; and statesmen by tacit consent leave the land free from Party politics. I see taller and stronger men and women, rosier and happier children; a race no longer narrow, squashed, and disproportionate; no longer smoke-dried and nerve-racked, with the driven, don't-care look of a town-ridden land. And surely the words "Old

England" are spoken by all voices with a new affection, as of a land no longer sucking its sustenance from other lands, but sound and sweet, the worthy heart once more of a great commonwealth of countries.

All this I seem to see, if certain things are done now and persevered in hereafter. But let none think that we can restore self-respect and the land-spirit to this country under the mere momentary pressure of our present-day need. Such a transformation cannot come unless we are genuinely ashamed that Britain should be a sponge; unless we truly wish to make her again sound metal, ringing true, instead of a splay-footed creature, dependent for vital nourishment on oversea supplies—a cockshy for every foe.

We are practically secured by Nature, yet have thrown security to the winds because we cannot feed ourselves! We have as good a climate and soil as any in the world, not indeed for pleasure, but for health and food, and yet, I am sure, we are rotting physically faster than any other people!

Let the nation put that reflection in its pipe and smoke it day by day; for only so shall we emerge from a bad dream and seize again on our birthright.

Let us dream a little of what we might become. Let us not crawl on with our stomachs to the ground, and not an ounce of vision in our heads for fear lest we be called visionaries. And let us rid our minds of one or two noxious superstitions. It is not true that country life need mean dull and cloddish life; it has in the past, because agriculture as been neglected for the false glamour of the towns, and village life left to seed down. There is no real reason why the villager should not have all he needs of social life and sane amusement; village life only wants organising. It is not true that country folk must be worse fed and worse plenished than town folk. This has only been so sometimes because a starved industry which was losing hope has paid starvation wages. It is not true that our soil and climate are of indifferent value for the growth of wheat. The contrary is the case. "The fact which has been lost sight of in the past twenty years must be insisted on nowadays, that England is naturally one of the best, if not the very best wheat-growing country in the world. Its climate and soil are almost ideal for the production of the heaviest crops": Professor R. H. Biffen. "The view of leading German agriculturists is that their soils and climate are distinctly inferior to those of Britain": Mr. T. H. Middleton, Assistant Secretary to the Board of Agriculture.

We have many mouths in this country, but no real excuse for not growing the wherewithal to feed them.

To break the chains of our lethargy and superstitions, let us keep before us a thought and a vision—the thought that, since the air is mastered and there are pathways under the sea, we, the proudest people in the world, will exist henceforth by mere merciful accident, until we grow our own food; and the vision of ourselves as a finer race in body and mind than we have ever yet been. And then let us be practical by all means; for in the practical measures of the present, spurred on by that thought, inspired by that vision, alone lies the hope and safety of the future.

What are those measures?

II

WHEAT

The measure which underlies all else is the ploughing up of permanent grass—the reconversion of land which was once arable, the addition to arable of land which has never been arable, so as to secure the only possible basis of success—the wheat basis.

I have before me a Report on the Breaking up of Grass Land in fifty-five counties for the winter of 1916-1917, which shows four successes for every failure. The Report says: "It has been argued during the past few months that it is hopeless to attempt to plough out old grass land in the expectation of adding to the nation's food. The experience of 1917 does not support this contention. It shows not only that the successes far outnumber the failures, but that the latter are to some extent preventable."

The Government's 1918 tillage programme for England and Wales was to increase (as compared with 1916), (1) the area under corn by 2,600,000 acres, (2) the area under potatoes and mangolds by 400,000 acres, (3) the arable land by 2,000,000 acres. I have it on the best authority that the Government hopes to better this in the forth-coming harvest. That shows what our farmers can do with their backs to the wall. It sometimes happens in this world that we act virtuously without in any way believing that virtue is its own reward. Most of our farmers are hoeing their rows in this crisis in the full belief that they are serving the country to the hurt of their own interests; they will not, I imagine, realise that they are laying the foundations of a future prosperity beyond their happiest dreams until the crisis is long past. All the more credit to them for a great effort. They by no means grasp at present the fact that with every acre they add to arable, with each additional acre of wheat, they increase their own importance and stability, and set the snowball of permanent prosperity in their industry rolling anew. Pasture was a policy adopted by men who felt defeat in their bones, saw bankruptcy round every corner. Those who best know seem agreed that after the war the price of wheat will not come down with a run. The world shortage of food and shipping will be very great, and the "new world's" surplus will be small. Let our farmers take their courage in their hands, play a bold game, and back their own horse for the next four or five seasons, and they will, if supported by the country, be in a position once more to defy competition. Let them have faith and go for the gloves and they will end by living without fear of the new worlds. "There is a tide in the affairs of men." This is the British farmer's tide, which, taken at the flood, leads on to fortune. But only if the British farmer intends that Britain shall feed herself; only if he farms the land of Britain so that acre by acre it yields the maximum of food. A hundred acres under potatoes feeds 420 persons; a hundred acres under wheat feeds 200 persons; a hundred acres of grass feeds fifteen persons. It requires no expert to see that the last is the losing horse; for increase of arable means also increase of winter food, and in the long run increase, not decrease, of live stock. In Denmark (1912) arable was to permanent grass as about 4 to 5; in the United Kingdom it was only as about 5 to 7. Yet in Denmark there were five cattle to every eight acres of grass, and in the United Kingdom only four cattle to every nine acres.

Let me quote Professor Biffen on the prospects of wheat: "In the United States the amount exported tends to fall. The results are so marked that we find American agricultural experts seriously considering the possibility of the United States having to become a wheat importing country in order to feed the rapidly growing population." When she does, that wheat will come from Canada; and "there are several other facts which lead one to question the statement so frequently made that Canada will shortly be the Empire's granary...." He thinks that the Argentine (which trebles her population every forty years) is an uncertain source; that Russia, where the population also increases with extreme rapidity, is still more uncertain; that neither India nor Australia are dependable fields of supply. "The world's crop continues to increase slowly, and concurrently the number of wheat consumers increases.... Prices have tended to rise of late years, a fact which may indicate that the world's consumption is increasing faster than its rate of production. There are now no vast areas of land comparable with those of North and South America awaiting the pioneer wheat growers, and consequently there is no likelihood of any repetition of the over-production characteristic of the period of 1874-1894....

"If as there is every reason to hope the problem of breeding satisfactory strong wheats" (for this country) "has been solved, then their cultivation should add about £1 to the value of the produce of every acre of wheat in the country....

"At a rough estimate the careful use of artificials might increase the average yield of the acre from four quarters up to five....

"England is one of the best, if not the very best wheat-growing country in the world."

That, shortly, is the wheat position for this country in the view of our most brilliant practical expert. I commend it to the notice of those who are faint-hearted about the future of wheat in Britain.

With these prospects and possibilities before him, and a fair price for wheat guaranteed him, is the British farmer going to let down the land to grass again when the war is over? The fair price for wheat will be the point on which his decision will turn. When things have settled down after the war, the fair price will be that at which the average farmer can profitably grow wheat, and such a price must be maintained—by bounty, if necessary. It never can be too often urged on politicians and electorate that they, who thwart a policy which makes wheat-growing firm and profitable, are knocking nails in the coffin of their country. We are no longer, and never shall again be, an island. The air is henceforth as simple an avenue of approach as Piccadilly is to Leicester Square. If we are ever attacked there will be no time to get our second wind, unless we can feed ourselves. And since we are constitutionally liable to be caught napping, we shall infallibly be brought to the German heel next time, if we are not self-supporting. But if we are, there will be no next time. An attempt on us will not be worth the cost. Further, we are running to seed physically from too much town-life and the failure of country stocks; we shall never stem that rot unless we re-establish agriculture on a large scale. To do that, in the view of nearly all who have thought this matter out, we must found our farming on wheat; grow four-fifths instead of one-fifth of our supply, and all else will follow.

In England and Wales 11,246,106 acres were arable land in 1917, and 15,835,375 permanent grass land. To reverse these figures, at least, is the condition of security, perhaps even of existence in the present and the only guarantee of a decent and safe future.

III

HOLDINGS

One expert pins faith to large farms; another to small holdings. How agreeable to think that both are right. We cannot afford to neglect any type of holding; all must be developed and supported, for all serve vital purposes. For instance, the great development of small holdings in Germany is mainly responsible for the plentiful supply of labour on the land there; "until measures can be devised for greatly increasing the area under holdings of less than 100 acres in Britain we are not likely to breed and maintain in the country a sufficient number of that class of worker which will be required if we are greatly to extend our arable land": Mr. T. H. Middleton, Assistant Secretary to the Board of Agriculture.

But I am not going into the pros and cons of the holdings question. I desire rather to point out here that a moment is approaching, which will never come again, for the resettling of the land.

A rough census taken in 1916 among our soldiers gave the astounding figure of 750,000 desirous of going on the land. That figure will shrink to a mere skeleton unless on demobilisation the Government is ready with a comprehensive plan. The men fall roughly into two classes: those who were already on the land; those who were not. The first will want to go back to their own districts, but not to the cottages and wages they had before the war. For them, it is essential to provide new cottages with larger gardens, otherwise they will go to the Dominions, to America, or to the towns. A fresh census should be taken and kept up to date, the wants of each man noted, and a definite attempt made now to earmark sites and material for building, to provide the garden plots, and plan the best and prettiest type of cottage. For lack of labour and material no substantial progress can be made with housing while the war is on, but if a man can see his cottage and his ground ready, in the air, he will wait; if he cannot, he will be off, and we shall have lost him. Wages are not to fall again below twenty-five shillings, and will probably stay at a considerably higher level. The cottage and the garden ground for these men will be the determining factor, and that garden ground should be at least an acre. A larger class by far will be men who were not on the land, but having tasted open-air life, think they wish to continue it. A fresh census of this class and their wants should be taken also. It will subdivide them into men who want the life of independent medium and small holders, with from 100 to 20 acres of land, and men who with 5 or 10 acres of their own are willing to supplement their living by seasonal work on the large farms. For all a cut-and-dried scheme providing land and homes is absolutely essential. If they cannot be assured of having these within a few months of their return to civil life, they will go either to the Dominions or back to the towns. One of them, I am told, thus forecasts their future wants: "When we're free we shall have a big spree in the town; we shall then take the first job that comes along; if it's an indoor job we shan't be able to stick it and shall want to get on the land." I am pretty sure he's wrong. He will want his spree, of course; but if he is allowed to go back to a town job he is not at all likely to leave it again. Men so soon get used to things, and the towns have a fierce grip. For this second class, no less than the first, it is vital to have the land ready, and the cottages estimated for. I think men of both these classes, when free, should be set at once to the building of their own homes and the preparation of their land. I think huts ought to be ready for them and their wives till their homes are habitable. A man who takes a hand in the building of his house, and the first work on his new holding, is far less likely to abandon his idea of settling on the land than a man who is simply dumped into a ready-made concern. That is human nature. Let him begin at the beginning, and while his house is going up be assisted and instructed. Frankly, I am afraid that in the difficulty of fixing on an ideal scheme and ideal ways of working it, we shall forget that the moment of demobilisation is unique. Any scheme, however rough and ready, which will fix men or their intention of settling on the land in Britain at the moment of demobilisation will be worth a hundred better-laid plans which have waited for perfection till that one precious moment is overpast. While doctors quarrel, or lay their heads together, the patient dies.

The Government, I understand, have adopted a scheme by which they can secure land. If they have not ascertained from these men what land they will want, and secured that land by the time the men are ready, that scheme will be of little use to them.

The Government, I gather, have decided on a huge scheme for urban and rural housing. About that I have this to say. The rural housing ought to take precedence of the urban, not because it is more intrinsically necessary, but because if the moment of demobilisation is let slip for want of rural cottages, we shall lose our very life blood, our future safety, perhaps our existence as a nation. We must seize on this one precious chance of restoring the land and guaranteeing our future. The towns can wait a little for their housing, the country cannot. It is a sort of test question for our leaders in every Party. Surely they will rise to the vital necessity of grasping this chance! If, when the danger of starvation has been staring us hourly in the face for years on end, and we have for once men in hundreds of thousands waiting and hoping to be settled on the land, to give us the safety of the future—if, in such circumstances, we cannot agree to make the most of that chance, it will show such lack of vision that I really feel we may as well throw up the sponge. If jealousy by towns of country can so blind public opinion to our danger and our chance, so that no precedence can be given to rural needs, well, then, frankly we are not fit to live as a nation.

I am told that Germany has seen to this matter. She does not mean to be starved in the future; she intends to keep the backbone of her country sound. She, who already grew 80 per cent. of her food, will grow it all. She, who already appreciated the dangers of a rampant industrialism, will take no further risks with the physique of her population. We who did not grow one-half of our food, and whose riotous industrialism has made far greater inroads on our physique; we who, though we have not yet suffered the privations of Germany, have been in far more real danger—we shall talk about it, say how grave the situation is, how "profoundly" we are impressed by the need to feed ourselves—and we shall act, I am very much afraid, too late.

There are times when the proverb: "Act in haste and repent at leisure" should be written "Unless you act in haste you will repent at leisure." This is such a time. We can take, of course, the right steps or the wrong steps to settle our soldiers on the land; but no wrong step we can take will be so utterly wrong as to let the moment of demobilisation slip. We have a good and zealous Minister of Agriculture, we have good men alive to the necessity, working on this job. If we miss the chance it will be because "interests" purblind, selfish and perverse, and a lethargic public opinion, do not back them; because we want to talk it out; because trade and industry think themselves of superior importance to the land. Henceforth trade and industry are of secondary importance in this country. There is only one thing of absolutely vital importance, and that is agriculture.

IV

INSTRUCTION

I who have lived most of my time on a farm for many years, in daily contact with farmer and labourer, do really appreciate what variety and depth of knowledge is wanted for good farming. It is a lesson to the armchair reformer to watch a farmer walking across the "home meadow" whence he can see a good way over his land. One can feel the slow wisdom working in his head. A halt, a look this way and that, a whistle, the call of some instruction so vernacular that only a native could understand; the contemplation of sheep, beasts, sky, crops; always something being noted, and shrewd deductions made therefrom. It is a great art, and, like all art, to be learned only with the sweat of the brow and a long, minute attention to innumerable details. You cannot play at farming, and you cannot "mug it up." One understands the contempt of the farmer born and bred for the book-skilled gentleman who tries to instruct his grandmother in the sucking of eggs. The farmer's knowledge, acquired through years of dumb wrestling with Nature, in his own particular corner, is his strength and—his weakness. Vision of the land at large, of its potentialities, and its needs is almost of necessity excluded. The practical farmers of our generation might well be likened unto sailing-ship seamen in an age when it has suddenly become needful to carry commerce by steam. They are pupils of the stern taskmaster bankruptcy; the children of the years from 1874-1897, when the nation had turned its thumb down on British farmers, and left them to fight, unaided, against extinction. They have been brought up to carry on against contrary winds and save themselves as best they could. Well, they have done it; and now they are being asked to reverse their processes in the interests of a country which left them in the lurch. Naturally they are not yet persuaded that the country will not leave them in the lurch again.

Instruction of the British farmer begins with the fortification of his will by confidence. When you ask him to plough up grass land, to revise the rotation of his crops, to grow wheat, to use new brands of corn, to plough with tractors, and to co-operate, you are asking a man deeply and deservedly cynical about your intentions and your knowledge. He has seen wheat fail all his life, he has seen grass succeed. Grass has saved him, and now he is asked to turn his back on it. Little wonder that he curses you for a meddling fool. "Prove it!" he says—and you cannot. You could if you had it in your power to show him that your guarantee of a fair price for wheat was "good as the Bank." Thus, the first item of instruction to the farmer consists in the definite alteration of public opinion towards the land by adoption of the sine quâ non that in future we will feed ourselves. The majority of our farmers do not think their interests are being served by the present revolution of farming. Patriotic fear for the country, and dread of D.O.R.A.—not quite the same thing—are driving them on. Besides, it is the townsmen of Britain, not the farmers, who are in danger of starvation, not merely now, but henceforth for evermore until we feed ourselves. If starvation really knocked at our doors, the only houses it would not enter would be the houses of those who grow food. The farmers in Germany are all right; they would be all right here. The townsmen of this country were entirely responsible for our present condition, and the very least they can do is to support their own salvation. But while with one corner of their mouths the towns are now shouting: "Grow food! Feed us, please!" with the other they are still inclined to add: "You pampered industry!" Alas! we cannot have it both ways.

The second point I want to make about instruction is the importance of youth. In America, where they contemplate a labour shortage of 2,000,000 men on their farms, they are using boys from sixteen to twenty-one, when their military age begins. Can we not do the same here? Most of our boys from fifteen to eighteen are now on other work. But the work they are doing could surely be done by girls or women. If we could put even a couple of hundred thousand boys of that age on the land it would be the solution of our present agricultural labour shortage, and the very best thing that could happen for the future of farming. The boys would learn at first hand; they would learn slowly and thoroughly; and many of them would stay on the land. They might be given specialised schooling in agriculture, the most important schooling we can give our rising generation, while all of them would gain physically. By employing women on the land, where we can employ boys of from fifteen to eighteen, we are blind-alleying. Women will not stay on the land in any numbers; few will wish that they should. Boys will, and every one would wish that they may.

The third point I want to make concerns the model farm. If we are to have resettlement on any large scale and base our farming on crops in future, the accessibility of the best practical advice is an absolute essential.

Till reformed education begins to take effect, the advice and aid of "model" farmers should be available in every district. Some recognised diploma might with advantage be given to farmers for outstanding merit and enterprise. No instruction provided from our advisory agricultural councils or colleges can have as much prestige and use in any district as the advice of the leading farmer who had been crowned as a successful expert. It is ever well in this country to take advantage of the competitive spirit which lies deep in the bones of our race. To give the best farmers a position and prestige to which other farmers can aspire would speed up effort everywhere. We want more competition in actual husbandry and less competition in matters of purchase and sale. And that brings us to the vital question of co-operation.

CO-OPERATION (SMALL HOLDINGS)

"The most important economic question for all nations in the past has been, and in the future will be, the question of a sufficient food supply, independent of imports.

"It is doubtful whether the replacement of German agriculture on a sound basis in the last ten years is to be ascribed in a greater measure to technical advance in agricultural methods, or to the development of the co-operative system. Perhaps it would be right to say that for the large farms it is due to the first, and for the smaller farms (three quarters of the arable land in Germany) to the second. For it is only through co-operation that the advantages of farming on a large scale are made possible for smaller farmers. The more important of those advantages are the regulated purchase of all raw materials and half-finished products (artificial manures, feeding stuffs, seeds, etc.), better prices for products, facilities for making use, in moderation, of personal credit at a cheap rate of interest, together with the possibility of saving and putting aside small sums of interest; all these advantages of the large farmer have been placed within the reach of the small farmers by local co-operative societies for buying, selling, and farming co-operatively, as well as by saving and other banks, all connected to central associations and central co-operative societies.

"Over two million small farmers are organised in Germany on co-operative lines."[E]

Nearly two million small farmers co-operated in Germany; and here-how many? The Registrar returns the numbers for 1916 at 1,427 small holders.

In the view of all authorities co-operation is essential for the success of small farmers and small holders; but it needs no brilliant intellect, nor any sweep of the imagination to see a truth plainer than the nose on a man's face.

"There is some reason to hope," says Mr. Middleton, "that after the war agriculturalists will show a greater disposition to co-operate; but we cannot expect co-operation to do as much for British agriculture as it has done for the Germans, who so readily join societies and support co-operative efforts."

So much the worse for us!

The Agricultural Organisation Society, the officially recognised agency for fostering the co-operative principle, has recently formed an Agricultural Wholesale Society with a large subscribed capital, for the purchase of all farming requirements, and the marketing of produce, to be at the disposal of all co-operated farmers, small holders, and allotment holders, whose societies are affiliated to the Agricultural Organisation. Society. This is a step of infinite promise. The drawing together of these three classes of workers on the land is in itself a matter of great importance. One of the chief complaints of small holders in the past has been that large holders regard them askance. The same, perhaps, applies to the attitude of the small holder to the allotment holder. That is all bad. Men and women on the land should be one big family, with interests, and sympathies in common and a neighbourly feeling.

A leaflet of the Agricultural Organisation Society thus describes a certain co-operative small holdings' society with seventeen members renting ninety acres. "It owns a team of horses, cart, horse-hoe, plough, ridger, harrow, Cambridge roller, marker; and hires other implements as required; it insures, buys, and sells co-operatively. This year (for patriotic reasons) wheat and potatoes form the chief crop, with sufficient oats, barley, beans and mangolds to feed the horses and the pigs, of which there are many. The society last year marketed more fat pigs than the rest of the village and adjoining farms put together.

"The land, on the whole, is undoubtedly better cultivated and cropped, and supports a far larger head of population per acre than the neighbouring large farms." Even allowing that the first statement may be disputed, the last is beyond dispute, and is the important thing to bear in mind about small holdings from the national point of view; for every extra man and woman on the land is a credit item in the bank book of the nation's future.

"In addition," says the leaflet, "there is a friendly spirit prevalent among the members, who are always willing to help each other, and at harvest time combine to gather in the crops."

With more land, not only some, but all the members of this little society could support themselves entirely on their holdings. "The members value their independence and freedom, but recognise the value of combined action and new ideas."

Now this is exactly what we want. For instance, these members have found out that the profit on potatoes when home-grown farmyard manure alone was used was only 14s. 6d. per acre; and that a suitable combination of artificial manures gave a profit of £14 12s. 6d. an acre, with double the yield. Mutual help and the spread of knowledge; more men and women on the land—this is the value of the agricultural co-operative movement, whose importance to this country it is impossible to over-estimate.

From letters of small holders I take the following remarks:—

"Of course it's absolutely necessary that the prospective small holder should have a thorough knowledge of farming."

"In regard to implements, you need as many of some sorts on a small holding as you do on a large farm. A small man can't afford to buy all, so he has to work at a disadvantage.... Then as to seeds, why not buy them wholesale, and sell them to the small holder, also manures, and many other things which the small holder has to pay through the nose for."

"Men with no actual knowledge of land work would rarely succeed whatever financial backing they might receive."

"About here small holdings are usually let to men who have been tradesmen or pitmen, and they of course cannot be expected to make the most of them."

"When you restrict a farmer to 50 acres he ought to be provided with ample and proper buildings for every kind of stock he wishes to keep."

These few remarks, which might be supplemented ad libitum, illustrate the difficulties and dangers which beset any large scheme of land settlement by our returning soldiers and others. Such a scheme is bound to fail unless it is based most firmly on co-operation, for, without that, the two absolute essentials—knowledge, with the benefit of practical advice and help; and assistance by way of co-operative finance, and co-operatively-owned implements, will be lacking.

Set the returning soldier down on the land to work it on his own and, whatever his good-will, you present the countryside with failure. Place at his back pooled labour, monetary help and knowledge, and, above all, the spirit of mutual aid, and you may, and I believe will, triumph over difficulties, which are admittedly very great.

VI

CO-OPERATION (ALLOTMENTS)

The growth of allotment gardens is a striking feature of our agricultural development under stimulus of the war. They say a million and a half allotment gardens are now being worked on. That is, no doubt, a papery figure; nor is it so much the number, as what is being done on them, that matters. Romance may have "brought up the nine-fifteen," but it will not bring up potatoes. Still, these new allotments without doubt add very greatly to our food supply, give hosts of our town population healthy work in the open air, and revive in them that "earth instinct" which was in danger of being utterly lost. The spade is a grand corrective of nerve strain, and the more town and factory workers take up allotment gardens, the better for each individual, and for us all as a race.

They say nearly all the ground available round our towns has already been utilised. But DORA, in her wild career, may yet wring out another hundred thousand acres. I wish her well in this particular activity. And the Government she serves with such devotion will betray her if, when DORA is in her grave—consummation devoutly to be wished—her work on allotment gardens is not continued. There is always a ring of land round a town, like a halo round the moon. As the town's girth increases, so should that halo; and even in time of peace, larger and larger, not less and less, should grow the number of town dwellers raising vegetables, fruit and flowers, resting their nerves and expanding lungs and muscles with healthy outdoor work.

"In no direction is the co-operative principle more adaptable or more useful than in the matter of Allotment Associations."

There are now allotment associations in many parts of the country. One at Winchester has over 1,000 tenant members. And round the great manufacturing towns many others have been formed.

To illustrate the advantages of such co-operation, let me quote a little from the Hon. Secretary of the Urmston Allotments Association, near Manchester: "Though the Urmston men had foremost in their mind the aim of producing payable crops ... they determined that their allotments should be convenient and comfortable to work, and pleasing to look upon.... It is a delusion often found among novices that ordinary ground takes a long time to get into decent order; and is an expensive business. But enlightened and energetic men working together can do wonderful things. They did them at Urmston. The ground was only broken up in March, 1916, but in the same season splendid crops of peas, potatoes and other vegetables were raised by the holders, the majority of whom had little or no previous experience of gardening.... So as to deal with the main needs of the members co-operatively in the most effective manner a Trading Committee was appointed to advise and make contracts.... Manure, lime, salt, and artificial manures have been ordered collectively; and seeds and other gardening requisites arranged for at liberal discounts."

Besides all this the association has fought the potato wart disease; had its soil analyzed; educated its members through literature and lectures; made roads and fences; looked after the appearance of its plots, and encouraged flower-growing. Finally, a neighbourly feeling of friendly emulation has grown up among its members. And this is their conclusion: "The advantages of co-operation are not confined to economy in time and money, for the common interest that binds all members to seek the success of the Association, also provides the means of developing and utilising the individual talents of the members for communal and national purposes."

They speak, indeed, like a book, and every word is true—which is not always the same thing.

The Agricultural Organization Society gives every assistance in forming these associations; and the more there are of them the greater will be the output of food, the strength and knowledge of the individual plot-holder, the stability of his tenure, and the advantage of the nation.

Mistrust and reserve between workers on the land, be they large farmers, small farmers, or plotholders is the result of combining husbandry with the habits and qualities of the salesman. If a man's business is to get the better of his neighbours on market days, it will be his pleasure to doubt them on all other days.

The co-operative system, by conducting purchase and sale impersonally, removes half the reason and excuse for curmudgeonery, besides securing better prices both at sale and purchase. To the disgust of the cynic, moral and material advantage here go hand in hand. Throughout agriculture co-operation will do more than anything else to restore spirit and economy to an industry which had long become dejected, suspicious and wasteful; and it will help to remove jealousy and distrust between townsmen and countrymen. The allotment holder, if encouraged and given fixity of tenure, or at all events the power of getting fresh ground if he must give up what he has—a vital matter—will become the necessary link between town and country, with mind open to the influence of both. The more he is brought into working contact with the small holder and the large farmer the better he will appreciate his own importance to the country and ensure theirs. But this contact can only be established through some central body, and by use of a wholesale society for trading and other purposes, such as has just been set up for all classes of co-operated agriculturalists.

Addressing a recent meeting of its members, the Chairman of the Agricultural Organisation Society, Mr. Leslie Scott, spoke thus:—"We have to cover the country" (with co-operative societies), "and we have got to get all the farmers in! If we can carry out any such scheme as this, which will rope in all the farmers of the country, what a magnificent position we shall be in! You will have your great trading organisation with its central wholesale society! You will have your organisation side with the Agricultural Organisation Society at the centre.... You will be able to use that side for all the ancillary purposes connected with farming; and do a great deal in the way of expert assistance. And through your electing the Board of Governors of the Agricultural Organisation Society, with the provincial branch Committees, you will have what is in effect a central Parliament in London.... You will be able to put before the country, both locally and here in London, the views of the farming community, and, those views will get from Government Departments an attention which the farming industry in the past has failed to get. You will command a power in the country."

And in a letter to Mr. Scott, read at the same meeting, the present Minister of Agriculture had this to say about co-operation:

"Farming is a business in which as in every other industry union is strength.... Every farmer should belong to a co-operative society.... Small societies like small farmers, must" (in their turn) "co-operate.... The word 'farmers' is intended to include all those who cultivate the land. In this sense allotment holders are farmers, and I trust that the union of all cultivators of the land in this sense will help to bridge the gap between town and country."

That townsman and countryman should feel their interests to be at bottom the same goes to the root of any land revival.

VII

VALEDICTORY

"There are many who contend that the nation will never again allow its rural industry to be neglected and discouraged as it was in the past; that the war has taught a lesson which will not soon be forgotten. This view of the national temperament is considered by others to be too confident. It is the firm conviction of this school that the consumer will speedily return to his old habit of indifference to national stability in the matter of food, and that Parliament acting at his bidding, will manifest equal apathy."

These words, taken from a leader in The Times of February 11th, 1918, bring me back to the starting point of these ragged reflections. There will be no permanent stablishing of our agriculture, no lasting advance towards safety and health, if we have not vision and a fixed ideal. The ruts of the past were deep, and our habit is to walk along without looking to left or right. A Liberalism worthy of the word should lift its head and see new paths. The Liberalism of the past, bent on the improvement of the people and the growth of good-will between nations, forgot in that absorption to take in the whole truth. Fixing its eyes on measures which should redeem the evils of the day, it did not see that those evils were growing faster than all possible remedy, because we had forgotten that a great community bountifully blessed by Nature has no business to exist parasitically on the earth produce of other communities; and because our position under pure free trade, and pure industrialism, was making us a tempting bait for aggression, and retarding the very good-will between nations which it desired so earnestly.

The human animal perishes if not fed. We have gone so far with our happy-go-lucky scheme of existence that it has become necessary to remind ourselves of that. So long as we had money we thought we could continue to exist. Not so. Henceforth till we feed ourselves again, we live on sufferance, and dangle before all eyes the apple of discord. A self-supporting Britain, free from this carking fear, would become once more a liberalising power. A Britain fed from overseas can only be an Imperialistic Junker, armed to the teeth, jealous and doubtful of each move by any foreigner; prizing quantity not quality; indifferent about the condition of his heart. Such a Britain dare not be liberal if it will.

The greatest obstacle to a true League of Nations, with the exception of the condition of Russia, will be the condition of Britain, till she can feed herself.

I believe in the principle of free trade, because it forces man to put his best leg foremost. But all is a question of degree in this world. It is no use starting a donkey, in the Derby, and bawling in its ear: "A fair field and no favour!" especially if all your money is on the donkey. All our money is henceforth on our agriculture till we have brought it into its own. And that can only be done at present with the help of bounty.

The other day a Canadian free trader said: "It all depends on what sort of peace we secure; if we have a crushing victory, I see no reason why Britain should not go on importing her food."

Fallacy—politically and biologically! The worst thing that could happen to us after the war would be a sense of perfect security, in which to continue to neglect our agriculture and increase our towns. Does any man think that a momentary exhaustion of our enemy is going to prevent that huge and vigorous nation from becoming strong again? Does he believe that we can trust a League of Nations—a noble project, for which we must all work—to prevent war till we have seen it successful for at least a generation? Does he consider that our national physique will stand another fifty years of rampant industrialism without fresh country stocks to breed from? Does he suppose that the use of the air and the underparts of the sea is more than just beginning?

Politically, our independence in the matter of food is essential to good will between the nations. Biologically, more country life is essential to British health. The improvement of town and factory conditions may do something to arrest degeneration, but in my firm conviction it cannot hope to do enough in a land where towns have been allowed to absorb seven-ninths of the population, and—such crowded, grimy towns!

Even from the economic point of view it will be far cheaper to restore the countryside and re-establish agriculture on a paying basis than to demolish and rebuild our towns till they become health resorts. And behind it all there is this: Are we satisfied with the trend of our modern civilisation? Are we easy in our consciences? Have not machines, and the demands of industry run away with our sense of proportion? Grant for a moment that this age marks the highest water so far of British advance. Are we content with that high-water mark? In health, happiness, taste, beauty, we are surely far from the ideal. I do not say that restoration of the land will work a miracle; but I do say that nothing we can do will benefit us so potently as the redress of balance between town and country life.

We are at the parting of the ways. The war has brought us realisation and opportunity. We can close our eyes again and drift, or we can move forward under the star of a new ideal. The principle which alone preserves the sanity of nations is the principle of balance. Not even the most enraged defender of our present condition will dare maintain that we have followed out that principle. The scales are loaded in favour of the towns, till they almost touch earth; unless our eyes are cleared to see that, unless our will is moved to set it right, we shall bump the ground before another two decades have slipped away, and in the mud shall stay, an invitation to any trampling heel.

I have tried to indicate general measures and considerations vital to the resettlement of the land, conscious that some of my readers will have forgotten more than I know, and that what could be said would fill volumes. But the thought which, of all others, I have wished to convey is this: Without vision we perish. Without apprehension of danger and ardour for salvation in the great body of this people there is no hope of anything save a momentary spurt, which will die away, and leave us plodding down the hill. There are two essentials. The farmer—and that means every cultivator of the land—must have faith in the vital importance of his work and in the possibility of success; the townsman must see and believe that the future of the country, and with it his own prosperity, is involved in the revival of our agriculture and bound up with our independence of oversea supply. Without that vision and belief in the townsman the farmer will never regain faith, and without that faith of the farmer agriculture will not revive.

Statesmen may contrive, reformers plan, farmers struggle on, but if there be not conviction in the body politic, it will be no use.

Resettlement of the land, and independence of outside food supply, is the only hope of welfare and safety for this country. Fervently believing that, I have set down these poor words.

1918.

[E] From an essay by the President of the German Agricultural Council, quoted by Mr. T. H. Middleton, of the Board of Agriculture, in his report on the recent development of German agriculture.

GROTESQUES

Κυνηδόν

I

The Angel Æthereal, on his official visit to the Earth in 1947, paused between the Bank and the Stock Exchange to smoke a cigarette and scrutinise the passers-by.

"How they swarm," he said, "and with what seeming energy—in such an atmosphere! Of what can they be made?"

"Of money, sir," replied his dragoman; "in the past, the present, or the future. Stocks are booming. The barometer of joy stands very high. Nothing like it has been known for thirty years; not, indeed, since the days of the Great Skirmish."

"There is, then, a connection between joy and money?" remarked the Angel, letting smoke dribble through his chiselled nostrils.

"Such is the common belief; though to prove it might take time. I will, however, endeavour to do this if you desire it, sir."

"I certainly do," said the Angel; "for a less joyous-looking crowd I have seldom seen. Between every pair of brows there is a furrow, and no one whistles."

"You do not understand," returned his dragoman; "nor indeed is it surprising, for it is not so much the money as the thought that some day you need no longer make it which causes joy."

"If that day is coming to all," asked the Angel, "why do they not look joyful?"

"It is not so simple as that, sir. To the majority of these persons that day will never come, and many of them know it—these are called clerks; to some amongst the others, even, it will not come—these will be called bankrupts; to the rest it will come, and they will live at Wimblehurst and other islands of the blessed, when they have become so accustomed to making money that to cease making it will be equivalent to boredom, if not torture, or when they are so old that they can but spend it in trying to modify the disabilities of age."

"What price joy, then?" said the Angel, raising his eyebrows. "For that, I fancy, is the expression you use?"

"I perceive, sir," answered his dragoman, "that you have not yet regained your understanding of the human being, and especially of the breed which inhabits this country. Illusion is what we are after. Without our illusions we might just as well be angels or Frenchmen, who pursue at all events to some extent the sordid reality known as 'le plaisir,' or enjoyment of life. In pursuit of illusion we go on making money and furrows in our brows, for the process is wearing. I speak, of course, of the bourgeoisie or Patriotic classes; for the practice of the Laborious is different, though their illusions are the same."

"How?" asked the Angel briefly.

"Why, sir, both hold the illusion that they will one day be joyful through the possession of money; but whereas the Patriotic expect to make it through the labour of the Laborious, the Laborious expect to make it through the labour of the Patriotic."

"Ha, ha!" said the Angel.

"Angels may laugh," replied his dragoman, "but it is a matter to make men weep."

"You know your own business best," said the Angel, "I suppose."

"Ah! sir, if we did, how pleasant it would be. It is frequently my fate to study the countenances and figures of the population, and I find the joy which the pursuit of illusion brings them is insufficient to counteract the confined, monotonous and worried character of their lives."

"They are certainly very plain," said the Angel.

"They are," sighed his dragoman, "and getting plainer every day. Take for instance that one," and he pointed to a gentleman going up the steps. "Mark how he is built. The top of his grizzled head is narrow, the bottom of it broad. His body is short and thick and square; his legs even thicker, and his feet turn out too much; the general effect is almost pyramidal. Again, take this one," and he indicated a gentleman coming down the steps, "you could thread his legs and body through a needle's eye, but his head would defy you. Mark his boiled eyes, his flashing spectacles, and the absence of all hair. Disproportion, sir, has become endemic."

"Can this not be corrected?" asked the Angel.

"To correct a thing," answered his dragoman, "you must first be aware of it, and these are not; no more than they are aware that it is disproportionate to spend six days out of every seven in a counting-house or factory. Man, sir, is the creature of habit, and when his habits are bad, man is worse."

"I have a headache," said the Angel; "the noise is more deafening than it was when I was here in 1910."

"Yes, sir; since then we have had the Great Skirmish, an event which furiously intensified money-making. We, like every other people, have ever since been obliged to cultivate the art of getting five out of two-and-two. The progress of civilisation has been considerably speeded up thereby, and everything but man has benefited; even horses, for they are no longer overloaded and overdriven up Tower Hill or any other."

"How is that," asked the Angel, "if the pressure of work is greater?"

"Because they are extinct," said his dragoman; "entirely superseded by electric and air traction, as you see."

"You appear to be inimical to money," the Angel interjected, with a penetrating look. "Tell me, would you really rather own one shilling than five and sixpence?"

"Sir," replied his dragoman, "you are putting the candidate before the caucus, as the saying is. For money is nothing but the power to purchase what one wants. You should rather be inquiring what I want."

"Well, what do you?" said the Angel.

"To my thinking," answered his dragoman, "instead of endeavouring to increase money when we found ourselves so very bankrupt, we should have endeavoured to decrease our wants. The path of real progress, sir, is the simplification of life and desire till we have dispensed even with trousers and wear a single clean garment reaching to the knees; till we are content with exercising our own limbs on the solid earth; the eating of simple food we have grown ourselves; the hearing of our own voices, and tunes on oaten straws; the feel on our faces of the sun and rain and wind; the scent of the fields and woods; the homely roof, and the comely wife unspoiled by heels, pearls, and powder; the domestic animals at play, wild birds singing, and children brought up to colder water than their fathers. It should have been our business to pursue health till we no longer needed the interior of the chemist's shop, the optician's store, the hairdresser's, the corset-maker's, the thousand and one emporiums which patch and prink us, promoting our fancies and disguising the ravages which modern life makes in our figures. Our ambition should have been to need so little that, with our present scientific knowledge, we should have been able to produce it very easily and quickly, and have had abundant leisure and sound nerves and bodies wherewith to enjoy nature, art, and the domestic affections. The tragedy of man, sir, is his senseless and insatiate curiosity and greed, together with his incurable habit of neglecting the present for the sake of a future which will never come."

"You speak like a book," said the Angel.

"I wish I did," retorted his dragoman, "for no book I am able to procure enjoins us to stop this riot, and betake ourselves to the pleasurable simplicity which alone can save us."

"You would be bored stiff in a week," said the Angel.

"We should, sir," replied his dragoman, "because from our schooldays we are brought up to be acquisitive, competitive, and restless. Consider the baby in the perambulator, absorbed in contemplating the heavens and sucking its own thumb. Existence, sir, should be like that."

"A beautiful metaphor," said the Angel.

"As it is, we do but skip upon the hearse of life."

"You would appear to be of those whose motto is: 'Try never to leave things as you find them,'" observed the Angel.

"Ah, sir!" responded his dragoman, with a sad smile, "the part of a dragoman is rather ever to try and find things where he leaves them."

"Talking of that," said the Angel dreamily, "when I was here in 1910, I bought some Marconi's for the rise. What are they at now?"

"I cannot tell you," replied his dragoman in a deprecating voice, "but this I will say: Inventors are not only the benefactors but the curses of mankind, and will be so long as we do not find a way of adapting their discoveries to our very limited digestive powers. The chronic dyspepsia of our civilisation, due to the attempt to swallow every pabulum which ingenuity puts before it, is so violent that I sometimes wonder whether we shall survive until your visit in 1984."

"Ah!" said the Angel, pricking his ears; "you really think there is a chance?"

"I do indeed," his dragoman answered gloomily. "Life is now one long telephone call—and what's it all about? A tour in darkness! A rattling of wheels under a sky of smoke! A never-ending game of poker!"

"Confess," said the Angel, "that you have eaten something which has not agreed with you?"

"It is so," answered his dragoman; "I have eaten of modernity, the damndest dish that was ever set to lips. Look at those fellows," he went on, "busy as ants from nine o'clock in the morning to seven in the evening. And look at their wives!"

"Ah! yes," said the Angel cheerily; "let us look at their wives," and with three strokes of his wings he passed to Oxford Street.

"Look at them!" repeated his dragoman, "busy as ants from ten o'clock in the morning to five in the evening."

"Plain is not the word for them," said the Angel sadly. "What are they after, running in and out of these shop-holes?"

"Illusion, sir. The romance of business there, the romance of commerce here. They have got into these habits and, as you know, it is so much easier to get in than to get out. Would you like to see one of their homes?"

"No, no," said the Angel, starting back and coming into contact with a lady's hat. "Why do they have them so large?" he asked, with a certain irritation.

"In order that they may have them small next season," replied his dragoman. "The future, sir; the future! The cycle of beauty and eternal hope, and, incidentally, the good of trade. Grasp that phrase and you will have no need for further inquiry, and probably no inclination."

"One could get American sweets in here, I guess," said the Angel, entering.

II

"And where would you wish to go to-day, sir?" asked his dragoman of the Angel who was moving his head from side to side like a dromedary in the Haymarket.

"I should like," the Angel answered, "to go into the country."

"The country!" returned his dragoman, doubtfully. "You will find very little to see there."

"Natheless," said the Angel, spreading his wings.

"These," gasped his dragoman, after a few breathless minutes, "are the Chilterns—they will serve; any part of the country is now the same. Shall we descend?"

Alighting on what seemed to be a common, he removed the cloud moisture from his brow, and shading his eyes with his hand, stood peering into the distance on every side. "As I thought," he said; "there has been no movement since I brought the Prime here in 1944; we shall have some difficulty in getting lunch."

"A wonderfully peaceful spot," said the Angel.

"True," said his dragoman. "We might fly sixty miles in any direction and not see a house in repair."

"Let us!" said the Angel. They flew a hundred, and alighted again.

"Same here!" said his dragoman. "This is Leicestershire. Note the rolling landscape of wild pastures."

"I am getting hungry," said the Angel. "Let us fly again."

"I have told you, sir," remarked his dragoman, while they were flying, "that we shall have the greatest difficulty in finding any inhabited dwelling in the country. Had we not better alight at Blackton or Bradleeds?"

"No," said the Angel. "I have come for a day in the fresh air."

"Would bilberries serve?" asked his dragoman; "for I see a man gathering them."

The Angel closed his wings, and they dropped on to a moor close to an aged man.

"My worthy wight," said the Angel, "we are hungry. Would you give us some of your bilberries?"

"Wot oh!" ejaculated the ancient party; "never 'eard yer comin'. Been flyin' by wireless, 'ave yer? Got an observer, I see," he added, jerking his grizzled chin at the dragoman. "Strike me, it's the good old dyes o' the Gryte Skirmish over agyne."

"Is this," asked the Angel, whose mouth was already black with bilberries, "the dialect of rural England?"

"I will interrogate him, sir," said his dragoman, "for in truth I am at a loss to account for the presence of a man in the country." He took the old person by his last button and led him a little apart. Returning to the Angel, who had finished the bilberries, he whispered:

"It is as I thought. This is the sole survivor of the soldiers settled on the land at the conclusion of the Great Skirmish. He lives on berries and birds who have died a natural death."

"I fail to understand," answered the Angel. "Where is all the rural population, where the mansions of the great, the thriving farmer, the contented peasant, the labourer about to have his minimum wage, the Old, the Merrie England of 1910?"

"That," responded his dragoman somewhat dramatically, extending his hand towards the old man, "that is the rural population, and he a cockney hardened in the Great Skirmish, or he could never have stayed the course."

"What!" said the Angel; "is no food grown in all this land!"

"Not a cabbage," replied his dragoman; "not a mustard and cress—outside the towns, that is."

"I perceive," said the Angel, "that I have lost touch with much that is of interest. Give me, I pray, a brief sketch of the agricultural movement."

"Why, sir," replied his dragoman, "the agricultural movement in this country since the days of the Great Skirmish, when all were talking of resettling the land, may be summed up in two words: 'Town Expansion.' In order to make this clear to you, however, I must remind you of the political currents of the past thirty years. You will not recollect that during the Great Skirmish, beneath the seeming absence of politics, there were germinating the Parties of the future. A secret but resolute intention was forming in all minds to immolate those who had played any part in politics before and during the important world-tragedy which was then being enacted, especially such as continued to hold portfolios, or persisted in asking questions in the House of Commons, as it was then called. It was not that people held them to be responsible, but nerves required soothing, and there is no anodyne, as you know, sir, equal to human sacrifice. The politician was, as one may say—'off.' No sooner, of course, was peace declared than the first real General Election was held, and it was with a certain chagrin that the old Parties found themselves in the soup. The Parties which had been forming beneath the surface swept the country; one called itself the Patriotic, and was called by its opponents the Prussian Party; the other called itself the Laborious, and was called by its opponents the Loafing Party. Their representatives were nearly all new men. In the first flush of peace, with which the human mind ever associates plenty, they came out on such an even keel that no Government could pass anything at all. Since, however, it was imperative to find the interest on a National Debt of £8,000,000,000, a further election was needed. This time, though the word Peace remained, the word Plenty had already vanished; and the Laborious Party, which, having much less to tax, felt that it could tax more freely, found itself in an overwhelming majority. You will be curious to hear, sir, of what elements this Party was composed. Its solid bulk were the returned soldiers, and the other manual workers of the country; but to this main body there was added a rump, of pundits, men of excellent intentions, brains, and principles, such as in old days had been known as Radicals and advanced Liberals. These had joined out of despair, feeling that otherwise their very existence was jeopardised. To this collocation—and to one or two other circumstances, as you will presently see, sir—the doom of the land must be traced. Now, the Laborious Party, apart from its rump, on which it would or could not sit—we shall never know now—had views about the resettlement of the land not far divergent from those held by the Patriotic Party, and they proceeded to put a scheme into operation, which, for perhaps a year, seemed to have a prospect of success. Many returned soldiers were established in favourable localities, and there was even a disposition to place the country on a self-sufficing basis in regard to food. But they had not been in power eighteen months when their rump—which, as I have told you, contained nearly all their principles—had a severe attack of these. 'Free Trade,'—which, say what you will, follows the line of least resistance and is based on the 'good of trade'—was, they perceived, endangered, and they began to agitate against bonuses on corn and preferential treatment of a pampered industry. The bonus on corn was in consequence rescinded in 1924, and in lieu thereof the system of small holdings was extended—on paper. At the same time the somewhat stunning taxation which had been placed upon the wealthy began to cause the break-up of landed estates. As the general bankruptcy and exhaustion of Europe became more and more apparent the notion of danger from future war began to seem increasingly remote, and the 'good of trade' became again the one object before every British eye. Food from overseas was cheapening once more. The inevitable occurred. Country mansions became a drug in the market, farmers farmed at a loss; small holders went bust daily, and emigrated; agricultural labourers sought the towns. In 1926 the Laborious Party, who had carried the taxation of their opponents to a pitch beyond the power of human endurance, got what the racy call 'the knock,' and the four years which followed witnessed the bitterest internecine struggle within the memory of every journalist. In the course of this strife emigration increased and the land emptied rapidly. The final victory of the Laborious Party, in 1930, saw them, still propelled by their rump, committed, among other things, to a pure town policy. They have never been out of power since; the result you see. Food is now entirely brought from overseas, largely by submarine and air service, in tabloid form, and expanded to its original proportions on arrival by an ingenious process discovered by a German. The country is now used only as a subject for sentimental poets, and to fly over, or by lovers on bicycles at week-ends."

"Mon Dieu!" said the Angel thoughtfully. "To me, indeed, it seems that this must have been a case of: 'Oh! What a surprise!'"

"You are not mistaken, sir," replied his dragoman; "people still open their mouths over this consummation. It is pre-eminently an instance of what will happen sometimes when you are not looking, even to the English, who have been most fortunate in this respect. For you must remember that all Parties, even the Pundits, have always declared that rural life and all that, don't you know, is most necessary, and have ever asserted that they were fostering it to the utmost. But they forgot to remember that our circumstances, traditions, education, and vested interests so favoured town life and the 'good of trade' that it required a real and unparliamentary effort not to take that line of least resistance. In fact, we have here a very good example of what I told you the other day was our most striking characteristic—never knowing where we are till after the event. But what with fog and principles, how can you expect we should? Better be a little town blighter with no constitution and high political principles, than your mere healthy country product of a pampered industry. But you have not yet seen the other side of the moon."

"To what do you refer?" asked the Angel.

"Why, sir, to the glorious expansion of the towns. To this I shall introduce you to-morrow, if such is your pleasure."

"Is London, then, not a town?" asked the Angel playfully.

"London?" cried his dragoman; "a mere pleasure village. To which real town shall I take you? Liverchester?"

"Anywhere," said the Angel, "where I can get a good dinner." So-saying, he paid the rural population with a smile and spread his wings.

III

"The night is yet young," said the Angel Æthereal on leaving the White Heart Hostel at Liverchester, "and I have had perhaps too much to eat. Let us walk and see the town."

"As you will, sir," replied his dragoman; "there is no difference between night and day, now that they are using the tides for the provision of electric power."

The Angel took a note of the fact. "What do they manufacture here?" he asked.

"The entire town," returned his dragoman, "which now extends from the old Liverpool to the old Manchester (as indeed its name implies), is occupied with expanding the tabloids of food which are landed in its port from the new worlds. This and the town of Brister, reaching from the old Bristol to the old Gloucester, have had the monopoly of food expansion for the United Kingdom since 1940."

"By what means precisely?" asked the Angel.

"Congenial environment and bacteriology," responded his dragoman. They walked for some time in silence, flying a little now and then in the dirtier streets, before the Angel spoke again:

"It is curious," he said, "but I perceive no difference between this town and those I remember on my visit in 1910, save that the streets are better lighted, which is not an unmixed joy, for they are dirty and full of people whose faces do not please me."

"Ah! sir," replied his dragoman, "it is too much to expect that the wonderful darkness which prevailed at the time of the Great Skirmish could endure; then, indeed, one could indulge the hope that the houses were all built by Wren, and the people all clean and beautiful. There is no poetry now."

"No!" said the Angel, sniffing, "but there is atmosphere, and it is not agreeable."

"Mankind, when herded together, will smell," answered his dragoman. "You cannot avoid it. What with old clothes, patchouli, petrol, fried fish and the fag, those five essentials of human life, the atmosphere of Turner and Corot are as nothing."

"But do you not run your towns to please yourselves?" said the Angel.

"Oh, no, sir! The resistance would be dreadful. They run us. You see, they are so very big, and have such prestige. Besides," he added, "even if we dared, we should not know how. For, though some great and good man once brought us plane-trees, we English are above getting the best out of life and its conditions, and despise light Frenchified taste. Notice the principle which governs this twenty-mile residential stretch. It was intended to be light, but how earnest it has all turned out! You can tell at a glance that these dwellings belong to the species 'house' and yet are individual houses, just as a man belongs to the species 'man,' and yet, as they say, has a soul of his own. This principle was introduced off the Avenue Road a few years before the Great Skirmish, and is now universal. Any person who lives in a house identical with another house is not known. Has anything heavier and more conscientious ever been seen?"

"Does this principle also apply to the houses of the working-man?" inquired the Angel.

"Hush, sir!" returned his dragoman, looking round him nervously; "a dangerous word. The LABORIOUS dwell in palaces built after the design of an architect called Jerry, with communal kitchens and baths."

"Do they use them?" asked the Angel with some interest.

"Not as yet, indeed," replied his dragoman; "but I believe they are thinking of it. As you know, sir, it takes time to introduce a custom. Thirty years is but as yesterday."

"The Japanese wash daily," mused the Angel.

"Not a Christian nation," replied his dragoman; "nor have they the dirt to contend with which is conspicuous here. Let us do justice to the discouragement which dogs the ablutions of such as know they will soon be dirty again. It was confidently supposed, at the time of the Great Skirmish, which introduced military discipline and so entirely abolished caste, that the habit of washing would at last become endemic throughout the whole population. Judge how surprised were we of that day when the facts turned out otherwise. Instead of the Laborious washing more, the Patriotic washed less. It may have been the higher price of soap, or merely that human life was not very highly regarded at the time. We cannot tell. But not until military discipline disappeared, and caste was restored, which happened the moment peace returned, did the survivors of the Patriotic begin to wash immoderately again, leaving the Laborious to preserve a level more suited to democracy."

"Talking of levels," said the Angel; "is the populace increasing in stature?"

"Oh, no, indeed!" responded his dragoman; "the latest statistics give a diminution of one inch and a half during the past generation."

"And in longevity?" asked the Angel.

"As to that, babies and old people are now communally treated, and all those diseases which are curable by lymph are well in hand."

"Do people, then, not die?"

"Oh, yes, sir! About as often as before. There are new complaints which redress the balance."

"And what are those?"

"A group of diseases called for convenience Scienticitis. Some think they come from the present food system; others from the accumulation of lymphs in the body; others, again, regard them as the result of dwelling on the subject—a kind of hypnotisation by death; a fourth school hold them traceable to town air; while a fifth consider them a mere manifestation of jealousy on the part of Nature. They date, one may say, with confidence, from the time of the Great Skirmish, when men's minds were turned with some anxiety to the question of statistics, and babies were at a premium."

"Is the population, then, much larger?"

"You mean smaller, sir, do you not? Not perhaps so much smaller as you might expect; but it is still nicely down. You see, the Patriotic Party, including even those Pontificals whose private practice most discouraged all that sort of thing, began at once to urge propagation. But their propaganda was, as one may say, brain-spun; and at once bumped up—pardon the colloquialism—against the economic situation. The existing babies, it is true, were saved; the trouble was rather that the babies began not to exist. The same, of course, obtained in every European country, with the exception of what was still, in a manner of speaking, Russia; and if that country had but retained its homogeneity, it would soon by sheer numbers have swamped the rest of Europe. Fortunately, perhaps, it did not remain homogeneous. An incurable reluctance to make food for cannon and impose further burdens on selves already weighted to the ground by taxes, developed in the peoples of each Central and Western land; and in the years from 1920 to 1930 the downward curve was so alarming in Great Britain that if the Patriotic Party could only have kept office long enough at a time they would, no doubt, have enforced conception at the point of the bayonet. Luckily or unluckily, according to taste, they did not; and it was left for more natural causes to produce the inevitable reaction which began to set in after 1930, when the population of the United Kingdom had been reduced to some twenty-five millions. About that time commerce revived. The question of the land had been settled by its unconscious abandonment, and people began to see before them again the possibility of supporting families. The ingrained disposition of men and women to own pets, together with 'the good of trade,' began once more to have its way; and the population rose rapidly. A renewed joy in life, and the assurance of not having to pay the piper, caused the slums, as they used to be called, to swarm once more, and filled the communal crèches. And had it not been for the fact that any one with physical strength, or love of fresh air, promptly emigrated to the Sister Nations on attaining the age of eighteen we might now, sir, be witnessing an overcrowding equal to that of the times before the Great Skirmish. The movement is receiving an added impetus with the approach of the Greater Skirmish between the Teutons and Mongolians, for it is expected that trade will boom and much wealth accrue to those countries which are privileged to look on with equanimity at this great new drama, as the editors are already calling it."

"In all this," said the Angel Æthereal, "I perceive something rather sordid."

"Sir," replied his dragoman earnestly, "your remark is characteristic of the sky, where people are not made of flesh and blood; pay, I believe, no taxes; and have no experience of the devastating consequences of war. I recollect so well when I was a young man, before the Great Skirmish began, and even when it had been going on several years, how glibly the leaders of opinion talked of human progress, and how blind they were to the fact that it has a certain connection with environment. You must remember that ever since that large and, as some still think, rather tragic occurrence environment has been very dicky and Utopia not unrelated to thin air. It has been perceived time and again that the leaders of public opinion are not always confirmed by events. The new world, which was so sapiently prophesied by rhetoricians, is now nigh thirty years old, and, for my part, I confess to surprise that it is not worse than it actually is. I am moralising, I fear, however, for these suburban buildings grievously encourage the philosophic habit. Rather let us barge along and see the Laborious at their labours, which are never interrupted now by the mere accident of night."

The Angel increased his speed till they alighted amid a forest of tall chimneys, whose sirens were singing like a watch of nightingales.

"There is a shift on," said the dragoman. "Stand here, sir; we shall see them passing in and out."

The Laborious were not hurrying, and went by uttering the words: "Cheer oh!" "So long!" and "Wot abaht it!"

The Angel contemplated them for a time before he said: "It comes back to me now how they used to talk when they were doing up my flat on my visit in 1910."

"Give me, I pray, an imitation," said his dragoman.

The Angel struck the attitude of one painting a door. "William," he said, rendering those voices of the past, "what money are you obtaining?"

"Not half, Alfred."

"If that is so, indeed, William, should you not rather leave your tools and obtain better money? I myself am doing this."

"Not half, Alfred."

"Round the corner I can obtain more money by working for fewer hours. In my opinion there is no use in working for less money when you can obtain more. How much does Henry obtain?"

"Not half, Alfred."

"What I am now obtaining is, in my opinion, no use at all."

"Not half, Alfred."

Here the Angel paused, and let his hand move for one second in a masterly exhibition of activity.

"It is doubtful, sir," said his dragoman, "whether you would be permitted to dilute your conversation with so much labour in these days; the rules are very strict."

"Are there, then, still Trades Unions?" asked the Angel.

"No, indeed," replied his dragoman; "but there are Committees. That habit which grew up at the time of the Great Skirmish has flourished ever since. Statistics reveal the fact that there are practically no adults in the country between the ages of nineteen and fifty who are not sitting on Committees. At the time of the Great Skirmish all Committees were nominally active; they are now both active and passive. In every industry, enterprise, or walk of life a small active Committee directs; and a large passive Committee, formed of everybody else, resists that direction. And it is safe to say that the Passive Committees are active and the Active Committees passive; in this way no inordinate amount of work is done. Indeed, if the tongue and the electric button had not usurped practically all the functions of the human hand, the State would have some difficulty in getting its boots blacked. But a ha'poth of visualisation is worth three lectures at ten shillings the stall, so enter, sir, and see for yourself."

Saying this, he pushed open the door.

In a shed, which extended beyond the illimitable range of the Angel's eye, machinery and tongues were engaged in a contest which filled the ozone with an incomparable hum. Men and women in profusion were leaning against walls or the pillars on which the great roof was supported, assiduously pressing buttons. The scent of expanding food revived the Angel's appetite.

"I shall require supper," he said dreamily.

"By all means, sir," replied his dragoman; "after work—play. It will afford you an opportunity to witness modern pleasures in our great industrial centres. But what a blessing is electric power!" he added. "Consider these lilies of the town, they toil not, neither do they spin—"

"Yet Solomon in all his glory," chipped in the Angel eagerly, "had not their appearance, you bet."

"Indeed they are an insouciant crowd," mused his dragoman. "How tinkling is their laughter! The habit dates from the days of the Great Skirmish, when nothing but laughter would meet the case."

"Tell me," said the Angel, "are the English satisfied at last with their industrial conditions, and generally with their mode of life in these expanded towns?"

"Satisfied? Oh dear, no, sir! But you know what it is: They are obliged to wait for each fresh development before they can see what they have to counteract; and, since that great creative force, 'the good of trade,' is always a little stronger than the forces of criticism and reform, each development carries them a little further on the road to—"

"Hell! How hungry I am again!" exclaimed the Angel. "Let us sup!"

IV

"Laughter," said the Angel Æthereal, applying his wineglass to his nose, "has ever distinguished mankind from all other animals with the exception of the dog. And the power of laughing at nothing distinguishes man even from that quadruped."

"I would go further, sir," returned his dragoman, "and say that the power of laughing at that which should make him sick distinguishes the Englishman from all other varieties of man except the negro. Kindly observe!" He rose, and taking the Angel by the waist, fox-trotted him among the little tables.

"See!" he said, indicating the other supper-takers with a circular movement of his beard, "they are consumed with laughter. The habit of fox-trotting in the intervals of eating has been known ever since it was introduced by Americans a generation ago, at the beginning of the Great Skirmish, when that important people had as yet nothing else to do; but it still causes laughter in this country. A distressing custom," he wheezed, as they resumed their seats, "for not only does it disturb the oyster, but it compels one to think lightly of the human species. Not that one requires much compulsion," he added, "now that music-hall, cinema, and restaurant are conjoined. What a happy idea that was of Berlin's, and how excellent for business! Kindly glance for a moment—but not more—at the left-hand stage."

The Angel turned his eyes towards a cinematograph film which was being displayed. He contemplated it for the moment without speaking.

"I do not comprehend," he said at last, "why the person with the arrested moustaches is hitting so many people with that sack of flour."

"To cause amusement, sir," replied his dragoman. "Look at the laughing faces around you."

"But it is not funny," said the Angel.

"No, indeed," returned his dragoman. "Be so good as to carry your eyes now to the stage on the right, but not for long. What do you see?"

"I see a very red-nosed man beating a very white-nosed man about the body."

"It is a real scream, is it not?"

"No," said the Angel drily. "Does nothing else ever happen on these stages?"

"Nothing. Stay! Revues happen!"

"What are revues?" asked the Angel.

"Criticisms of life, sir, as it would be seen by persons inebriated on various intoxicants."

"They should be joyous."

"They are accounted so," his dragoman replied; "but for my part, I prefer to criticise life for myself, especially when I am drunk."

"Are there no plays, no operas?" asked the Angel from behind his glass.

"Not in the old and proper sense of these words. They disappeared towards the end of the Great Skirmish."

"What food for the mind is there, then?" asked the Angel, adding an oyster to his collection.

"None in public, sir, for it is well recognised, and has been ever since those days, that laughter alone promotes business and removes the thought of death. You cannot recall, as I can, sir, the continual stream which used to issue from theatres, music-halls, and picture-palaces in the days of the Great Skirmish, nor the joviality of the Strand and the more expensive restaurants. I have often thought," he added with a touch of philosophy, "what a height of civilisation we must have reached to go jesting, as we did, to the Great Unknown."

"Is that really what the English did at the time of the Great Skirmish?" asked the Angel.

"It is," replied his dragoman solemnly.

"Then they are a very fine people, and I can put up with much about them which seems to me distressing."

"Ah! sir, though, being an Englishman, I am sometimes inclined to disparage the English, I am yet convinced that you could not fly a week's journey and come across another race with such a peculiar nobility, or such an unconquerable soul, if you will forgive my using a word whose meaning is much disputed. May I tempt you with a clam?" he added, more lightly. "We now have them from America—in fair preservation, and very nasty they are, in my opinion."

The Angel took a clam.

"My Lord!" he said, after a moment of deglutition.

"Quite so!" replied his dragoman. "But kindly glance at the right-hand stage again. There is a revue on now. What do you see?"

The Angel made two holes with his forefingers and thumbs and, putting them to his eyes, bent a little forward.

"Tut, tut!" he said; "I see some attractive young females with very few clothes on, walking up and down in front of what seem to me, indeed, to be two grown-up men in collars and jackets as of little boys. What precise criticism of life is this conveying?"

His dragoman answered in reproachful accents:

"Do you not feel, sir, from your own sensations, how marvellously this informs one of the secret passions of mankind? Is there not in it a striking revelation of the natural tendencies of the male population? Remark how the whole audience, including your august self, is leaning forward and looking through their thumb-holes?"

The Angel sat back hurriedly.

"True," he said, "I was carried away. But that is not the criticism of life which art demands. If it had been, the audience, myself included, would have been sitting back with their lips curled dry, instead of watering."

"For all that," replied his dragoman, "it is the best we can give you; anything which induces the detached mood of which you spoke, has been banned from the stage since the days of the Great Skirmish; it is so very bad for business."

"Pity!" said the Angel, imperceptibly edging forward; "the mission of art is to elevate."

"It is plain, sir," said his dragoman, "that you have lost touch with the world as it is. The mission of art—now truly democratic—is to level—in principle up, in practice down. Do not forget, sir, that the English have ever regarded æstheticism as unmanly, and grace as immoral; when to that basic principle you add the principle of serving the taste of the majority, you have perfect conditions for a sure and gradual decrescendo."

"Does taste, then, no longer exist?" asked the Angel.

"It is not wholly, as yet, extinct, but lingers in the communal kitchens and canteens, as introduced by the Young Men's Christian Association in the days of the Great Skirmish. While there is appetite there is hope, nor is it wholly discouraging that taste should now centre in the stomach; for is not that the real centre of man's activity? Who dare affirm that from so universal a foundation the fair structure of æstheticism shall not be rebuilt? The eye, accustomed to the look of dainty dishes and pleasant cookery, may once more demand the architecture of Wren, the sculpture of Rodin, the paintings of—dear me—whom? Why, sir, even before the days of the Great Skirmish, when you were last on earth, we had already begun to put the future of æstheticism on a more real basis, and were converting the concert-halls of London into hotels. Few at the time saw the far-reaching significance of that movement, or realised that æstheticism was to be levelled down to the stomach, in order that it might be levelled up again to the head, on true democratic principles."

"But what," said the Angel, with one of his preternatural flashes of acumen, "what if, on the other hand, taste should continue to sink and lose even its present hold on the stomach? If all else has gone, why should not the beauty of the kitchen go?"

"That indeed," sighed his dragoman, placing his hand on his heart, "is a thought which often gives me a sinking sensation. Two liqueur brandies," he murmured to the waiter. "But the stout heart refuses to despair. Besides, advertisements show decided traces of æsthetic advance. All the great painters, poets, and fiction writers are working on them; the movement had its origin in the propaganda demanded by the Great Skirmish. You will not recollect the war poetry of that period, the patriotic films, the death cartoons, and other remarkable achievements. We have just as great talents now, though their object has not perhaps the religious singleness of those stirring times. Not a food, corset, or collar which has not its artist working for it! Toothbrushes, nutcrackers, babies' baths—the whole caboodle of manufacture—are now set to music. Such themes are considered subliminal if not sublime. No, sir, I will not despair; it is only at moments when I have dined poorly that the horizon seems dark. Listen—they have turned on the 'Kalophone,' for you must know that all music now is beautifully made by machine—so much easier for every one."

The Angel raised his head, and into his eyes came the glow associated with celestial strains.

"The tune," he said, "is familiar to me."

"Yes, sir," answered his dragoman, "for it is 'The Messiah' in ragtime. No time is wasted, you notice; all, even pleasure, is intensively cultivated, on the lines of least resistance, thanks to the feverishness engendered in us by the Great Skirmish, when no one knew if he would have another chance, and to the subsequent need for fostering industry. But whether we really enjoy ourselves is perhaps a question to answer which you must examine the English character."

"That I refuse to do," said the Angel.

"And you are wise, sir, for it is a puzzler, and many have cracked their heads over it. But have we not been here long enough? We can pursue our researches into the higher realms of art to-morrow."

A beam from the Angel's lustrous eyes fell on a lady at the next table. "Yes, perhaps we had better go," he sighed.

V

"And so it is through the fields of true art that we shall walk this morning?" said the Angel Æthereal.

"Such as they are in this year of Peace 1947," responded his dragoman, arresting him before a statue; "for the development of this hobby has been peculiar since you were here in 1910, when the childlike and contortionist movement was just beginning to take hold of the British."

"Whom does this represent?" asked the Angel.

"A celebrated publicist, recently deceased at a great age. You see him unfolded by this work of multiform genius, in every aspect known to art, religion, nature, and the population. From his knees downwards he is clearly devoted to nature, and is portrayed as about to enter his bath. From his waist to his knees he is devoted to religion—mark the complete disappearance of the human aspect. From his neck to his waist he is devoted to public affairs; observe the tweed coat, the watch chain, and other signs of practical sobriety. But the head is, after all, the crown of the human being, and is devoted to art. This is why you cannot make out that it is a head. Note its pyramidal severity, its cunning little ears, its box-built, water-tightal structure. The hair you note to be in flames. Here we have the touch of beauty—the burning shrub. In the whole you will observe that aversion from natural form and the single point of view, characteristic of all twentieth-century æsthetics. The whole thing is a very great masterpiece of childlike contortionism. To do things as irresponsibly as children and contortionists—what a happy discovery of the line of least resistance in art that was! Mark, by the way, this exquisite touch about the left hand."

"It appears to be deformed," said the Angel, going a step nearer.

"Look closer still," returned his dragoman, "and you will see that it is holding a novel of the great Russian, upside down. Ever since that simple master who so happily blended the childlike with the contortionist became known in this country they have been trying to go him one better, in letters, in painting, in sculpture, and in music, refusing to admit that he was the last cry; and until they have beaten him this movement simply cannot cease; it may therefore go on for ever, for he was the limit. That hand symbolises the whole movement."

"How?" said the Angel.

"Why, sir, somersault is its mainspring. Did you never observe the great Russian's method? Prepare your characters to do one thing, and make them very swiftly do the opposite. Thus did that terrific novelist demonstrate his overmastering range of vision and knowledge of the depths of human nature. Since his characters never varied this routine in the course of some eight thousand pages, people have lightly said that he repeated himself. But what of that? Consider what perfect dissociation he thereby attained between character and action; what nebulosity of fact; what a truly childlike and mystic mix-up of all human values hitherto known! And here, sir, at the risk of tickling you, I must whisper." The dragoman made a trumpet of his hand: "Fiction can only be written by those who have exceptionally little knowledge of ordinary human nature, and great fiction only by such as have none at all."

"How is that?" said the Angel, somewhat disconcerted.

"Surprise, sir, is the very kernel of all effects in art, and in real life people will act as their characters and temperaments determine that they shall. This dreadful and unmalleable trait would have upset all the great mystic masters from generation to generation if they had only noticed it. But did they? Fortunately not. These greater men naturally put into their books the greater confusion and flux in which their extraordinary selves exist! The nature they portray is not human, but super- or subter-human, which you will. Who would have it otherwise?"

"Not I," said the Angel. "For I confess to a liking for what is called the 'tuppence coloured.' But Russians are not as other men, are they?"

"They are not," said his dragoman, "but the trouble is, sir, that since the British discovered him, every character in our greater fiction has a Russian soul, though living in Cornwall or the Midlands, in a British body under a Scottish or English name."

"Very piquant," said the Angel, turning from the masterpiece before him. "Are there no undraped statues to be seen?"

"In no recognisable form. For, not being educated to the detached contemplation which still prevailed to a limited extent even as late as the days of the Great Skirmish, the populace can no longer be trusted with such works of art; they are liable to rush at them, for embrace, or demolition, as their temperaments may dictate."

"The Greeks are dead, then," said the Angel.

"As door-nails, sir. They regarded life as a thing to be enjoyed—a vice you will not have noticed in the British. The Greeks were an outdoor people, who lived in the sun and the fresh air, and had none of the niceness bred by the life of our towns. We have long been renowned for our delicacy about the body; nor has the tendency been decreased by constituting Watch Committees of young persons in every borough. These are now the arbiters of art, and nothing unsuitable to the child of seven passes their censorship."

"How careful!" said the Angel.

"The result has been wonderful," remarked his dragoman. "Wonderful!" he repeated, dreamily. "I suppose there is more smouldering sexual desire and disease in this country than in any other."

"Was that the intention?" asked the Angel.

"Oh! no, sir! That is but the natural effect of so remarkably pure a surface. All is within instead of without. Nature has now wholly disappeared. The process was sped up by the Great Skirmish. For, since then, we have had little leisure and income to spare on the gratification of anything but laughter; this and the 'unco-guid' have made our art-surface glare in the eyes of the nations, thin and spotless as if made of tin."

The Angel raised his eyebrows. "I had hoped for better things," he said.

"You must not suppose, sir," pursued his dragoman, "that there is not plenty of the undraped, so long as it is vulgar, as you saw just now upon the stage, for that is good business; the line is only drawn at the danger-point of art, which is always very bad business in this country. Yet even in real life the undraped has to be grotesque to be admitted; the one fatal quality is natural beauty. The laugh, sir, the laugh—even the most hideous and vulgar laugh—is such a disinfectant. I should, however, say in justice to our literary men, that they have not altogether succumbed to the demand for cachinnations. A school, which first drew breath before the Great Skirmish began, has perfected itself, till now we have whole tomes where hardly a sentence would be intelligible to any save the initiate; this enables them to defy the Watch Committees, with other Philistines. We have writers who mysteriously preach the realisation of self by never considering anybody else; of purity through experience of exotic vice; of courage through habitual cowardice; and of kindness through Prussian behaviour. They are generally young. We have others whose fiction consists of autobiography interspersed with philosophic and political fluencies. These may be of any age from eighty odd to the bitter thirties. We have also the copious and chatty novelist; and transcribers of the life of the Laborious, whom the Laborious never read. Above all, we have the great Patriotic school, who put the national motto first, and write purely what is good for trade. In fact, we have every sort, as in the old days."

"It would appear," said the Angel, "that the arts have stood somewhat still."

"Except for a more external purity, and a higher internal corruption," replied his dragoman.

"Are artists still noted for their jealousies?" asked the Angel.

"They are, sir; for that is inherent in the artistic temperament, which is extremely touchy about fame."

"And do they still get angry when those gentlemen—the—"

"Critics," his dragoman suggested. "They get angry, sir; but critics are usually anonymous, and from excellent reasons; for not only are the passions of an angry artist very high, but the knowledge of an angry critic is not infrequently very low, especially of art. It is kinder to save life, where possible."

"For my part," said the Angel, "I have little regard for human life, and consider that many persons would be better buried."

"That may be," his dragoman retorted with some irritation; "'errare est humanum.' But I, for one, would rather be a dead human being any day than a live angel, for I think they are more charitable."

"Well," said the Angel genially, "you have the prejudice of your kind. Have you an artist about the place, to show me? I do not recollect any at Madame Tussaud's."

"They have taken to declining that honour. We could see one in real life if we went to Cornwall."

"Why Cornwall?"

"I cannot tell you, sir. There is something in the air which affects their passions."

"I am hungry, and would rather go to the Savoy," said the Angel, walking on.

"You are in luck," whispered his dragoman, when they had seated themselves at a table covered with prawns; "for at the next on your left is our most famous exponent of the mosaic school of novelism."

"Then here goes!" replied the Angel. And, turning to his neighbour, he asked pleasantly: "How do you do, sir? What is your income?"

The gentleman addressed looked up from his prawn, and replied wearily: "Ask my agent. He may conceivably possess the knowledge you require."

"Answer me this, at all events," said the Angel, with more dignity, if possible: "How do you write your books? For it must be wonderful to summon around you every day the creatures of your imagination. Do you wait for afflatus?"

"No," said the author; "er—no! I—er—" he added weightily, "sit down every morning."

The Angel rolled his eyes and, turning to his dragoman, said in a well-bred whisper: "He sits down every morning! My Lord, how good for trade!"

VI

"A glass of sherry, dry, and ham sandwich, stale, can be obtained here, sir," said the dragoman; "and for dessert, the scent of parchment and bananas. We will then attend Court 45, where I shall show you how fundamentally our legal procedure has changed in the generation that has elapsed since the days of the Great Skirmish."

"Can it really be that the Law has changed? I had thought it immutable," said the Angel, causing his teeth to meet with difficulty: "What will be the nature of the suit to which we shall listen?"

"I have thought it best, sir, to select a divorce case, lest you should sleep, overcome by the ozone and eloquence in these places."

"Ah!" said the Angel: "I am ready."

The Court was crowded, and they took their seats with difficulty, and a lady sitting on the Angel's left wing.

"The public will frequent this class of case," whispered his dragoman. "How different when you were here in 1910!"

The Angel collected himself: "Tell me," he murmured, "which of the grey-haired ones is the judge?"

"He in the bag-wig, sir," returned his dragoman; "and that little lot is the jury," he added, indicating twelve gentlemen seated in two rows.

"What is their private life?" asked the Angel.

"No better than it should be, perhaps," responded his dragoman facetiously; "but no one can tell that from their words and manner, as you will presently see. These are special ones," he added, "and pay income tax, so that their judgment in matters of morality is of considerable value."

"They have wise faces," said the Angel. "Which is the prosecutor?"

"No, no!" his dragoman answered, vividly: "This is a civil case. That is the plaintiff with a little mourning about her eyes and a touch of red about her lips, in the black hat with the aigrette, the pearls, and the fashionably sober clothes."

"I see her," said the Angel: "an attractive woman. Will she win?"

"We do not call it winning, sir; for this, as you must know, is a sad matter, and implies the breaking-up of a home. She will most unwillingly receive a decree, at least, I think so," he added; "though whether it will stand the scrutiny of the King's Proctor we may wonder a little, from her appearance."

"King's Proctor?" said the Angel. "What is that?"

"A celestial Die-hard, sir, paid to join together again those whom man have put asunder."

"I do not follow," said the Angel fretfully.

"I perceive," whispered his dragoman, "that I must make clear to you the spirit which animates our justice in these matters. You know, of course, that the intention of our law is ever to penalise the wrong-doer. It therefore requires the innocent party, like that lady there, to be exceptionally innocent, not only before she secures her divorce, but for six months afterwards."

"Oh!" said the Angel. "And where is the guilty party?"

"Probably in the south of France," returned his dragoman, "with the new partner of his affections. They have a place in the sun; this one a place in the Law Courts."

"Dear me!" said the Angel. "Does she prefer that?"

"There are ladies," his dragoman replied, "who find it a pleasure to appear, no matter where, so long as people can see them in a pretty hat. But the great majority would rather sink into the earth than do this thing."

"The face of this one is most agreeable to me; I should not wish her to sink," said the Angel warmly.

"Agreeable or not," resumed his dragoman, "they have to bring their hearts for inspection by the public if they wish to become free from the party who has done them wrong. This is necessary, for the penalisation of the wrong-doer."

"And how will he be penalised?" asked the Angel naïvely.

"By receiving his freedom," returned his dragoman, "together with the power to enjoy himself with his new partner, in the sun, until, in due course, he is able to marry her."

"This is mysterious to me," murmured the Angel. "Is not the boot on the wrong leg?"

"Oh! sir, the law would not make a mistake like that. You are bringing a single mind to the consideration of this matter, but that will never do. This lady is a true and much-wronged wife; that is—let us hope so!—to whom our law has given its protection and remedy; but she is also, in its eyes, somewhat reprehensible for desiring to avail herself of that protection and remedy. For, though the law is now purely the affair of the State and has nothing to do with the Appointed, it still secretly believes in the religious maxim: 'Once married, always married,' and feels that however much a married person is neglected or ill-treated, she should not desire to be free."

"She?" said the Angel. "Does a man never desire to be free?"

"Oh, yes! sir, and not infrequently."

"Does your law, then, not consider him reprehensible in that desire?"

"In theory, perhaps; but there is a subtle distinction. For, sir, as you observe from the countenances before you, the law is administered entirely by males, and males cannot but believe in the divine right of males to have a better time than females; and, though they do not say so, they naturally feel that a husband wronged by a wife is more injured than a wife wronged by a husband."

"There is much in that," said the Angel. "But tell me how the oracle is worked—for it may come in handy!"

"You allude, sir, to the necessary procedure? I will make this clear. There are two kinds of cases: what I may call the 'O.K.' and what I may call the 'rig.' Now in the 'O.K.' it is only necessary for the plaintiff, if it be a woman, to receive a black eye from her husband and to pay detectives to find out that he has been too closely in the company of another; if it be a man, he need not receive a black eye from his wife, and has merely to pay the detectives to obtain the same necessary information."

"Why this difference between the sexes?" asked the Angel.

"Because," answered his dragoman, "woman is the weaker sex, things are therefore harder for her."

"But," said the Angel, "the English have a reputation for chivalry."

"They have, sir."

"Well—" began the Angel.

"When these conditions are complied with," interrupted his dragoman, "a suit for divorce may be brought, which may or may not be defended. Now, the 'rig,' which is always brought by the wife, is not so simple, for it must be subdivided into two sections: 'Ye straight rig' and 'Ye crooked rig.' 'Ye straight rig' is where the wife cannot induce her husband to remain with her, and discovering from him that he has been in the close company of another, wishes to be free of him. She therefore tells the Court that she wishes him to come back to her, and the Court will tell him to go back. Whereon, if he obey, the fat is sometimes in the fire. If, however, he obeys not, which is the more probable, she may, after a short delay, bring a suit, adducing the evidence she has obtained, and receive a decree. This may be the case before you, or, on the other hand, it may not, and will then be what is called 'Ye crooked rig.' If that is so, these two persons, having found that they cannot live in conjugal friendliness, have laid their heads together for the last time, and arranged to part; the procedure will now be the same as in 'Ye straight rig.' But the wife must take the greatest care to lead the Court to suppose that she really wishes her husband to come back; for, if she does not, it is collusion. The more ardent her desire to part from him, the more care she must take to pretend the opposite! But this sort of case is, after all, the simplest, for both parties are in complete accord in desiring to be free of each other, so neither does anything to retard that end, which is soon obtained."

"About that evidence?" said the Angel. "What must the man do?"

"He will require to go to an hotel with a lady friend," replied his dragoman; "once will be enough. And, provided they are called in the morning, there is no real necessity for anything else."

"H'm!" said the Angel. "This, indeed, seems to me to be all around about the bush. Could there not be some simple method which would not necessitate the perversion of the truth?"

"Ah, no!" responded his dragoman. "You forget what I told you, sir. However unhappy people may be together, our law grudges their separation; it requires them therefore to be immoral, or to lie, or both, before they can part."

"Curious!" said the Angel.

"You must understand, sir, that when a man says he will take a woman, and a woman says she will take a man, for the rest of their natural existence, they are assumed to know all about each other, though not permitted, of course, by the laws of morality to know anything of real importance. Since it is almost impossible from a modest acquaintanceship to make sure whether they will continue to desire each other's company after a completed knowledge, they are naturally disposed to go it 'blind,' if I may be pardoned the expression, and will take each other for ever on the smallest provocations. For the human being, sir, makes nothing of the words 'for ever,' when it sees immediate happiness before it. You can well understand, therefore, how necessary it is to make it very hard for them to get untied again."

"I should dislike living with a wife if I were tired of her," said the Angel.

"Sir," returned his dragoman confidentially, "in that sentiment you would have with you the whole male population. And, I believe, the whole of the female population would feel the same if they were tired of you, as the husband."

"That!" said the Angel, with a quiet smile.

"Ah! yes, sir; but does not this convince you of the necessity to force people who are tired of each other to go on living together?"

"No," said the Angel, with appalling frankness.

"Well," his dragoman replied soberly, "I must admit that some have thought our marriage laws should be in a museum, for they are unique; and, though a source of amusement to the public, and emolument to the profession, they pass the comprehension of men and angels who have not the key of the mystery."

"What key?" asked the Angel.

"I will give it you, sir," said his dragoman: "The English have a genius for taking the shadow of a thing for its substance. 'So long,' they say, 'as our marriages, our virtue, our honesty, and happiness seem to be, they are.' So long, therefore, as we do not dissolve a marriage it remains virtuous, honest and happy though the parties to it may be unfaithful, untruthful, and in misery. It would be regarded as awful, sir, for marriage to depend on mutual liking. We English cannot bear the thought of defeat. To dissolve an unhappy marriage is to recognise defeat by life, and we would rather that other people lived in wretchedness all their days than admit that members of our race had come up against something too hard to overcome. The English do not care about making the best out of this life in reality so long as they can do it in appearance."

"Then they believe in a future life?"

"They did to some considerable extent up to the 'eighties of the last century, and their laws and customs were no doubt settled in accordance therewith, and have not yet had time to adapt themselves. We are a somewhat slow-moving people, always a generation or two behind our real beliefs."

"They have lost their belief, then?"

"It is difficult to arrive at figures, sir, on such a question. But it has been estimated that perhaps one in ten adults now has some semblance of what may be called active belief in a future existence."

"And the rest are prepared to let their lives be arranged in accordance with the belief of that tenth?" asked the Angel, surprised. "Tell me, do they think their matrimonial differences will be adjusted over there, or what?"

"As to that, all is cloudy; and certain matters would be difficult to adjust without bigamy; for general opinion and the law permit the remarriage of persons whose first has gone before."

"How about children?" said the Angel; "for that is no inconsiderable item, I imagine."

"Yes, sir, they are a difficulty. But here, again, my key will fit. So long as the marriage seems real, it does not matter that the children know it isn't and suffer from the disharmony of their parents."

"I think," said the Angel acutely, "there must be some more earthly reason for the condition of your marriage laws than those you give me. It's all a matter of property at bottom, I suspect."

"Sir," said his dragoman, seemingly much struck, "I should not be surprised if you were right. There is little interest in divorce where no money is involved, and our poor are considered able to do without it. But I will never admit that this is the reason for the state of our divorce laws. No, no; I am an Englishman."

"Well," said the Angel, "we are wandering. Does this judge believe what they are now saying to him?"

"It is impossible to inform you, for judges are very deep and know all that is to be known on these matters. But of this you may be certain: if anything is fishy to the average apprehension, he will not suffer it to pass his nose."

"Where is the average apprehension?" asked the Angel.

"There, sir," said his dragoman, pointing to the jury with his chin, "noted for their common sense."

"And these others with grey heads who are calling each other friend, though they appear to be inimical?"

"Little can be hid from them," returned his dragoman; "but this case, though defended as to certain matters of money, is not disputed in regard to the divorce itself. Moreover, they are bound by professional etiquette to serve their clients through thin and thick."

"Cease!" said the Angel; "I wish to hear this evidence, and so does the lady on my left wing."

His dragoman smiled in his beard, and made no answer.

"Tell me," remarked the Angel, when he had listened, "does this woman get anything for saying she called them in the morning?"

"Fie, sir!" responded his dragoman; "only her expenses to the Court and back. Though indeed, it is possible that after she had called them, she got half a sovereign from the defendant to impress the matter on her mind, seeing that she calls many people every day."

"The whole matter," said the Angel with a frown, "appears to be in the nature of a game; nor are the details as savoury as I expected."

"It would be otherwise if the case were defended, sir," returned his dragoman; "then, too, you would have had an opportunity of understanding the capacity of the human mind for seeing the same incident to be both black and white; but it would take much of your valuable time, and the Court would be so crowded that you would have a lady sitting on your right wing also, and possibly on your knee. For, as you observe, ladies are particularly attached to these dramas of real life."

"If my wife were a wrong one," said the Angel, "I suppose that, according to your law, I could not sew her up in a sack and place it in the water?"

"We are not now in the days of the Great Skirmish," replied his dragoman somewhat coldly. "At that time any soldier who found his wife unfaithful, as we call it, could shoot her with impunity and receive the plaudits and possibly a presentation from the populace, though he himself may not have been impeccable while away—a masterly method of securing a divorce. But, as I told you, our procedure has changed since then; and even soldiers now have to go to work in this roundabout fashion."

"Can he not shoot the paramour?" asked the Angel.

"Not even that," answered his dragoman. "So soft and degenerate are the days. Though, if he can invent for the paramour a German name, he will still receive but a nominal sentence. Our law is renowned for never being swayed by sentimental reasons. I well recollect a case in the days of the Great Skirmish, when a jury found contrary to the plainest facts sooner than allow that reputation for impartiality to be tarnished."

"Ah!" said the Angel absently; "what is happening now?"

"The jury are considering their verdict. The conclusion is, however, foregone, for they are not retiring. The plaintiff is now using her smelling salts."

"She is a fine woman," said the Angel emphatically.

"Hush, sir! The judge might hear you."

"What if he does?" asked the Angel in surprise.

"He would then eject you for contempt of Court."

"Does he not think her a fine woman, too?"

"For the love of justice, sir, be silent," entreated his dragoman. "This concerns the happiness of three, if not of five lives. Look! She is lifting her veil; she is going to use her handkerchief."

"I cannot bear to see a woman cry," said the Angel, trying to rise; "please take this lady off my left wing."

"Kindly sit tight!" murmured his dragoman to the lady, leaning across behind the Angel's back. "Listen, sir!" he added to the Angel: "The jury are satisfied that what is necessary has taken place. All is well; she will get her decree."

"Hurrah!" said the Angel in a loud voice.

"If that noise is repeated, I will have the Court cleared."

"I am going to repeat it," said the Angel firmly; "she is beautiful!"

His dragoman placed a hand respectfully over the Angel's mouth. "Oh, sir!" he said soothingly, "do not spoil this charming moment. Hark! He is giving her a decree nisi, with costs. To-morrow it will be in all the papers, for it helps to sell them. See! She is withdrawing; we can now go." And he disengaged the Angel's wing.

The Angel rose quickly and made his way towards the door. "I am going to walk out with her," he announced joyously.

"I beseech you," said his dragoman, hurrying beside him, "remember the King's Proctor! Where is your chivalry? For he has none, sir—not a little bit!"

"Bring him to me; I will give it him!" said the Angel, kissing the tips of his fingers to the plaintiff, who was vanishing in the gloom of the fresh air.

VII

In the Strangers' room of the Strangers' Club the usual solitude was reigning when the Angel Æthereal entered.

"You will be quiet here," said his dragoman, drawing up two leather chairs to the hearth, "and comfortable," he added, as the Angel crossed his legs. "After our recent experience, I thought it better to bring you where your mind would be composed, since we have to consider so important a subject as morality. There is no place, indeed, where we could be so completely sheltered from life, or so free to evolve from our inner consciousness the momentous conclusions of the armchair moralist. When you have had your sneeze," he added, glancing at the Angel, who was taking snuff, "I shall make known to you the conclusions I have formed in the course of a chequered career."

"Before you do that," said the Angel, "it would perhaps be as well to limit the sphere of our inquiry."

"As to that," remarked his dragoman, "I shall confine my information to the morals of the English since the opening of the Great Skirmish, in 1914, just a short generation of three and thirty years ago; and you will find my theme readily falls, sir, into the two main compartments of public and private morality. When I have finished you can ask me any questions."

"Proceed!" said the Angel, letting his eyelids droop.

"Public morality," his dragoman began, "is either superlative, comparative, positive, or negative. And superlative morality is found, of course, only in the newspapers. It is the special prerogative of leader-writers. Its note, remote and unchallengeable, was well struck by almost every organ at the commencement of the Great Skirmish, and may be summed up in a single solemn phrase: 'We will sacrifice on the altar of duty the last life and the last dollar—except the last life and dollar of the last leader-writer.' For, as all must see, that one had to be preserved, to ensure and comment on the consummation of the sacrifice. What loftier morality can be conceived? And it has ever been a grief to the multitude that the lives of those patriots and benefactors of their species should, through modesty, have been unrevealed to such as pant to copy them. Here and there the lineaments of a tip-topper were discernible beneath the disguise of custom; but what fair existences were screened! I may tell you at once, sir, that the State was so much struck at the time of the Great Skirmish by this doctrine of the utter sacrifice of others that it almost immediately adopted the idea, and has struggled to retain it ever since. Indeed, only the unaccountable reluctance of 'others' to be utterly sacrificed has ensured their perpetuity."

"In 1910," said the Angel, "I happened to notice that the Prussians had already perfected that system. Yet it was against the Prussians that this country fought?"

"That is so," returned his dragoman; "there were many who drew attention to the fact. And at the conclusion of the Great Skirmish the reaction was such that for a long moment even the leader-writers wavered in their selfless doctrines; nor could continuity be secured till the Laborious Party came solidly to the saddle in 1930. Since then the principle has been firm but the practice has been firmer, and public morality has never been altogether superlative. Let us pass to comparative public morality. In the days of the Great Skirmish this was practised by those with names, who told others what to do. This large and capable body included all the preachers, publicists, and politicians of the day, and in many cases there is even evidence that they would have been willing to practise what they preached if their age had not been so venerable or their directive power so invaluable."

"In-valuable," murmured the Angel; "has that word a negative signification?"

"Not in all cases," said his dragoman with a smile; "there were men whom it would have been difficult to replace, though not many, and those perhaps the least comparatively moral. In this category, too, were undoubtedly the persons known as conchies."

"From conch, a shell?" asked the Angel.

"Not precisely," returned his dragoman; "and yet you have hit it, sir, for into their shells they certainly withdrew, refusing to have anything to do with this wicked world. Sufficient unto them was the voice within. They were not well treated by an unfeeling populace."

"This is interesting to me," said the Angel. "To what did they object?"

"To war," replied his dragoman. "'What is it to us,' they said, 'that there should be barbarians like these Prussians, who override the laws of justice and humanity?'—words, sir, very much in vogue in those days. 'How can it affect our principles if these rude foreigners have not our views, and are prepared, by cutting off the food supplies of this island, to starve us into submission to their rule? Rather than turn a deaf ear to the voice within we are prepared for general starvation; whether we are prepared for the starvation of our individual selves we cannot, of course, say until we experience it. But we hope for the best, and believe that we shall go through with it to death, in the undesired company of all who do not agree with us.' And it is certain, sir, that some of them were capable of this; for there is, as you know, a type of man who will die rather than admit that his views are too extreme to keep himself and his fellow-men alive."

"How entertaining!" said the Angel. "Do such persons still exist?"

"Oh! yes," replied the dragoman; "and always will. Nor is it, in my opinion, altogether to the disadvantage of mankind, for they afford a salutary warning to the human species not to isolate itself in fancy from the realities of existence and extinguish human life before its time has come. We shall now consider the positively moral. At the time of the Great Skirmish these were such as took no sugar in their tea and invested all they had in War Stock at five per cent. without waiting for what were called Premium Bonds to be issued. They were a large and healthy group, more immediately concerned with commerce than the war. But the largest body of all were the negatively moral. These were they who did what they crudely called 'their bit,' which I may tell you, sir, was often very bitter. I myself was a ship's steward at the time, and frequently swallowed much salt water, owing to the submarines. But I was not to be deterred, and would sign on again when it had been pumped out of me. Our morality was purely negative, if not actually low. We acted, as it were, from instinct, and often wondered at the sublime sacrifices which were being made by our betters. Most of us were killed or injured in one way or another; but a blind and obstinate mania for not giving in possessed us. We were a simple lot." The dragoman paused and fixed his eyes on the empty hearth. "I will not disguise from you," he added, "that we were fed-up nearly all the time; and yet—we couldn't stop. Odd, was it not?"

"I wish I had been with you," said the Angel, "for—to use that word without which you English seem unable to express anything—you were heroes."

"Sir," said his dragoman, "you flatter us by such encomium. We were, I fear, dismally lacking in commercial spirit, just men and women in the street having neither time nor inclination to examine our conduct and motives, nor to question or direct the conduct of others. Purely negative beings, with perhaps a touch of human courage and human kindliness in us. All this, however, is a tale of long ago. You can now ask me any questions, sir, before I pass to private morality."

"You alluded to courage and kindliness," said the Angel: "How do these qualities now stand?"

"The quality of courage," responded his dragoman, "received a set-back in men's estimation at the time of the Great Skirmish, from which it has never properly recovered. For physical courage was then, for the first time, perceived to be most excessively common; it is, indeed, probably a mere attribute of the bony chin, especially prevalent in the English-speaking races. As to moral courage, it was so hunted down that it is still somewhat in hiding. Of kindliness there are, as you know, two sorts: that which people manifest towards their own belongings; and that which they do not as a rule manifest towards every one else."

"Since we attended the Divorce Court," remarked the Angel with deliberation, "I have been thinking. And I fancy no one can be really kind unless they have had matrimonial trouble, preferably in conflict with the law."

"A new thought to me," observed his dragoman attentively; "and yet you may be right, for there is nothing like being morally outcast to make you feel the intolerance of others. But that brings us to private morality."

"Quite!" said the Angel, with relief. "I forgot to ask you this morning how the ancient custom of marriage was now regarded in the large?"

"Not indeed as a sacrament," replied his dragoman; "such a view was becoming rare already at the time of the Great Skirmish. Yet the notion might have been preserved but for the opposition of the Pontifical of those days to the reform of the Divorce Laws. When principle opposes common sense too long, a landslide follows."

"Of what nature, then, is marriage now?"

"Purely a civil, or uncivil, contract, as the case may be. The holy state of judicial separation, too, has long been unknown."

"Ah!" said the Angel, "that was the custom by which the man became a monk and the lady a nun, was it not?"

"In theory, sir," replied his dragoman, "but in practice not a little bit, as you may well suppose. The Pontifical, however, and the women, old and otherwise, who supported them, had but small experience of life to go on, and honestly believed that they were punishing those still-married but erring persons who were thus separated. These, on the contrary, almost invariably assumed that they were justified in free companionships, nor were they particular to avoid promiscuity! So it ever is, sir, when the great laws of Nature are violated in deference to the Higher Doctrine."

"Are children still born out of wedlock?" asked the Angel.

"Yes," said his dragoman, "but no longer considered responsible for the past conduct of their parents."

"Society, then, is more humane?"

"Well, sir, we shall not see the Millennium in that respect for some years to come. Zoos are still permitted, and I read only yesterday a letter from a Scottish gentleman pouring scorn on the humane proposal that prisoners should be allowed to see their wives once a month without bars or the presence of a third party; precisely as if we still lived in the days of the Great Skirmish. Can you tell me why it is that such letters are always written by Scotsmen?"

"Is it a riddle?" asked the Angel.

"It is indeed, sir."

"Then it bores me. Speaking generally, are you satisfied with current virtue now that it is a State matter, as you informed me yesterday?"

"To tell you the truth, sir, I do not judge my neighbours; sufficient unto myself is the vice thereof. But one thing I observe, the less virtuous people assume themselves to be, the more virtuous they commonly are. Where the limelight is not, the flower blooms. Have you not frequently noticed that they who day by day cheerfully endure most unpleasant things, while helping their neighbours at the expense of their own time and goods, are often rendered lyrical by receiving a sovereign from some one who would never miss it, and are ready to enthrone him in their hearts as a king of men? The truest virtue, sir, must be sought among the lowly. Sugar and snow may be seen on the top, but for the salt of the earth one must look to the bottom."

"I believe you," said the Angel. "It is probably harder for a man in the limelight to enter virtue than for the virtuous to enter the limelight. Ha, ha! Is the good old custom of buying honour still preserved?"

"No, sir; honour is now only given to such as make themselves too noisy to be endured, and saddles the recipient with an obligation to preserve public silence for a period not exceeding three years. That maximum sentence is given for a dukedom. It is reckoned that few can survive so fearful a term."

"Concerning the morality of this new custom," said the Angel, "I feel doubtful. It savours of surrender to the bully and the braggart, does it not?"

"Rather to the bore, sir; not necessarily the same thing. But whether men be decorated for making themselves useful, or troublesome, the result in either case is to secure a comparative inertia, which has ever been the desideratum; for you must surely be aware, sir, how a man's dignity weighs him down."

"Are women also rewarded in this way?"

"Yes, and very often; for although their dignity is already ample, their tongues are long, and they have little shame and no nerves in the matter of public speaking."

"And what price their virtue?" asked the Angel.

"There is some change since the days of the Great Skirmish," responded his dragoman. "They do not now so readily sell it, except for a wedding ring; and many marry for love. Women, indeed, are often deplorably lacking in commercial spirit; and though they now mix in commerce, have not yet been able to adapt themselves. Some men even go so far as to think that their participation in active life is not good for trade and keeps the country back."

"They are a curious sex," said the Angel; "I like them, but they make too much fuss about babies."

"Ah! sir, there is the great flaw. The mother instinct—so heedless and uncommercial! They seem to love the things just for their own sakes."

"Yes," said the Angel, "there's no future in it. Give me a cigar."

VIII

"What, then, is the present position of 'the good'?" asked the Angel Æthereal, taking wing from Watchester Cathedrome towards the City Tabernacle.

"There are a number of discordant views, sir," his dragoman whiffled through his nose in the rushing air; "which is no more novel in this year of Peace 1947 than it was when you were here in 1910. On the far right are certain extremists, who believe it to be what it was—omnipotent, but suffering the presence of 'the bad' for no reason which has yet been ascertained; omnipresent, though presumably absent where 'the bad' is present; mysterious, though perfectly revealed; terrible, though loving; eternal, though limited by a beginning and an end. They are not numerous, but all stall-holders, and chiefly characterised by an almost perfect intolerance of those whose views do not coincide with their own; nor will they suffer for a moment any examination into the nature of 'the good,' which they hold to be established for all time, in the form I have stated, by persons who have long been dead. They are, as you may imagine, somewhat out of touch with science, such as it is, and are regarded by the community at large rather with curiosity than anything else."

"The type is well known in the sky," said the Angel. "Tell me: Do they torture those who do not agree with them?"

"Not materially," responded his dragoman. "Such a custom was extinct even before the days of the Great Skirmish, though what would have happened if the Patriotic or Prussian Party had been able to keep power for any length of time we cannot tell. As it is, the torture they apply is purely spiritual, and consists in looking down their noses at all who have not their belief and calling them erratics. But it would be a mistake to underrate their power, for human nature loves the Pontifical, and there are those who will follow to the death any one who looks down his nose, and says: 'I know!' Moreover, sir, consider how unsettling a question 'the good' is, when you come to think about it and how unfatiguing the faith which precludes all such speculation."

"That is so," said the Angel thoughtfully.

"The right centre," continued his dragoman, "is occupied by the small yet noisy Fifth Party. These are they who play the cornet and tambourine, big drum and concertina, descendants of the Old Prophet, and survivors of those who, following a younger prophet, joined them at the time of the Great Skirmish. In a form ever modifying with scientific discovery they hold that 'the good' is a superman, bodiless yet bodily, with a beginning but without an end. It is an attractive faith, enabling them to say to Nature: 'Je m'en fiche de tout cela. My big brother will look after me Pom!' One may call it anthropomorphia, for it seems especially soothing to strong personalities. Every man to his creed, as they say; and I would never wish to throw cold water on such as seek to find 'the good' by closing one eye instead of two, as is done by the extremists on the right."

"You are tolerant," said the Angel.

"Sir," said his dragoman, "as one gets older, one perceives more and more how impossible it is for man not to regard himself as the cause of the universe, and for certain individual men not to believe themselves the centre of the cause. For such to start a new belief is a biological necessity, and should by no means be discouraged. It is a safety-valve—the form of passion which the fires of youth take in men after the age of fifty, as one may judge by the case of the prophet Tolstoy and other great ones. But to resume: In the centre, of course, are situated the enormous majority of the community, whose view is that they have no view of what 'the good' is."

"None?" repeated the Angel Æthereal, somewhat struck.

"Not the faintest," answered his dragoman. "These are the only true mystics; for what is a mystic if not one with an impenetrable belief in the mystery of his own existence? This group embraces the great bulk of the Laborious. It is true that many of them will repeat what is told them of 'the good' as if it were their own view, without compunction, but this is no more than the majority of persons have done from the beginning of time."

"Quite," admitted the Angel; "I have observed that phenomenon in the course of my travels. We will not waste words on them."

"Ah, sir!" retorted his dragoman, "there is more wisdom in these persons than you imagine. For, consider what would be the fate of their brains if they attempted to think for themselves. Moreover, as you know, all definite views about 'the good' are very wearing, and it is better, so this great majority thinks, to let sleeping dogs lie than to have them barking in its head. But I will tell you something," the dragoman added: "These innumerable persons have a secret belief of their own, old as the Greeks, that good fellowship is all that matters. And, in my opinion, taking 'the good' in its limited sense, it is an admirable creed."

"Oh! cut on!" said the Angel.

"My mistake, sir!" said his dragoman. "On the left centre are grouped that increasing section whose view is that since everything is very bad, 'the good' is ultimate extinction—'Peace, perfect peace,' as the poet says. You will recollect the old tag: 'To be or not to be.' These are they who have answered that question in the negative; pessimists masquerading to an unsuspecting public as optimists. They are no doubt descendants of such as used to be called 'Theosophians,' a sect which presupposed everything and then desired to be annihilated; or, again, of the Christian Scientites, who simply could not bear things as they were, so set themselves to think they were not, with some limited amount of success, if I remember rightly. I recall to mind the case of a lady who lost her virtue, and recovered it by dint of remembering that she had no body."

"Curious!" said the Angel. "I should like to question her; let me have her address after the lecture. Does the theory of reincarnation still obtain?"

"I do not wonder, sir, that you are interested in the point, for believers in that doctrine are compelled, by the old and awkward rule that 'Two and two make four,' to draw on other spheres for the reincarnation of their spirits."

"I do not follow," said the Angel.

"It is simple, however," answered his dragoman, "for at one time on earth, as is admitted, there was no life. The first incarnation, therefore—an amœba, we used to be told—enclosed a spirit, possibly from above. It may, indeed, have been yours, sir. Again, at some time on this earth, as is admitted, there will again be no life; the last spirit will therefore flit to an incarnation, possibly below; and again, sir, who knows, it may be yours."

"I cannot jest on such a subject," said the Angel, with a sneeze.

"No offence," murmured his dragoman. "The last group, on the far left, to which indeed I myself am not altogether unaffiliated, is composed of a small number of extremists, who hold that 'the good' is things as they are—pardon the inevitable flaw in grammar. They consider that what is now has always been, and will always be; that things do but swell and contract and swell again, and so on for ever and ever; and that, since they could not swell if they did not contract, since without the black there could not be the white, nor pleasure without pain, nor virtue without vice, nor criminals without judges; even contraction, or the black, or pain, or vice, or judges, are not 'the bad,' but only negatives; and that all is for the best in the best of all possible worlds. They are Voltairean optimists masquerading to an unsuspecting population as pessimists. 'Eternal Variation' is their motto."

"I gather," said the Angel, "that these think there is no purpose in existence?"

"Rather, sir, that existence is the purpose. For, if you consider, any other conception of purpose implies fulfilment, or an end, which they do not admit, just as they do not admit a beginning."

"How logical!" said the Angel. "It makes me dizzy! You have renounced the idea of climbing, then?"

"Not so," responded his dragoman. "We climb to the top of the pole, slide imperceptibly down, and begin over again; but since we never really know whether we are climbing or sliding, this does not depress us."

"To believe that this goes on for ever is futile," said the Angel.

"So we are told," replied his dragoman, without emotion. "We think, however, that the truth is with us, in spite of jesting Pilate."

"It is not for me," said the Angel, with dignity, "to argue with my dragoman."

"No, sir, for it is always necessary to beware of the open mind. I myself find it very difficult to believe the same thing every day. And the fact is that whatever you believe will probably not alter the truth, which may be said to have a certain mysterious immutability, considering the number of efforts men have made to change it from time to time. We are now, however, just above the City Tabernacle, and if you will close your wings we shall penetrate it through the clap-trap-door which enables its preachers now and then to ascend to higher spheres."

"Stay!" said the Angel; "let me float a minute while I suck a peppermint, for the audiences in these places often have colds." And with that delicious aroma clinging to them they made their entry through a strait gate in the roof and took their seats in the front row, below a tall prophet in eyeglasses, who was discoursing on the stars. The Angel slept heavily.

"You have lost a good thing, sir," said his dragoman reproachfully, when they left the Tabernacle.

"In my opinion," the Angel playfully responded, "I won a better, for I went nap. What can a mortal know about the stars?"

"Believe me," answered his dragoman, "the subject is not more abstruse than is generally chosen."

"If he had taken religion I should have listened with pleasure," said the Angel.

"Oh! sir, but in these days such a subject is unknown in a place of worship. Religion is now exclusively a State affair. The change began with discipline and the Education Bill in 1918, and has gradually crystallised ever since. It is true that individual extremists on the right make continual endeavours to encroach on the functions of the State, but they preach to empty houses."

"And the Deity?" said the Angel: "You have not once mentioned Him. It has struck me as curious."

"Belief in the Deity," responded his dragoman, "perished shortly after the Great Skirmish, during which there was too active and varied an effort to revive it. Action, as you know, sir, always brings reaction, and it must be said that the spiritual propaganda of those days was so grossly tinged with the commercial spirit that it came under the head of profiteering and earned for itself a certain abhorrence.

For no sooner had the fears and griefs brought by the Great Skirmish faded from men's spirits than they perceived that their new impetus towards the Deity had been directed purely by the longing for protection, solace, comfort, and reward, and not by any real desire for 'the good' in itself. It was this truth, together with the appropriation of the word by Emperors, and the expansion of our towns, a process ever destructive of traditions, which brought about extinction of belief in His existence."

"It was a large order," said the Angel.

"It was more a change of nomenclature," replied his dragoman. "The ruling motive for belief in 'the good' is still the hope of getting something out of it—the commercial spirit is innate."

"Ah!" said the Angel, absently. "Can we have another lunch now? I could do with a slice of beef."

"An admirable idea, sir," replied his dragoman; "we will have it in the White City."

IX

"What in your opinion is the nature of happiness?" asked the Angel Æthereal, as he finished his second bottle of Bass, in the grounds of the White City. The dragoman regarded his angel with one eye.

"The question is not simple, sir, though often made the subject of symposiums in the more intellectual journals. Even now, in the middle of the twentieth century, some still hold that it is a by-product of fresh air and good liquor. The Old and Merrie England indubitably procured it from those elements. Some, again, imagine it to follow from high thinking and low living, while no mean number believe that it depends on women."

"Their absence or their presence?" asked the Angel, with interest.

"Some this and others that. But for my part, it is not altogether the outcome of these causes."

"Is this now a happy land?"

"Sir," returned his dragoman, "all things earthly are comparative."

"Get on with it," said the Angel.

"I will comply," responded his dragoman reproachfully, "if you will permit me first to draw your third cork. And let me say in passing that even your present happiness is comparative, or possibly superlative, as you will know when you have finished this last bottle. It may or may not be greater; we shall see."

"We shall," said the Angel, resolutely.

"You ask me whether this land is happy; but must we not first decide what happiness is? And how difficult this will be you shall soon discover. For example, in the early days of the Great Skirmish, happiness was reputed non-existent; every family was plunged into anxiety or mourning; and, though this to my own knowledge was not the case, such as were not pretended to be. Yet, strange as it may appear, the shrewd observer of those days was unable to remark any indication of added gloom. Certain creature comforts, no doubt, were scarce, but there was no lack of spiritual comfort, which high minds have ever associated with happiness; nor do I here allude to liquor. What, then, was the nature of this spiritual comfort, you will certainly be asking. I will tell you, and in seven words: People forgot themselves and remembered other people. Until those days it had never been realised what a lot of medical men could be spared from the civil population; what a number of clergymen, lawyers, stockbrokers, artists, writers, politicians, and other persons, whose work in life is to cause people to think about themselves, never would be missed. Invalids knitted socks and forgot to be unwell; old gentlemen read the papers and forgot to talk about their food; people travelled in trains and forgot not to fall into conversation with each other; merchants became special constables and forgot to differ about property; the House of Lords remembered its dignity and forgot its impudence; the House of Commons almost forgot to chatter. The case of the working man was the most striking of all—he forgot he was the working man. The very dogs forgot themselves, though that, to be sure, was no novelty, as the Irish writer demonstrated in his terrific outburst: 'On my doorstep.' But time went on, and hens in their turn forgot to lay, ships to return to port, cows to give enough milk, and Governments to look ahead, till the first flush of self-forgetfulness which had dyed peoples' cheeks—"

"Died on them," put in the Angel, with a quiet smile.

"You take my meaning, sir," said his dragoman, "though I should not have worded it so happily. But certainly the return to self began, and people used to think: 'This war is not so bloody as I thought, for I am getting better money than I ever did, and the longer it lasts the more I shall get, and for the sake of this I am prepared to endure much.' The saying "Beef and beer, for soon you must put up the shutters," became the motto of all classes. 'If I am to be shot, drowned, bombed, ruined, or starved to-morrow,' they said, 'I had better eat, drink, marry, and buy jewelry to-day.' And so they did, in spite of the dreadful efforts of one bishop and two gentlemen who presided over the important question of food. They did not, it is true, relax their manual efforts to accomplish the defeat of their enemies, or 'win the war,' as it was somewhat loosely called; but they no longer worked with their spirits, which, with a few exceptions, went to sleep. For, sir, the spirit, like the body, demands regular repose, and in my opinion is usually the first of the two to snore. Before the Great Skirmish came at last to its appointed end the snoring from spirits in this country might have been heard in the moon. People thought of little but money, revenge, and what they could get to eat, though the word 'sacrifice' was so accustomed to their lips that they could no more get it off them than the other forms of lip-salve, increasingly in vogue. They became very merry. And the question I would raise is this: By which of these two standards shall we assess the word 'happiness'? Were these people happy when they mourned and thought not of self; or when they married and thought of self all the time?"

"By the first standard," replied the Angel, with kindling eyes. "Happiness is undoubtedly nobility."

"Not so fast, sir," replied his dragoman; "for I have frequently met with nobility in distress; and, indeed, the more exalted and refined the mind, the unhappier is frequently the owner thereof, for to him are visible a thousand cruelties and mean injustices which lower natures do not perceive."

"Hold!" exclaimed the Angel: "This is blasphemy against Olympus, 'The Spectator,' and other High-Brows."

"Sir," replied his dragoman gravely, "I am not one of those who accept gilded doctrines without examination; I read in the Book of Life rather than in the million tomes written by men to get away from their own unhappiness."

"I perceive," said the Angel, with a shrewd glance, "that you have something up your sleeve. Shake it out!"

"My conclusion is this, sir," returned his dragoman, well pleased: "Man is only happy when he is living at a certain pressure of life to the square inch; in other words, when he is so absorbed in what he is doing, making, saying, thinking, or dreaming, that he has lost self-consciousness. If there be upon him any ill—such as toothache or moody meditation—so poignant as to prevent him losing himself in the interest of the moment, then he is not happy. Nor must he merely think himself absorbed, but actually be so, as are two lovers sitting under one umbrella, or he who is just making a couplet rhyme."

"Would you say, then," insinuated the Angel, "that a man is happy when he meets a mad bull in a narrow lane? For there will surely be much pressure of life to the square inch."

"It does not follow," responded his dragoman; "for at such moments one is prone to stand apart, pitying himself and reflecting on the unevenness of fortune. But if he collects himself and meets the occasion with spirit he will enjoy it until, while sailing over the hedge, he has leisure to reflect once more. It is clear to me," he proceeded, "that the fruit of the tree of knowledge in the old fable was not, as has hitherto been supposed by a puritanical people, the mere knowledge of sex, but symbolised rather general self-consciousness; for I have little doubt that Adam and Eve sat together under one umbrella long before they discovered they had no clothes on. Not until they became self-conscious about things at large did they become unhappy."

"Love is commonly reputed by some, and power by others, to be the keys of happiness," said the Angel, regardless of his grammar.

"Duds," broke in his dragoman. "For love and power are only two of the various paths to absorption, or unconsciousness of self; mere methods by which men of differing natures succeed in losing their self-consciousness, for he who, like Saint Francis, loves all creation, has no time to be conscious of loving himself, and he who rattles the sword and rules like Bill Kaser, has no time to be conscious that he is not ruling himself. I do not deny that such men may be happy, but not because of the love or the power. No, it is because they are loving or ruling with such intensity that they forget themselves in doing it."

"There is much in what you say," said the Angel thoughtfully. "How do you apply it to the times and land in which you live?"

"Sir," his dragoman responded, "the Englishman never has been, and is not now, by any means so unhappy as he looks, for, where you see a furrow in the brow, or a mouth a little open, it portends absorption rather than thoughtfulness—unless, indeed, it means adenoids—and is the mark of a naturally self-forgetful nature; nor should you suppose that poverty and dirt which abound, as you see, even under the sway of the Laborious, is necessarily deterrent to the power of living in the moment; it may even be a symptom of that habit. The unhappy are more frequently the clean and leisured, especially in times of peace, when they have little to do save sit under mulberry trees, invest money, pay their taxes, wash, fly, and think about themselves. Nevertheless, many of the Laborious also live at half-cock, and cannot be said to have lost consciousness of self."

"Then democracy is not synonymous with happiness?" asked the Angel.

"Dear sir," replied his dragoman, "I know they said so at the time of the Great Skirmish. But they said so much that one little one like that hardly counted. I will let you into a secret. We have not yet achieved democracy, either here or anywhere else. The old American saying about it is all very well, but since not one man in ten has any real opinion of his own on any subject on which he votes, he cannot, with the best will in the world, put it on record. Not until he learns to have and record his own real opinion will he truly govern himself for himself, which is, as you know, the test of true democracy."

"I am getting fuddled," said the Angel. "What is it you want to make you happy?"

His dragoman sat up: "If I am right," he purred, "in my view that happiness is absorption, our problem is to direct men's minds to absorption in right and pleasant things. An American making a corner in wheat is absorbed and no doubt happy, yet he is an enemy of mankind, for his activity is destructive. We should seek to give our minds to creation, to activities good for others as well as for ourselves, to simplicity, pride in work, and forgetfulness of self in every walk of life. We should do things for the sheer pleasure of doing them, and not for what they may or may not be going to bring us in, and be taught always to give our whole minds to it; in this way only will the edge of our appetite for existence remain as keen as a razor which is stropped every morning by one who knows how. On the negative side we should be brought up to be kind, to be clean, to be moderate, and to love good music, exercise, and fresh air."

"That sounds a bit of all right," said the Angel. "What measures are being taken in these directions?"

"It has been my habit, sir, to study the Education Acts of my country ever since that which was passed at the time of the Great Skirmish; but, with the exception of exercise, I have not as yet been able to find any direct allusion to these matters. Nor is this surprising when you consider that education is popularly supposed to be, not for the acquisition of happiness, but for the good of trade or the promotion of acute self-consciousness through what we know as culture. If by any chance there should arise a President of Education so enlightened as to share my views, it would be impossible for him to mention the fact for fear of being sent to Colney Hatch."

"In that case," asked the Angel, "you do not believe in the progress of your country?"

"Sir," his dragoman replied earnestly, "you have seen this land for yourself and have heard from me some account of its growth from the days when you were last on earth, shortly before the Great Skirmish; it will not have escaped your eagle eye that this considerable event has had some influence in accelerating the course of its progression; and you will have noticed how, notwithstanding the most strenuous intentions at the close of that tragedy, we have yielded to circumstance and in every direction followed the line of least resistance."

"I have a certain sympathy with that," said the Angel, with a yawn; "it is so much easier."

"So we have found; and our country has got along, perhaps, as well as one could have expected, considering what it has had to contend with: pressure of debt; primrose paths; pelf; party; patrio-Prussianism; the people; pundits; Puritans; proctors; property; philosophers; the Pontifical; and progress. I will not disguise from you, however, that we are far from perfection; and it may be that on your next visit, thirty-seven years hence, we shall be further. For, however it may be with angels, sir, with men things do not stand still; and, as I have tried to make clear to you, in order to advance in body and spirit, it is necessary to be masters of your environment and discoveries instead of letting them be masters of you. Wealthy again we may be; healthy and happy we are not, as yet."

"I have finished my beer," said the Angel Æthereal, with finality, "and am ready to rise. You have nothing to drink! Let me give you a testimonial instead!" Pulling a quill from his wing, he dipped it in the mustard and wrote: "A Dry Dog—No Good For Trade" on his dragoman's white hat. "I shall now leave the earth," he added.

"I am pleased to hear it," said his dragoman, "for I fancy that the longer you stay the more vulgar you will become. I have noticed it growing on you, sir, just as it does on us."

The Angel smiled. "Meet me by sunlight alone," he said, "under the left-hand lion in Trafalgar Square at this hour of this day, in 1984. Remember me to the waiter, will you? So long!" And, without pausing for a reply, he spread his wings, and soared away.

"L'homme moyen sensuel! Sic itur ad astra!" murmured his dragoman enigmatically, and, lifting his eyes, he followed the Angel's flight into the empyrean.

John Galsworthy — A Short Biography

John Galsworthy, eldest son of John Galsworthy (1817-1904), a solicitor and company director of Old Jewry, London, and Blanche Bailey (1835-1915), daughter of Charles Bartleet, a needlemaker in Redditch. His father's ancestors originated in Wembury, near Plymouth in England, and Galsworthy, for whom family origins were of significant importance, maintained a close connection with Devon. His more immediate family were considerably wealthy and well established in the shipping industry, and owned a fine estate in Kingston-upon-Thames called Parkfield, where Galsworthy was born on the 14th August 1867. At the age of nine he began education at Saugeen, a Bournemouth preparatory school, before starting at Harrow school in 1881 where he remained until 1886, distinguishing himself as an athlete.

His education at Harrow being successful enough to gain him entrance to Oxford, he began at New College to read law and gained a second-class degree with honours in 1889. Following Lincoln's Inn he was called to the bar in 1890. Despite this recognition he realised that he was not keen to actually begin practising law and so he resolved instead to look after the family's shipping business while specialising himself in Marine Law. This decision saw him take to the seas to destinations such as Vancouver, Island and South AFrica, though it was at the age of twenty-five on one particular journey to Australia, motivated by an (unfulfilled) intention to meet Robert Louis Stevenson on Samoa that he would being to realise fully his literary interests: though he was not considering becoming a writer at this time, his enjoyment of literature was enough to encourage an attempt at meeting a great writer and eventually enabled one of the most significant encounters of his life. He made the journey with his friend Edward Sanderson and, though he missed Stevenson, he met Joseph Conrad, a fellow future author famed for his novels which were often nautically themed. At the time Conrad was the first mate of the sailing-ship Torrens moored in the harbour of Adelaide, Australia; still very much focused on his ship-borne career, he was yet to begin his writing in earnest.

Indeed, though neither knew at the time, both Conrad and Galsworthy were at similar junctures in their lives, their time spent as sea acting as a transitional period during which each found their literary calling. It is perhaps owing to this unknown common ground that they became close friends. During his time on the Torrens Galsworthy recorded several details, offering a frank and valuable characterisation of Conrad while also illuminating his own experiences as a student of Marine Law.

"I supposed to be studying navigation for the Admiralty Bar, would every day work out the position of the ship with the captain. On one side of the saloon table we would sit and check our observations with those of Conrad, who from the other side of the table would look at us a little quizzically."

On his return to England and the cessation of his nautical voyaging, Galsworthy began an affair with the wife of his first cousin, Major Arthur John Galsworthy. Ada Nemesis Pearson Cooper (1864-1956), the daughter of Emanuel Copper, an obstetrician from Norwich, remained married to the Major for ten years and the affair remained secret for its duration. In order to conceal the affair they took considerable pains to avoid suspicion. One such tactic was to stay in a secluded farmhouse called Wingstone in the village on Manaton on Dartmoor, in Devon. In Galsworthy's decision to choose Devon as the location for their clandestine rendezvous we see evidence of Galsworthy's affection for the place of his father's origin. It was only when, in 1905, she divorced the Major that their affair became known following their marriage on 23rd September of that year.

Galsworthy now took to writing sometime after having met Conrad and his career began in earnest when, in 1897, his first work, From the Four Winds, a volume of short stories, was published under the pseudonym John Sinjohn. He succeeded this in 1898 with Jocelyn, his first novel, and then his second in 1900, Villa Rubein. In 1901 he published a second volume of short stories, A Man of Devon, which was the last of his work to be published under pseudonym. The first of his work to be published under his own name was The Island Pharisees in 1904, a novel of social observation, seasoned with flashes of satire and propaganda. His decision to write under his own name is arguably owing to the recent death of his father, either as a mark of respect to his name or because now he was able to publish freely without incurring the possibility of paternal disappointment at his choice of career. It also marked a shift in his professionalism; he had hitherto published with small, independent publishers, but The Island Pharisees was published by Heinemann, a far more established House and one with whom he remained for the duration of his writing career.

He arguably cemented his position and maturity as a writer when, in 1906, he saw the publication of both his first major play, The Silver Box, and the novel The Man of Property. Each was published to considerable critical acclaim, and to achieve both in such a short space of time was impressive. the Silver Box concerns the imbalance in the justice system with regards to criminals of differing class by contrasting the treatment of a poor thief and a rich thief, both of whom stole silver cigarette cases but for very different reasons. The complexity of individual experience when not dealt with in public is highlighted and questioned in a bravely critical manner; despite the clear issues it raises with class and privilege, the final night was attended by the Price and Princess of Wales. The Man of Property was the first novel in the famous The Forsyte Saga, a trilogy of novels with an 'interlude' between each one, written between 1906 and 1921. Dealing with the questions of status, class and materialism, The Man of Property introduces us to the Forsyte family, particularly Soames Forsyte, who is acutely aware of his status as 'new money' and equally keen to assert himself as a wealthy man. Jealous of his wife and desperate to own things in order to confirm his wealth to those observing him, he engineers a plan to keep his wife from her friends which backfires spectacularly when, instead of cutting her off, all Soames achieves is enabling her to have an affair. This drives Soames to terrible actions with terrible consequences, which Galsworthy depicts with confidence.

Very typically Edwardian, the novel focuses on conflict between property and art, and to a certain degree much of its emotional power is drawn from Galsworthy's own life, particularly his affair with Ada. Their rendezvous in the countryside of Devon mirror the manner in which Forsyte seeks to relocate his wife and; though theirs was a much healthier relationship, there are clear similarities. By examining the fragile nature of the class system and those moving within it Galsworthy offered an important perspective on the relationships between material wealth, personal happiness and obsession, and the manner in which these change over time. His contemporaries widely regarded the publication of this novel as marking the end of Victorianism. His friend Conrad praised it as "indubitably a piece of art" and, though the notoriously risqué D.H. Lawrence lamented the novel's timidity in the face of sexuality and sensuality, he considered it potentially "a very great novel, a very great satire".

Though he continued to write both plays and novels, it was his work as a playwright for which he was most celebrated by his contemporaries. Indeed, his next novel, The Country House, seems uncharacteristically unfocused, its satirical view of those belonging to the country set comparatively unremarkable and weakly characterised, while at times the tone of satire becomes one of ironic detachment. In 1909 he published Fraternity, an exploration of of the various connections between urban society and the social classes therein, though its representation of lower-class Londoners is utterly unconvincing and ill-informed. Remaining with the subject of the landed gentry and the society surrounding it, in 1915 he published The Freelands, which does not stray far from conservative discussions of capitalism, the rural economy and their interrelationship.

His drama, however, featured a convincingly muted realism, directed at a relatively small, educated and politically-aware audience. His social agenda is prevalent here too, and is represented in a simple and static manner producing arresting instances of high drama. This talent for creating moments of captivating theatre is complimented by an instinctual sense of balance enabling his narratives to vacillate between their emotional high- and low-points, ultimately reaching conclusive equilibrium. This is particularly evident in one of his most popular plays, Strife, published in 1909 and examining the antagonists in a strike at a Cornish tin mine. In this, and in 1910's Justice, he approaches his subject with sympathy, irony and balance, which establishes a position of narrative authority while garnering the audiences trust that he is representing his characters and their motives justly. Justice condemns the use of solitary confinement in prisons, a reformist agenda which caught the liberality of his contemporary audiences along with the home secretary, Winston Churchill. Despite he was careful to disassociate himself with politics and professed himself apolitical, he and his work were nevertheless aligned with the views of the Liberal establishment. He spent much of the duration of the First World War working in a field hospital in France as an orderly having been passed over for military service.

Despite the popularity and brilliance of his work, it was only in 1920 that he had his first true commercial success with The Skin Game, a melodrama dealing with ethics, property and class. The play was adapted by Alfred Hitchcock in 1931. Galsworthy, meanwhile, had turned down a knighthood in 1918, considering his work not sufficient to be made a knight of the realm. He did, however, accept the Belgian Palmes d'Or in the following year. In 1920 he published the second novel in the Forsyte Saga, In Chancery, in which he resumes many of the themes of the first novel, focusing on the marital disharmony between Soames Forsyte and his wife. Katherine Mansfield considered it "a fascinating, brilliant book" in her review in The Atheneum. Then, in 1921, he was elected as the PEN International Literary Club's first president. The concluding novel to The Forsyte Saga, To Let was published in 1921 with a kind of peace being found between Forsyte and his now-ex wife, though he is left contemplating his losses and his greed. More ironic treatment of class confusions followed in Loyalties, bringing with it more popular success which lasted until 1926 and Escape, the last of his popular plays. Though he enjoyed popular success it was inconsistent and relatively small. His Collected Plays was published in 1929.

Over the course of time the appreciation of his work has gradually shifted from his plays to his novels, and particularly the detail and intricacy of his chronicle of English social difference, tension and pretension in The Forsyte Saga. Its success encouraged Galsworthy to revisit Soames Forsyte in a second trilogy, A Modern Comedy, which follows Soames's obsessive love of his daughter Fleur. In its three volumes, The White Monkey (1924), The Silver Spoon (1936) and Swan Song (1928) he examines the English commercial upper-middle class and its ideologies, its instinct to possess as its only way of distinguishing itself manifested in the poisonous materialism of Soames. Interestingly, this emergent social class which he so vehemently criticises is the very class from which he emerged. He witnessed first-hand its insularity, its chauvinism, its restrictive and oppressive morality, its stubborn imperialism and its materialism, and it is this experience which enables him to write so comfortably about it. Swan Song is widely considered among the best of Galsworthy's writing for the depth of its exploration of society and its heightened emotional subtlety. In 1929 he was appointed to the Order of Merit, despite having turned down a knighthood earlier. He spent his last years writing a third trilogy, End of the Chapter, beginning in 1931 with Maid in Waiting, Flowering Wilderness in 1932 and concluding with Over The River in 1933. These are significantly less coherent works and are indicative of his deteriorating health. Indeed, in 1932 he was awarded the Nobel Prize, though he was too ill to attend the ceremony.

Throughout the course of his career he received honorary degrees from the universities of St Andrews (1922), Manchester (1927), Dublin (1929), Cambridge (1930), Sheffield (1930), Oxford (1931), and Princeton (1931). In 1926 New College, Oxford, elected him as an honourary fellow. In photographs he is portrayed as handsome, fastidiously dressed and dignified. He was unusually compassionate and this saw him involved in several charitable and humane causes throughout the course of his life, including penal reforms, attacks on theatrical censorship and campaigning for animal rights. Though he spent the majority of the final seven years of his life at his home in Bury, West Sussex, it was at his home in Hampstead, London, that he died of a brain tumour on 31st January, 1933, six weeks after having been too ill to attend the ceremony in honour of his receiving the Nobel Prize. According to demands made in his will he was cremated and his ashes scattered over the South Downs from an aeroplane. Also in his will was his wish to leave cottages to several of his astonished tenants. He is memorialised in Highgate 'New' Cemetery and in the cloisters of New College, Oxford, where he was an honourary fellow.

John Galsworthy – A Concise Bibliography

From the Four Winds, 1897 (as John Sinjohn)
Jocelyn, 1898 (as John Sinjohn)
Villa Rubein, 1900 (as John Sinjohn)
A Man of Devon, 1901 (as John Sinjohn)
The Island Pharisees, 1904
The Silver Box, 1906 (his first play)
The Man of Property, 1906 – First book of The Forsyte Saga (1922)
The Country House, 1907
A Commentary, 1908

Fraternity, 1909

A Justification for the Censorship of Plays, 1909

Strife, 1909

Fraternity, 1909

Joy, 1909

Justice, 1910

A Motley, 1910

The Spirit of Punishment, 1910

Horses in Mines, 1910

The Patrician, 1911

The Little Dream, 1911

The Pigeon, 1912

The Eldest Son, 1912

Quality, 1912

Moods, Songs, and Doggerels, 1912

For Love of Beasts, 1912

The Inn of Tranquillity, 1912

The Dark Flower, 1913

The Fugitive, 1913

The Mob, 1914

The Freelands, 1915

The Little Man, 1915

A Bit o' Love, 1915

A Sheaf, 1916

The Apple Tree, 1916

The Foundations, 1917

Beyond, 1917

Five Tales, 1918

Indian Summer of a Forsyte, 1918 – First interlude of The Forsyte Saga

Saint's Progress, 1919

Addresses in America, 1912

In Chancery, 1920 – Second book of The Forsyte Saga

Awakening, 1920 – Second interlude of The Forsyte Saga

The Skin Game, 1920

To Let, 1921 – Third book of The Forsyte Saga

A Family Man, 1922

The Little Man, 1922

Loyalties, 1922

Windows, 1922

Captures, 1923

Abracadabra, 1924

The Forest, 1924

Old English, 1924

The White Monkey, 1924 – First book of A Modern Comedy

The Show, 1925

Escape, 1926

The Silver Spoon, 1926 – Second book of A Modern Comedy

Verses New and Old, 1926

Castles in Spain, 1927
A Silent Wooing, 1927 – First Interlude of A Modern Comedy
Passers By, 1927 – Second Interlude of A Modern Comedy
Swan Song, 1928 – Third book of A Modern Comedy
The Manaton Edition, 1923–26 (collection, 30 vols.)
Exiled, 1929
The Roof, 1929
On Forsyte 'Change, 1930
Two Essays on Conrad, 1930
Soames and the Flag, 1930
The Creation of Character in Literature, 1931 (The Romanes Lecture for 1931).
Maid in Waiting, 1931 – First book of End of the Chapter (1934)
Forty Poems, 1932
Flowering Wilderness, 1932 – Second book of End of the Chapter
Autobiographical Letters of Galsworthy: A Correspondence with Frank Harris, 1933
One More River (originally Over the River), 1933 – Third book of End of the Chapter
The Grove Edition, 1927–34 (collection, 27 Vols.)
Collected Poems, 1934
Punch and Go, 1935
The Life and Letters, 1935
The Winter Garden, 1935
Forsytes, Pendyces and Others, 1935
Selected Short Stories, 1935
Glimpses and Reflections, 1937

www.ingramcontent.com/pod-product-compliance
Lightning Source LLC
Chambersburg PA
CBHW071405170626
46811CB00003B/1268